BOUNTIFUL LEGACIES

THE POUSTINIA SERIES, BOOK 3

KATHLEEN MCKEE

First Edition: February 2017
Revised: December 2021

Cover design by Robin Ludwig Design Inc.
www.gobookcoverdesign.com

ISBN-10: 154309189X
ISBN-13: 978-1543091892

Printed in the United States of America

"What you leave behind is not what is engraved in stone monuments but what is woven into the lives of others."
— Pericles

ALSO BY KATHLEEN MCKEE

The Poustinia Series:

Poustinia: A Novel

Joyful Encounters

Bountiful Legacies

No Gifts to Bring

(*Prequel to the Aspen Notch Mystery Series*)

The Aspen Notch Mystery Series:

Murder in Aspen Notch

The Garden Shop Mystery

A Cameo Appearance

Below the Landscape

Bedlam in the Blizzard

The Ghost of Ridgeton Manor

A Specter of Truth

Living with a Springer Spaniel:

Pete and Me

Honest reviews of my books help bring them to the attention of other readers. If you enjoyed Bountiful Legacies, *please post a brief review on Amazon and Goodreads. It's unbelievably important, and I'd be so grateful.*

CHAPTER 1

The first notable snowfall in January started as soft flakes at daybreak, cradling the frozen grass and tree limbs in its embracing coverlet. Charlie and I awoke at the crack of dawn, then watched the storm intensify while we sipped our morning coffee at the kitchen table. "I told you this would be a big one," Charlie said, with a hint of excitement in his voice.

"What makes you so sure?" I asked. "It could fizzle out like the last snow forecast. After all the hype, we had only an inch or two."

Charlie shook his head. "Nope. It's going to be a whopper this time. I told Leon I'd help him clear the monastery drive and shovel the paths today."

"Let Leon do the shoveling. He's younger than you, so you can do the plowing in the truck."

"We'll see," Charlie replied.

I didn't bother arguing because Charlie would do what he wanted. Although technically still newlyweds, I'd already learned that he had a stubborn streak, especially when he became fixed on an idea. Despite our upwardly mobile ages, Charlie and I married at the end of the summer, I retired from the publishing firm where I worked for 40 years, and we sold the house that had been my home for just about as long. We bought land from the Sisters at the Monastery of St. Carmella, then settled into our new modular home just before Thanksgiving.

As difficult as I found it to transition from the suburbs to the rural countryside, I considered that a breeze compared to my evolution from Victoria Sullivan, VP of Human Resources, to Vicki Munley, wife of Charlie Munley, and managing director of *Rock Creek Farm*, a non-profit educational enterprise recently started by the Sisters at the monastery. We didn't actually have a working farm yet, but we hoped to plant our first crops in the spring.

"You'll need a hot breakfast if you're going out in the snow," I said, trying to motivate myself to start my day. "How about some bacon and eggs?"

"That sounds good," Charlie agreed. "I'll make another pot of coffee."

"You're just lucky I went to the grocery store yesterday," I remarked as I opened the refrigerator. "Based on your weather prediction, I figured I'd better stock up."

"Good thinking," Charlie nodded.

With the snow falling rapidly by the time I plated our breakfast, Charlie and I again settled at the kitchen table, while Harvey, our mutt, caught the scent of sizzling bacon. In a flash, he awoke from his snooze and sat at my feet. "No begging," I admonished, to no avail, since Charlie already had given Harvey a few morsels from his dish.

"He's going to need something to warm his innards, too," Charlie noted. The two of them had become inseparable pals.

"Harvey won't go out in this snow," I said.

"Sure, he will. Won't you, boy?" Harvey wagged his tail in agreement.

We had barely finished eating when Leon arrived in the truck, and I opened the back door to welcome him. "Come on in and have a cup of coffee. Do you want any breakfast?"

"Morning, Vicki. I already ate, but I'll gladly take some of Charlie's brew." Leon took off his boots, placed them on the mat by the door, and joined us at the kitchen table.

"How are the roads?" I asked.

"Getting slick," Leon replied. "The plows haven't gone out yet, but it's snowing darn hard. The wind's starting to pick up, too, so I hope you don't have to go anywhere today."

"I planned to work on a grant," I said, "unless you guys need my help."

"No, ma'am," Leon replied. "Joe's already started clearing the paths, and I'll join him, though I thought Charlie could work on plowing the drive."

The Sisters hired Leon to work as groundskeeper for the monastery last summer. The job had been Charlie's for more than 10 years, but Charlie decided to move to St. Louis when the nuns transferred his sister-in-law, Sister Tony, there. After only two months, Charlie realized his mistake, so he returned to the monastery—and proposed to me.

Leon, previously a homeless veteran who suffered from PTSD, didn't think he'd have the stamina to hold down a steady job. Living in one of the cabins that the Sisters designated as a poustinia—a place of solitude and prayer—had been remarkably transformative, and Leon thrived in his new environment. He told me that the kindness and support of the Sisters brought back his spirit.

Interestingly, the same thing happened to Charlie after the death of his first wife, Stella. The two men must have shared a bond of brotherhood, because Leon and Charlie had become good friends. Leon took another sip of coffee and said, "I can't get tired of the view from your kitchen window."

"I love my new home," I replied, following his gaze. "I'm so glad we decided to hold off on the sunroom at the back of the house, and put in the picture window instead. The panorama of the fields and woods delights me."

"You can't see much with the blowing snow," Charlie said as he began putting on his boots. "Let's get moving, or we won't get ahead of the storm."

"I'll start a pot of soup so you'll have something to warm you up when you can take a break," I remarked.

"Sounds good," Leon agreed as he put his mug in the sink. "It's mighty cold out there."

Charlie took his cell phone off the charger and put it in his pocket before bundling up in his jacket and scarf. He called to Harvey when he opened the back door. "Are you coming, boy?" Harvey stuck his nose out, then settled back under the table.

"I told you," I teased as I gave Charlie a kiss.

"Smart dog," Leon chuckled. "Let's go."

CHAPTER 2

J cleared and wiped the table, then put a package of chicken breasts into a large pot of water. While that simmered, I finished loading the dishwasher, then set up my laptop on the kitchen table. I had just started the grant application when Amanda called.

I met Amanda on my first visit to the monastery almost two years ago when we each stayed in a poustinia. At the time, she had recently graduated from high school and went through a rather rebellious stage, though I saw the strengths that she tried to hide, and invited her to spend the summer working as a temp at my firm and living with me. Later, through a surprising twist of fate, we learned that Amanda was Charlie's granddaughter.

After she completed culinary school last year, the Sisters hired Amanda as the chef at the newly established *Monastery Restaurant and Inn*. The nuns converted an unused wing of the monastery to a B&B for those who might enjoy solitude with a more comfortable ambiance than a rustic cabin in the woods, and the restaurant provided meals for the guests, as well as the general public.

Last summer, Amanda and Joe Henderson, a young man she met in her culinary program, became engaged, and he often helped her at the monastery restaurant during his free time. Joe, a pastry chef at

Jake's Diner, rented a poustinia for his living quarters, while Amanda had a room in the B&B. I assumed they'd find an apartment in town once they married.

"What are you doing?" Amanda asked when I picked up the call.

"Making a pot of soup and writing a grant," I replied. "What about you?"

"Nothing," Amanda said. "We're closed. In fact, even Jake decided not to open the diner today. The plows haven't been out yet, and Joe told us the roads are a mess."

"I wondered how Joe could manage to help Leon and GP with the shoveling," I remarked, using Amanda's acronym for Charlie, since she called him GP, short for grandpop. "At least, you'll have some companionship."

"Maybe," Amanda replied. "I shoveled a bit, but came in to get warm."

"Do you have to cook anything for the Sisters?" I asked.

"No. They decided to have a snow day. That's what they call it when they just relax and enjoy the day. Sister Cheryl told me to take the day off."

"That's great," I said. "You don't have very many breaks."

"Right, but it's kind of boring since I'm the only one in this whole wing of the monastery."

"You could watch a movie or read a book," I suggested.

"Yeah, I know, but I don't feel like doing either. Do you want some company?"

"Sure," I agreed. "You can de-bone the chicken and finish making the soup for me. The guys plan to head over here when they need to warm up, so you could call GP on his cell phone, and ask him to pick you up in the truck."

"Cool. That'll work. I'll see you in a bit."

By the time the plowing crew and Amanda arrived, I had skimmed the fat off the stock while the chicken cooled. I'd just started cutting up celery when they all traipsed through the back door, with their boots and jackets covered with snow. "Twelve inches already," Charlie announced, "and it's not about to let up anytime soon."

"I heard on the news that it's a winter nor'easter," Amanda said, "and we could get two to three feet."

"Oh, my gosh," I exclaimed. "I hope we don't lose power."

"I hooked up our generator yesterday," Charlie noted, "so we'll be OK. The nuns have a permanent back-up system, and they'll be fine, too, but poor Leon and Joe will need their battery lanterns and a couple of extra blankets."

"Nonsense," I said. "They can stay here. We have a guest room, as well as a futon in the den. In the meantime, why don't you boys warm up by the gas fireplace in the living room? Amanda can help me finish the soup."

DESPITE THE SLIGHTLY AL *dente* celery, everyone declared the chicken noodle soup a winner. The men bundled up again and continued their battle with the snowstorm, though Amanda stayed with me to make a hearty stew for supper. I began browning the beef cubes, while Amanda prepared the vegetables.

I thought it quite nice that Amanda and I had some time together because we didn't often have a whole afternoon to chat.

Between packing, moving, then unpacking everything, as well as starting my work for the Sisters, I had so many distractions that I could barely stay focused.

Charlie and I gratefully accepted the help that Amanda and Joe provided during our move. Joe gave Charlie a hand with all of the boxes, while Amanda assisted me with her design strategy in the house, since she had such an amazing talent for decorating. Now, our home felt cozy and inviting.

"It looks pretty good in here," Amanda commented as she peeled and sliced an onion. "Joe and I decided that we'd like to do the same thing as you and GP. You know, like get a piece of land and put a house on it, then we'd be neighbors."

"I thought you and Joe would want to live in town," I said. "Do you actually think you'd prefer to stay in the sticks?"

"We like it here," Amanda replied. "Besides, it'll be really neat when we have the farm up and running because we'd like to raise our family here."

"How are the wedding plans coming along?" I asked.

"I don't know. We have a new wrinkle."

I added flour and more seasonings to my pot of meat, and stirred that around before creating a gravy with the beef broth. "What's the problem?" I questioned.

Amanda gave me a strange look before replying, "You were at the nuns' Christmas dinner. Didn't you hear my dad announce that he and Hannah intend to get married?"

Amanda and her dad, Steve Angeli, had both struggled to come to terms with her mother's death a few years back. Steve dealt with his grief by retreating to his books and his teaching at the university; Amanda acted out.

"Of course," I said, "but why should that influence your plans? Besides, you gave your approval before he told everyone else the news."

"I like Hannah," Amanda said. "The whole thing's kind of strange and all, but we get along great. Anyway, Dad's now talking about having a double wedding. Don't you think that's weird?"

"How does Joe feel about it?" I queried.

"He doesn't care, because he thinks my dad's cool, and he likes Hannah, too. Unfortunately, he's not sure his mom will be able to come because she fell off the wagon again."

"Oh, no! She was doing so well, even helping out at the homeless shelter."

Joe's dad left his family years ago, and Joe's mother struggled with an alcohol addiction throughout Joe's life. Had it not been for the intervention of Father Jim, the priest who ran the soup kitchen and homeless shelter in the city, Joe would never have been able to go to culinary school, or get his life together.

Amanda put the carrots, onions, and celery into the pot and began peeling the potatoes, then turned to me as she said, "Father Jim got her into a program, and we hope she'll be better by spring, but you just don't know. Anyway, I have to give Dad an answer soon, so what do you think?"

Amanda's question made me pause since we'd learned just a little more than a year ago that Amanda's dad was Charlie's son. After Charlie's first wife died in a car accident, Charlie had put his son up for adoption because he didn't have the resources to care for him. If Steve hadn't brought Amanda to the monastery poustinia to distance her from dysfunctional friends, we might never have discovered the relationship between Charlie and Steve.

Finally, I said, "Your wedding day's very special. Your dad will be there no matter what, and your mom will be with you in spirit. Even though you still grieve for your mother, your father has found that he can finally open his heart to another woman, to Hannah. Ultimately, only you can decide the answer to your question."

"It's just too weird," Amanda replied.

"Not really," I stated. "Your dad will symbolically give you away as the bride, so if you decided to have a double wedding, you could have some type of similar custom where you give him away."

"I hadn't thought about that," Amanda said. "It could be kind of cool, so I'll ask Joe what he thinks. Would you like a cup of tea?"

"Sure," I nodded as I put the peeled potatoes in the pot, "and I have some cookies in the cabinet. Did you tell any of the Sisters that you intended to come over here?"

Amanda shook her head. "I didn't think about it. I mean, it's not like they're going to go looking for me."

"They might. Give them a call, then you can help me with the grant application I'm writing. I'm trying to get funding for educational programs at *Rock Creek Farm*."

Last summer, Sister Cathy and I had discovered a hidden passage in the basement of the monastery. She wanted to learn more about the wealthy couple who bequeathed their estate to the Sisters, and I, just plain curious, enjoyed solving puzzles. Our sleuthing resulted in an amazing find.

Jonas Willard Smithfield and his wife, Hildegarde, well respected citizens in the highest echelons of society during the 1920's, purchased their country estate and built a mansion. Surprisingly, Cathy and I discovered that JW, as we called him, actually ran a bootleg operation during the time of Prohibition. Finding the vintage still put the monastery on the National Historic Register, which triggered the Sisters' decision to set up a non-profit organization to oversee it, and they asked me to serve as the executive director.

I put a lid on the stew, and brought our mugs of tea to the kitchen table. Amanda, chatting with Sister Cheryl, put her on speaker mode. Once she brought me into the conversation, I asked, "How are you faring with the storm?"

"We're fine here," she said, "but we're concerned about our neighbors, the Holtzes. The power went out for much of the county, and I don't think they have a generator."

"Did you try reaching them by phone?" I queried.

"There's no answer," Cheryl replied. "Maybe they went to stay with one of their kids, but I doubt it because Joe told us the roads are terrible."

"Do you think Charlie might be able to drive over there with the plow?" I questioned.

"That's what we were thinking. Can you get hold of him?"

"Yes," I replied. "He has his cell phone, so I'll ask him to go check on them."

"Tell Charlie that they can stay in the B&B tonight, and as long as needed. Cable and internet are out, but at least we have lights and heat."

"That's a good idea," I said. "Leon and Joc will come here tonight and, probably Amanda, too."

"If GP brings the Holtzes to the B&B," Amanda added, "Joe and I can stay with them. It's kind of eerie to be in that wing by yourself."

"That would be great," Cheryl replied. "You might need to cook dinner for them."

"We have a big pot of stew on the stove," I said. "I'll have Charlie bring them here for supper, then he can take them to the monastery. We'll keep you posted with whatever they decide."

CHAPTER 3

usk had descended by the time Charlie, Joe, and Leon arrived with Mr. and Mrs. Holtz. I'd met the Holtzes last year when we helped them harvest their apple orchards, though I didn't know them well, but remembered them as friendly, kindly neighbors, somewhat older than Charlie and I, perhaps in their early-70's. While removing their boots and hanging their jackets on the hooks by the back door, they introduced themselves as Gunther and Pauline, and thanked us for our hospitality.

"You must be frozen," I said. "Let's go sit by the fireplace in the living room so you can all warm up."

"We don't want to impose," Pauline replied. "We accepted the Sisters' invitation since we can pay for our accommodations at the B&B, but Charlie insisted that we come here first."

"It's not an imposition at all," I noted. "We have dinner already prepared, and I just added a few more potatoes to the pot. Besides, you're saving Amanda from having to go home and cook another meal."

"That's very kind of you," Pauline said. "I made a loaf of bread this morning. Gunther, did you bring the bread?"

"Yes, it's under the tarp in the truck. I'll get it after I warm up a bit."

"Awesome," Amanda grinned. "That will go great with our stew. I'll set the table and make a salad."

Pauline looked around, admiring everything she saw. "Your home is lovely. It's hard to believe it was prefabricated. Gunther and I watched those big trucks come down the road with sections of the house. Didn't we say we couldn't imagine how it would hold up, Gunther?"

"That we did," he nodded.

"Well, you'd never know it now," Pauline stated. "It looks sturdier than our place. Of course, we live in Gunther's old family homestead. His grandfather built the house in the early 1920's."

"That's about the time that the Smithfields built the mansion the Sisters live in," I said.

"Just after," Pauline noted. "Did you know that Gunther's grandmother was a servant at the mansion? I told Gunther that we needed to stay in the B&B so we'd get a better sense of his family history, and this storm gave us the perfect opportunity."

"That's amazing," I replied. "I've tried to research everything I can find to learn more about JW Smithfield and his wife, Hildegarde. Did you know that he had a secret passageway in the basement of the mansion? Apparently, Mr. Smithfield was a bootlegger."

"I don't know anything about the husband, but Gunther's grandmother and Hildegarde were close friends, which is how Gunther's grandfather obtained the land for the orchard. Fact is, I think the Smithfields gave them 35 acres of their estate. Isn't that right, Gunther?"

Gunther nodded. "Yep, I think so."

"Of course, we don't own that much land now," Pauline said. "Over the years, Gunther's parents sold off some of it, and the county took some to build the road. Eminent domain, they called it, which I consider a bunch of baloney, if you ask me."

Although Pauline rambled, she'd caught my attention. I wanted to learn more about Gunther's grandmother and her relationship with

Hildegarde, so I asked, "What was your grandmother's name, Gunther?"

"Adele. We named our oldest daughter after her."

"How nice," I smiled. "Can you tell me more about Adele and Hildegarde? It might give me a better understanding of the early days of the monastery."

"I know they were both from Germany and about the same age," Pauline said. "Funny you should ask about them, because just this morning, I told Gunther that this would be a perfect day to start cleaning out the attic. In fact, that's where we were when the Sisters called us, knee deep in dust, and couldn't get to the phone, though we went downstairs when the power went off. Anyway, I found a lovely wooden box. Guess what was in it."

"I don't know," I replied. "Adele's wedding gown?"

"No, I think it might be Hildegarde's diary."

"Oh, my!" I exclaimed. "Do you think I could see it sometime?"

"You're in luck," Pauline smiled. "We brought it with us so we could show the Sisters. You put it in the truck, didn't you, Gunther?"

"That I did," Gunther nodded.

"Please go get it, Gunther," Pauline said, "and bring in the bread while you're at it."

Charlie offered to assist, so he and Gunther went to the kitchen to put on their boots. While they donned their jackets, Amanda announced that she had dinner ready. "We'll be right back," Charlie said, "so save some for us."

I ushered everyone around the table. Amanda managed to make room for all seven of us by bringing in three folding chairs from the den. When the men returned, Charlie handed the bread to Amanda to slice, while Gunther gently placed the box on the floor near the row of boots.

Amanda brought two large bowls of steaming stew to the center of the table, along with the crusty bread and salad. Once everyone took their seats and we said grace, I invited everyone to serve themselves. "Did you notice any sign of the storm letting up?" I asked Charlie.

"I listened to the weather report on the truck's radio when we went to pick up the Holtzes," he said. "We'll still get a few more inches tonight, but it should end by mid-morning."

"You must be exhausted after working out there all day," I noted, reaching for the butter.

Charlie agreed that the three of them admitted to feeling tired since they'd tried to keep the paths to the poustinias and the main drive of the monastery cleared. "They're not great," he noted, "but they're passable."

"We had a good routine because we all shoveled, then we'd warm up in the truck while we plowed," Joe explained.

"Charlie wasn't supposed to do any shoveling," I sighed.

"I had to do my part," Charlie shrugged. "Besides, use it or lose it, I say. I even caught some of the football playoffs on the truck's radio. At least, Leon and Joe can now get to their cabins."

"Not tonight, they won't," I said firmly. "Leon, you can stay in our guest room, though Amanda has plans for Joe."

"Right," Amanda said. "Joe, we'll go to the B&B with the Holtzes, and serve them breakfast in the morning."

Joe had no problem with Amanda's arrangements. In fact, he offered to drive Amanda and the Holtzes to the monastery in the truck, then pick up Charlie and Leon in the morning. "I'm sure Jake will have to close the diner again tomorrow, and I thought that neighbors might need help plowing."

"I'd help," Gunther said, "but my son borrowed our plow. We would've gone to their house, but they lost power, too. Besides, Pauline's been itching to stay at the B&B, and she says she wants a romantic evening, whatever that means."

"It means just the two of us, without having to play with the grandkids," Pauline said. "This man can drive you crazy," she murmured to me.

"I understand completely," I chuckled. When we finished eating, I began to clear the table, saying, "We have apple pie for dessert. It's not homemade, but it's one of Charlie's favorites. Would anyone also want a cup of hot tea?"

Amanda poured the tea, while I cut and distributed the pie. "How long did it take to put the house together?" Pauline asked. I supposed she'd never seen a modular home.

"Surprisingly, less than two months," I replied. "Charlie stayed in it a couple of days a week once they put on the roof and installed the doors and windows. Of course, they hadn't finished the plumbing and electric but, at least, he could oversee the interior work."

"I wouldn't have thought they'd let you do that," Gunther said, raising an eyebrow.

"We had an agreement to take early ownership," I stated, "because Charlie had to supervise the volunteers helping to fence the fields. He and Leon also began repairing the Smithfield's machine barn across the drive."

"I noticed that when we arrived," Gunther stated, "though I never saw it before."

"It was part of the original Smithfield estate," I explained, "but the woods covered it, so Leon and some other volunteers worked to clear out the underbrush and some of the trees."

"Where are you getting all of these volunteers?" Gunther asked.

"Father Jim, the priest who often visits the monastery, encouraged some people to help Leon and Charlie," I said. "He runs a soup kitchen and homeless shelter in the city."

"So, when did you actually move in?" Pauline asked.

"Right before Thanksgiving," I replied. "I'd hoped that we could start giving tours this fall, but didn't anticipate the amount of work it would take. Now, we think we'll be ready by spring."

"What kind of tours?" Pauline questioned.

"Mr. Smithfield made liquor in that old machine barn during the years of Prohibition," I explained, "and there's a tunnel that connects the barn to the basement in the monastery." Pauline and Gunther looked fascinated.

"Once we get everything fixed up," Charlie noted, "We'll offer historical tours about bootlegging, then show folks the vintage bowling alley under the Sisters' living quarters."

"Oh, my goodness," Pauline said. "Who'd have thought? Will you be in charge of this for the nuns?"

"Yes," I replied. "They hired me to be the director. We also hope to have a working farm, with educational programs for children and adults. It's all a little overwhelming, but I'm excited to get started. Actually, I planned to work on a grant today but, once the internet went down, I couldn't retrieve the documents I needed."

"Further reason for us to continue cleaning out our attic, Gunther," Pauline stated emphatically. "We probably have more stuff up there from Hildegarde to Adele, so the Munleys might be able to use it somehow on the tours."

"That would be marvelous," I exclaimed, "because there's hardly anything left of the Smithfields in the mansion. We think that the early Sisters must have tossed it all."

"We'll do what we can to help," Pauline said. "Won't we, Gunther?"

Gunther nodded his agreement. "Sure will. We share a lot of history with this place."

On that note, I told Amanda that I'd clean up if she and Joe wanted to take the Holtzes to the B&B. As they donned their boots, Pauline thanked me for the delicious dinner, and I complimented her on her tasty bread. "I'm glad we brought it," she said. "No use leaving it to get stale on the kitchen counter."

"What about your box?" I asked.

"We might as well keep it here," Pauline said. "You didn't get a chance to look at the diary, and I'm sure the Sisters wouldn't read it tonight."

"Probably not," I agreed. "If you'd like, I can call and ask them if I can read it."

"I don't see why you'd need to bother them at this hour," Pauline replied. "Besides, they put you in charge, so we'll just tell them about it in the morning."

"Let's get going, folks," Amanda urged. "Your romantic evening is dwindling away." We all laughed as the four of them trudged their way through the deep snow to the truck.

CHAPTER 4

*L*eon gave Harvey his bowl of kibbles, then took him out after he ate, while I cleaned the table and put away the few leftovers. Charlie loaded the dishwasher and washed the big pot, leaving it to drain in the sink. By the time Leon returned with Harvey, we had the kitchen in good shape. "Did Harvey do his business?" I asked as Leon hung his jacket on the hook by the back door.

Leon laughed. "It took him a while to find the right spot because some of the drifts are over his head."

"I don't think Harvey would've ventured out if you hadn't taken him," I said. "Thank you."

"You're a wimp, Harvey-boy," Charlie teased, "though I don't blame you." Harvey wagged his tail and stood by the pantry until Charlie gave him a treat.

"Sorry to say there's no TV tonight," I noted. "Internet's out."

"That's OK by me," Leon said. "I'm bushed. Do you mind if I hit the sack?"

"Not at all. Let me get you a towel and washcloth, and I think we have an extra toothbrush in the bathroom cabinet."

After I helped Leon get settled in the guest room, I returned to the kitchen to see that Charlie had moved the box with Hildegarde's diary to the table. I figured he knew I'd want to take a look at it this evening, and I suggested that he join me, but Charlie, too, decided to make it an early night. Before he went to the bedroom, I remarked, "I'm glad you brought the Holtzes over to our place. I enjoyed getting to know them better."

"They're good people," Charlie said. "Gunther hangs out at the firehouse every so often. He told me he needs to get away sometimes, and I can't say that I blame him."

"I know what you mean," I chuckled. "Pauline does like to talk. In fact, I thought she might make a great tour guide. She's interested in history, and I'll bet she could tell a good story. She certainly knows how to take charge."

"God help us," Charlie grinned. "I'll leave that decision in your hands since you're pretty good at finding the right person for the job."

Charlie's expression made me laugh. "I'll think about it a little more. In the meantime, you can sleep on it."

"Don't stay up too late," Charlie said, giving me a kiss.

"I'll be in shortly. Sweet dreams!"

I RAN my fingers along the top and sides of the ornate wooden box as I admired its beautiful craftsmanship. Most likely some type of jewelry box from Germany, I thought Hildegarde might have brought it with her when she immigrated to the United States. I lifted the simple latch on the front, and put the diary on the table.

The cover, still intact, looked sturdy, but well-used, and the first page had bold script to identify the book as the *Diary of Hildegarde Smithfield*. As I flipped through it, I noticed that Hildegarde had written the first 20 pages or so in German, with dates from 1915 to 1916, so I needed to ask Gunther if he'd translate those for me.

Beginning in 1917, Hildegarde wrote in English. I knew that she and JW married in 1913, and figured that she'd gained confidence to speak and write in her new second language. The diary may have given her a way to practice writing skills since she had very few spelling or grammar errors.

January 10, 1917
I received a package in the mail today from dear Mama and Papa. I miss them so much. They sent our long-awaited Christmas gifts, perhaps traveling by slow boat. I hope that our presents to my family arrived in time to be placed by their Yule log. Jonas said he posted them well before the Advent season. I can imagine Mama's Tannenbaum, beautifully decorated with apples, and nuts, and fine glass ornaments. Oh, how different it is in America. We had no tree for Christmas, though der Weihnachtsmann still arrived. I will continue to show Jonas my traditions. Some day he will understand. He promises to buy land so that we can build a house in the countryside. We will have plenty of fir trees and we can plant grapes for a vineyard, then it will seem more like home.

January 12, 1917
Jonas returned from his business trip last evening, and we opened our gifts from Mama and Papa. It was wonderful to receive the box of hand-painted ornaments created by our town's master craftsman, and I will save them for our country home. Mama knitted a lovely scarf and hat for Jonas, but I do not think he liked them. For me, she made a pretty apron with embroidered flowers. Jonas laughed and said that I should give it to one of our servants. That made me angry, and I told him that it was very special to me. Even though Mama and Papa are wealthy, they do not forget the things that are important. I hope that Greta loves the doll. These are the things that have meaning.

I wondered if Hildegarde had a younger sister named Greta, and scrolled through the earlier section of the diary written in German to see several references of her. I needed to learn more about Greta, as well as the meaning of *der Weihnachtsmann*. I supposed that Tannenbaum meant a Christmas tree, given its context in the passage, but I'd have to wait until we had our internet connection restored, or ask Gunther in the morning.

February 8, 1917

Nearly a month has gone by since I last wrote in my diary. We have had a cold winter with many ice storms, so it is very dreary. Perhaps I am lonely because Jonas has many trips for business. I should be proud of him, but I get tearful instead. I am sad so much. Last night we had a dinner party for two of Jonas' friends and their wives. The women were very rude, complaining about everything from the arrangement of our table to the way our servants treated them. Jonas said we will replace the domestics. I think that is not what we should do. Jonas told me that I should be kind to the wives of his friends because they can teach me how to behave in society, but I don't want to act like them.

February 15, 1917

Jonas departed this morning for another business trip, and he will be gone a month. I don't know if I am happy or sad, but mostly I am sad because we had many disagreements this week, and he was not very loving. Even Greta does not take to him when he is so angry. Perhaps I am the cause. I don't want to do the things he tells me to do, so I cry and I argue. I should be a better wife. That is what Mama would tell me. I wish I could talk to her, but she is so far away.

March 2, 1917

I finally received a letter from Mama, though I do not understand why it takes so very long to arrive. It must be due to the dreadful war in Germany. I know Mama is worried about Friedrich, but my brother is very strong. He will survive even though he was drafted into the Army. As children, he protected me, and he will now protect my family. Just like Friedrich, Jonas is older than I am. Maybe that is why I fell in love with Jonas. I thought he would take care of me, but he is never home.

March 23, 1917

At last, Jonas has returned home, and I am trying to be a dutiful wife. Perhaps my spirit will improve when spring arrives, but it is still chilly and bleak. Jonas told me that there is more talk about war for America. Many are upset because a German submarine torpedoed an American steamer trav-

eling through a safe zone near Holland, and more than 20 innocent crew
members lost their lives. I don't understand why there is hatred and conflict
in this world. Can people not live together in peace?

I read Hildegarde's diary through to April of 1917, until my eyelids had a weight of their own. I learned that JW often went away on business, and left Hildegarde alone in a city unfamiliar to her. Unhappy in this new environment, she yearned to return home to Germany. I felt certain that she worried about her family, especially her older brother who had to go to war. With those thoughts, I closed the diary and put it back in its box.

I tried to entice Harvey to go outside one more time, but he didn't budge from his favorite spot under the kitchen table. I turned out the lights and went to bed, thinking all the while about Hildegarde. I could only imagine how I'd have felt at that age to be uprooted from my home, and often left alone to fend for myself.

Hildegarde, probably not much older than Amanda when she married JW and came to the United States, had little or no say in the household decisions. It made me think that we'd see sparks flying if Joe ever spoke to Amanda as JW seemed to speak to Hildegarde.

Somehow, Hildegarde would have to find the courage to become a woman of strength and conviction.

CHAPTER 5

I awoke to the raucous sound of a snow shovel scraping the pavement. The day had barely dawned, and I had no interest in greeting it so early since I preferred to stay snuggled under the covers with Charlie. He opened his eyes, and I moved into his embrace. "Leon's probably up and about already," Charlie murmured groggily.

"It seems so," I said, "but I need another hour's sleep."

"Me, too," Charlie agreed.

We both dozed until the shoveling sounds woke us again, and I reminded Charlie that we should show more hospitality to our guest. I took a quick shower, while Charlie dressed and went to make the coffee, and by the time I finished dressing and made it to the kitchen, Charlie called Leon to come in and get warm.

Apparently, Leon had taken Harvey out with him, and they both shivered when they returned to the warmth of the kitchen. I fed Harvey, while Charlie poured the coffee, then the three of us sat with our steaming mugs at the table. The view from our picture window captured a beautiful scene of winter's glory with snow still falling lightly and the western sky beginning to brighten.

"Don't try opening your front door," Leon grinned. "The snow drift is up to your shoulders."

"That's another reason we need a front porch," I said. "We should make that our first addition in the spring."

"You need a garage, too," Leon advised. "Your car is under a huge mound of snow, and you won't get that out for a few days."

"A garage is another priority," Charlie agreed. "I figured we'd get through this winter first, but never expected a storm like this. It's one for the records."

I told the guys that I didn't plan to go anywhere, though I could try to unearth my car while they continued their plowing. "We'll get to it later," Charlie stated. "I thought you might want to go over to the monastery to help Amanda entertain the Holtzes, since their home probably still doesn't have power, so they could end up having to stay at the B&B for a few days."

"Surely it won't take that long to dig out from the storm," I commented.

"Yes, it will," Charlie replied. "We had almost three feet of snow, and there might even be some trees down with the wind we had. They'll get the city up and running first, then work on the towns. Lone houses in the rural areas will be last. That's why I considered it so important to get our generator working."

"I guess the internet's not up yet either," I noted. "Isn't it amazing that we don't know what to do when there's no wi-fi or electricity? I'd intended to continue reading Hildegarde's diary, but I can take it over to the monastery. Besides, I need Gunther to translate the first section."

"I thought you'd stay up all night reading it," Charlie said. "How far did you get?"

"Only a couple of months into 1917." I told Charlie and Leon about my first impressions of Hildegarde as a young and inexperienced woman when she began her diary. "She sure didn't seem very comfortable in her role among the wealthy trend-setters in the higher echelons of American society."

"Didn't she come from money?" Charlie asked.

"From what I've learned, Hildegarde's parents operated a

successful vineyard and winery but, in the diary, she said they stayed true to their heritage. I guess she meant that they didn't wield their power over others."

"So, JW's acting high and mighty?" Leon queried.

"That's what I think," I replied. "I hope Hildegarde doesn't turn out to be a wimp."

"I can't imagine that," Charlie said. "You found references at the historical society that she did a lot of entertaining at the mansion, even hosting the First Lady. I think you need to keep reading."

"I suppose so," I agreed, "but her whining is annoying. I did learn that she had an older brother named Friedrich who was drafted into the war in Germany. I'd also like to know more about Greta because Hildegarde mentioned her several times."

"Maybe a servant?" Charlie questioned.

"I don't think so. Perhaps a younger sister. Greta's name also showed up in the German section of the diary. I'm hoping that Gunther can shed some light on the mystery girl, and some of the other words I didn't understand."

When he finished his coffee, Leon said he wanted to make progress shoveling the drift at the front door. Charlie offered to help, and I told them I'd work on breakfast. By the time they returned, we enjoyed pancakes and sausages, and a fresh round of hot coffee until Joe arrived.

"Amanda wants you to come over to the monastery today," Joe said, "and the Holtzes want you to bring the box with the diary."

"I'm already planning on it," I replied. "Did Gunther and Pauline enjoy their evening at the B&B?"

"I guess so," Joe nodded. "They're going to stay another night. Are you guys ready to go?"

I FOUND the Holtzes chatting with Sister Marian and Sister Cathy in the parlor when I arrived. I gave the wooden box to Pauline, then took off my parka and boots as I remarked, "Good morning, everyone. The storm is finally beginning to wane. I hope you all had a warm and cozy night."

"I slept like a log," Pauline giggled. "In fact, I told Gunther this morning that we need to get a comforter like the one on the bed in our room. It's marvelous. Wherever did you find it?"

"I think Amanda bought it at the outlet mall," Cathy said.

"We need to buy one of those, Gunther," Pauline stated with an emphatic nod of her head.

"Ours is fine," Gunther said. "You've never had a problem with it before."

"That old quilt? It doesn't even compare. We'll get one of these as soon as they've cleared the roads." Gunther probably knew better than to respond.

"I'm glad you brought the box," Pauline stated, "because I just told the Sisters about it. Did you have a chance to finish the diary last night?"

"I only read a little of what Hildegarde wrote in English, and I hope Gunther can translate the first section, written in German."

"My German's a little rusty," Gunther said. "I don't know if I can remember much."

"Sure, you can, Gunther," Pauline argued. "You taught the kids German when they were little."

"It's been a long time, but I'll take a stab at it," he replied.

Pauline removed Hildegarde's diary from the box, then handed it to Sister Marian. Marian flipped through it, with Cathy looking over her shoulder. "This is amazing," Sister Cathy said. "Tell us what you've learned so far."

I mentioned that I hadn't progressed very far the previous evening since we'd all made it an early night. Then, I reiterated what I had told Charlie and Leon at breakfast about the words I didn't understand. I showed them the quotations about Tannenbaum, Greta, and *der Weihnachtsmann,* and asked Gunther to explain their meaning.

"Tannenbaum is easy," Gunther said. "It's the Christmas tree. You've probably sung the familiar carol at some point in your life."

We all nodded while the tune popped into our heads. Gunther

continued, "Literally translated, *der Weihnachtsmann*, is the Christmas man. Here we call him Santa Claus."

"OK. Now I get the gist," I said. "Hildegarde wrote that *der Weihnachtsmann* had come to their home at Christmas."

"In my family," Gunther noted, "we celebrated *Christkind* who would bring the Christmas gifts. Other regions of Germany have a similar tradition, but *der Weihnachtsmann* delivers the presents."

"How interesting," I said. "So, I guess the Smithfields celebrated Christmas with a visit from Santa Claus. That seems strange for an adult couple, but not unlikely since Hildegarde wrote that she wanted to teach JW about her family's customs."

Sister Cathy found the reference in the diary. "It also says here that Greta got a doll. As far as we know, the Smithfields had no children."

"Exactly," I nodded, "so I wondered if she had a younger sister, and the Smithfields sent her a doll for Christmas, but then I learned that Hildegarde had only an older brother named Friedrich, who was drafted into the war."

Cathy handed the diary to Gunther and said, "See if you can tell us about Greta."

Gunther began to read silently. When he stumbled across anything of interest in his translation, he would mention it out loud. "It says here that they bought a suitable brownstone home in the city during the early part of 1914. They have a kitchen servant and a butler."

"Does Hildegarde seem lonely?" I asked.

"No," Gunther replied. "She speaks often of being in love. She says that Jonas is very kind to her, but she wanted to learn English because she couldn't communicate with the staff."

Gunther skipped ahead to 1915. "Jonas hired a tutor for Hildegarde, and she had English lessons every afternoon. Ah, you are going to be very surprised. Hildegarde is pregnant."

"Oh, my gosh," Cathy said. "Sister Tony told us they had no children."

"Here it says that the child is a girl," Gunther said. "Her name is

Greta, and she was born on November 19, 1915."

"So, Hildegarde's parents sent the doll for little Greta," I noted, "and that's why Santa brought the Christmas gifts. It all makes sense now."

"Not entirely," Marian replied. "I'm pretty sure that the Smith-fields didn't have a child when they built this mansion. Is there any reference to Greta in 1916?"

Gunther continued reading before saying, "Yes, there's a nanny for Greta. Hildegarde wanted to travel with Jonas on his business trips, but she's not permitted because of the baby, so she's not happy about it. She also mentioned that she'll now write in English, as she no longer needs the tutor."

"You'll have to continue with it, Vicki," Cathy said, "so you can tell us more about Greta."

I thought that the Sisters might want to keep the diary at the monastery, but Sister Marian suggested that I should read it first since it could give me some ideas for grants or tours. Pauline agreed, saying, "I don't need the diary back, but I'd like you to tell me anything of interest that pertained to Adele, Gunther's grandmother."

"She was a servant here at the mansion?" Marian asked.

"Yes," Pauline replied. "I'd hoped that you might show us the servants' quarters during our visit. Isn't that right, Gunther?"

"We can show you right now," Marian said. "In fact, Sister Dolores and Sister Julie are in the community room. Perhaps they'll join us because they slept in the servants' quarters as postulants, so they can tell you much more than Cathy and I can. You're welcome to come along, Vicki."

I told the Sisters that I'd take a rain check since I wanted to ask Amanda if she needed any help in the kitchen, especially since Charlie, Leon, and Joe had planned to join us for lunch.

"Sister Cheryl's lending a hand, as well, since we may have more guests," Marian remarked. "I told Charlie to invite anyone from town who might need a hot meal or a place to get warm."

The Sisters' generosity didn't surprise me, because I knew they always thought of others first.

CHAPTER 6

$\mathcal{I}$ found Amanda and Sister Cheryl working on a garden salad when I met them in the kitchen, and noticed that they'd prepared three large pans of lasagna, which they'd placed on a counter. After greeting them, I explained that Marian took the Holtzes for a tour of the old servants' quarters on the third floor, and they'd all join us shortly. "Why so much food?" I asked, looking around.

"We need to feed the home guard and the Sisters in the infirmary, as well as any guests who arrive," Sister Cheryl said. "Luckily, Amanda had all of the ingredients on hand. We also have two chuck roasts and a ham baking in the ovens. Those should last us through dinner service, and maybe even provide enough leftovers for sandwiches tomorrow."

We set up the buffet table, and Amanda lit the chafing fuel to keep the lasagna warm. Cheryl prepared the trays for the infirmary, then delivered the cart. By the time she returned, Charlie, Joe, and Leon had come to the dining room. Apparently, they'd presented the nuns' message, because Joe said, "I think a number of people who were plowing will stop by for lunch."

"That's good," Amanda grinned. "Maybe we can make some money, after all."

Sister Cheryl disagreed. "We can't charge for lunch today because people haven't had a hot meal in the past 24 hours. I do want to let them know that they can stay here with their families until their homes have electricity."

"You won't be bored, that's for sure," I told Amanda.

"How can I entertain all of those people?" Amanda asked. She didn't look very happy about the Sisters' decision.

"We'll all do it together," Cheryl replied in a gentle tone. "Now, let's get people seated so they can start eating."

Charlie and I ate with Leon and one of his buddies from the fire-house. Although they'd filled their plates, I noticed that Charlie didn't have much of an appetite. "Have you made any progress with the plowing?" I asked.

"Yes," Charlie nodded. "We focused on the parking lots for all of the businesses in town, so they can open once the power comes on." I knew the importance of that, since small business owners often lived hand-to-mouth. Every day that they had to remain closed meant less income for their livelihood.

"County plows tackled the main roads," Leon added. "Once the residents shoveled out, they worked with us or went to help elderly neighbors."

Charlie sneezed several times in response. "What's that all about?" I asked.

"I think I'm getting a cold," Charlie muttered.

"Yeah, he's been hacking in the truck all morning," Leon said. "Joe and I wanted to take him home, but the stubborn old coot wouldn't listen."

"I'm not leaving you guys with all of the work," Charlie stated, shaking his head.

"You might be contagious," I argued. "Do you want the whole work crew to come down with what you have?"

"Of course not, but I'm not sick. I just have a tickle."

In the end, we convinced Charlie that he and I should go home. I suggested that he might want to retrieve some of his birdhouse equipment from the nuns' basement in case he became bored. Charlie liked building birdhouses in his spare time, and he'd stored numerous cartons of his craft materials when he went to St. Louis. With all that we needed to do to get settled, he hadn't yet brought his supplies to our place.

"I don't have a workshop yet," Charlie said with another sneeze.

"What's wrong with the den?" I asked.

"I didn't think you'd want me to mess it up." He changed his tune when he saw my reaction. "Yeah, that'll work," he said.

When we finished eating, the men went to the basement to retrieve some of Charlie's items, and I went to Amanda's table to explain that Charlie didn't feel well. "I think we need to go home," I stated.

"Traitor," Amanda grumbled.

"Is he OK?" Sister Cheryl asked.

"He's coming down with a cold or something," I said, "but I don't want others to catch it. He's getting some of his birdhouse things from the basement, and that might keep him occupied, because he's sure grumpy about not being involved in the snow cleanup."

"It's better to nip it in the bud," Cheryl said.

"That's what I think," I agreed.

I told Amanda to call me later if she wanted to talk, then gave my farewells to the Holtzes and the other Sisters. "You should take the diary with you," Pauline suggested.

"Thank you. I'll let you know what I learn about Adele."

LEON HELPED Charlie carry in the couple of cartons he'd brought home, and they piled them in the den. I put the box with the diary on the kitchen table, then let Harvey out for a pit stop. Before Leon returned to plowing, I invited him to stay the night again. He thanked me, but preferred to go to his cabin regardless of when the power came on. We could hear Charlie coughing, so I figured Leon wanted to avoid the germs, and I knew he liked his privacy.

Charlie, going through his boxes when I went to check on him in the den, had set up the card table, and had begun laying out pieces of wood already cut to size. I felt his forehead and cheeks, then said, "I think you have a fever. Would you like me to make you a hot toddy?"

"I guess so. I have to admit that I don't feel too good."

I put on the kettle to boil some water, made a cup of hot tea for each of us, then added honey, cinnamon, and whiskey to Charlie's mug. Charlie, resting in the recliner, took a sip of my brew, and asked, "Are you trying to put me under?" Apparently, I'd made a rather strong concoction.

"Maybe I put in too much whiskey," I chuckled. "Think of it as JW's moonshine."

"Very funny. I see you didn't make any for yourself."

"I might have some later since I don't want to catch what you have, but I want a clear head this afternoon. I'll bring the diary in here and read it while you take a snooze."

"I'd like that," Charlie mumbled. "He took another swig when he began to cough again.

"You don't have just a cold," I said. "A cold with a fever is the flu."

"It came on me really fast," Charlie replied.

"I know," I nodded. "Unfortunately, you'll have to just ride it out, at least for now." By the time I returned to the den with my tea and the diary, Charlie had already fallen asleep in the chair, so I began to read Hildegarde's entries from where I had left off the night before.

April 16, 1917

Jonas has been home for nearly a month, and I have tried to show him that I am a good wife. He is happy that his steel factories are making a profit since the railroads are converting iron to steel, and Jonas says that we will be very rich. I don't care about the money because I want that we have a happy family. When I told Jonas about Friedrich in the war, he said that Germany is not doing well, and that I should worry about Friedrich's safety. I do not

want to think about that. Friedrich is my only brother, and I have no other
siblings, so I will pray that he is safe.

May 1, 1917
Jonas has dismissed our servants because he was very angry that Helen let
me help in the kitchen. I like to cook, and I found solace when making dishes
from recipes my mother taught me. Jonas says that I must act like the women
in society. He hired a new cook and a new manservant, but the nanny may
stay as Greta likes her. I do not like Anna, the new cook, since she does not
permit me to enter the kitchen. How can I be a good wife when I am upset so
often?

June 8, 1917
I am happy that Jonas left for his business trip. Sometimes I wonder if he
sleeps with another woman. Is it possible that it is always his work that takes
him away? I know that he loves Greta very much, because he spends time
with her as much as he can when he is at home. I can see that Greta loves
him so much more than she loves me. Of course, I am the one who must
punish her if she is naughty. Jonas brings her gifts from his travels, but he
says I will have none until I behave as a woman in society.

I wanted to shake Hildegarde for acting like a spoiled child, and
tried to put myself in her shoes, though I couldn't understand the
difficulty of adjusting to a wealthy lifestyle. In my mind, JW didn't
help matters, especially if he had an affair, but Hildegarde hadn't done
anything to lift herself out of the sadness she felt. On the other hand, I
wondered if Hildegarde could have experienced an actual clinical
depression, since her melancholy seemed to coincide with the birth of
their child. Perhaps she had postpartum depression, a condition
rarely recognized or discussed until more recent years.

Charlie's cough started again, and he felt quite feverish. I gave him
some Tylenol, then led him to our bed so I could cover him with
blankets. He moaned when I placed a cool washcloth to his head and
neck. It didn't seem to break his fever, but he fell back into a deep
sleep.

I brought the diary into the kitchen, and made a fresh cup of tea. As I settled myself at the table, Amanda called to say that power had returned for people in town, but not the rural areas, and she hoped they, too, could soon go home. "How's GP doing?" she asked.

"He's pretty sick," I replied. "His fever spiked a little while ago."

"It's weird," Amanda said, "because he seemed fine yesterday."

"I know. He felt tired this morning, but I just figured all of the shoveling caused that. Now, I think he has the flu."

"Do you need anything?" Amanda questioned.

"No, we'll finish up the chicken noodle soup later, since I'll let him sleep for a while. Do you have a crowd there?"

"We did," Amanda replied, "but most went home a little while ago. After lunch, the nuns invited everyone to their community room where they put in a DVD and we watched a movie, so we had fun."

"That was nice," I said. "Are the Holtzes still there?"

"Yeah, they're going to stay another night. Joe's staying in the B&B again, but I think Leon's going to his cabin because he doesn't want to catch whatever GP has."

"Couldn't he stay at the B&B?" I asked.

"Sister Marian invited him, but he wants to go back to his place, so she gave him a couple of blankets."

"I suppose he just needs some alone time," I noted. "He'll be fine."

"Do you want me to have Joe bring me over after supper?" Amanda questioned. "I can help you."

"No, thanks. I don't want you to catch whatever it is that GP has. I'll continue reading Hildegarde's diary, then go to bed early."

"OK," Amanda sighed, "but call me if you need anything."

CHAPTER 7

I slept on the futon in the den so I could hear Charlie if he awoke during the night. I gave him two extra strength Tylenol around midnight, and that seemed to bring down his fever a bit. Except for his coughing, he had slept fairly well, though I heard him puttering around the kitchen after I finally roused the next morning. "What are you doing up and about?" I asked when I went to check on him. He had on his robe and slippers, which indicated to me that he still felt sick.

"I'm just going to make the coffee," Charlie said.

"I can do that. Have a seat, and I'll get you some orange juice." While the coffee brewed, I poured his juice, then handed him a vitamin and two more Tylenol. As I made myself a cup of tea, I asked, "How are you feeling?"

"Lousy, but better than yesterday."

"You shouldn't go out today," I remarked. "I could make hot Cream of Wheat for breakfast."

"Yeah, I'd like that. Did Leon stay here last night?"

"No," I replied. "He wanted to go to his own place."

"Does he have electricity yet?" Charlie questioned.

"Not that I know of. They had power in town by late afternoon, but not out here, so the Holtzes stayed another night at the B&B. Amanda called to see how you're doing. She wanted to help last night, but I told her not to come."

"Good," Charlie said. "I don't want her to catch whatever this is."

"That's what I thought," I agreed.

Charlie had another fit of coughing and I felt his forehead. "You still have a fever," I noted.

"That's probably why I'm so achy. After breakfast, I'll go back to bed for a while."

"Do you want me to call the doctor?" I asked.

"Nah, I'll be fine."

While Charlie slept, I dressed, freshened up the guest bedroom and bath, and did a load of wash. Then, I settled down with Hilde-garde's diary.

September 5, 1917

Jonas took Greta and me to the seashore for the Labor Day weekend, and it was wonderful. We had perfect weather, and the sound of the waves lifted my spirits. We could even see the ocean from our room. Each afternoon, we took Greta to the beach, and she made castles in the sand. In the evenings, all three of us walked the boardwalk, then Greta enjoyed riding the carousel. Jonas and I made love when Greta fell asleep at night. It was the first time in a long while that I felt amorous. In the mornings, Jonas and I had coffee on the veranda while Greta played with her doll, and I told him some of the things that have troubled me. He seemed to listen.

September 18, 1917

Jonas told me of a German girl who works as a servant for one of his friends. He thinks I should interview her to see if she would be a suitable addition to our staff. When I asked if it would make his friend angry, Jonas told me that he had already made arrangements, but he wanted to first know if I would like her. Adele is near to my age, and Jonas thought it would make me less homesick if I found someone who speaks my language. Jonas said that I must communicate in English first, but I may still converse in my own tongue.

The girl's name is Adele Goetz, and she is fluent in English. I will interview
her on Friday.

September 22, 1917
I interviewed Adele yesterday afternoon, and I liked her very much. Her
family sent her to the United States just before the war. She had been here
only a few months when she learned about the death of her entire family.
What sadness she has endured, yet she is happy about all that she has
achieved. I spoke to Jonas about her at supper last night, and told him that I
thought Adele would be a suitable servant, but I want more than that. I need
a friend who understands my culture and my heritage. If Jonas cannot accept
that Adele would be more than a servant, then I do not wish the transaction.
Jonas wants me to have a German friend, so Adele will begin employment
with us on October 1. I felt very amorous again last night.

Besides my relief that JW had become more attentive to Hildegarde, I noticed that she seemed to have found her voice. By telling
JW that she felt lonely and uncomfortable in her new environment,
he no longer had to guess what fueled her negative emotions.

It surprised me that Jonas understood Hildegarde's need for a
connection to her culture. Actually, I gave him credit for that because,
typically, a woman of high social standing wouldn't fraternize with
the servants. Perhaps he realized that he'd receive additional benefits
by providing more support to his wife.

I heard Charlie hacking in the bedroom, so I went to check on
him. Finding him awake, but still feverish, I brought more Tylenol,
and a cold glass of root beer, though I kicked myself for not having
any cough medicine on hand. Even if the drug store in town had
opened, snow still shrouded my car, so I needed to go outside and
start cleaning it off, not that I felt so inclined.

I sat with Charlie until he drifted into a fitful sleep, then called
Amanda to ask if Joe could drive to the drug store in town, if it had
opened, and talk to the pharmacist about what over-the-counter
medication would manage Charlie's symptoms. "I feel certain he has
the flu," I said, "so he needs something for his cough and congestion,

and something to bring down his fever. Joe can tell them to put it on my tab."

"I'll text Joe right away," Amanda replied. "Are you sure you don't need me there? I really want to help."

"I'm positive. This is a nasty bug, and I hope I don't get it, nor anyone else we came in contact with."

"That would be awful," Amanda agreed, "but can't we do anything?"

"The medications would be a big help and, honestly, if someone could dig out my car, I'd really appreciate it. I might need to take GP to the doctor tomorrow, and I want to make sure my car will start."

"We'll take care of it for you," Amanda assured me. "Don't worry about a thing."

"Thanks, Sweetie. I appreciate it."

I HAD to admit that I did feel worried. I'd certainly had the flu in my lifetime and, as a virus, I knew it had to run its course, but it had been a long time, if ever, that I had to take care of someone I loved. I also knew that the flu could have serious consequences for children and the elderly, and Charlie approached his senior years.

Joe arrived just before dark with a bag of medications from the drug store, as well as a couple of ham-on-rye sandwiches and a large bottle of ginger ale from Amanda. "Did you talk to the pharmacist?" I asked.

"Yep," Joe nodded. "He told me you did the right thing with the Tylenol, so he sent more of that, and picked out some cough medicine and chest rub to break up the congestion. He said if Charlie's not better in the morning, you should bring him to the doctor."

"That's what I thought," I nodded, "because he has a really deep cough."

"I'll clear off your car now," Joe stated, "and make sure it starts."

"I really appreciate it, Joe."

"You call us if you need anything, even through the night."

"I will," I promised. Actually, it gave me great comfort to have Joe and Amanda nearby.

I let Harvey out to do his business, then looked through the bag that Joe had brought. When Charlie awoke, I gave him cough medicine and rubbed the menthol salve on his chest. He didn't want anything to eat, though he asked for the ginger ale, so I brought him that, then stayed with him until he fell asleep again.

When I returned to the kitchen, I nibbled on half of a ham sandwich, and made myself a cup of tea. I felt tired and didn't have much of an appetite, though I fed Harvey. Too early to go to bed, I continued where I'd left off in Hildegarde's diary.

October 15, 1917

I am happy that Adele is here with me while Jonas is away on business. After Jonas told Adele that she must keep the house clean and help Anna in the kitchen, he gave me the duty to now supervise the servants. Adele understands why I do not like Anna. Anna makes Adele do more than her share of work, so I will divide the duties more evenly and speak to Anna about it. If she is not satisfied, Anna can find other employment.

October 29, 1917

Adele told me of a custom she learned since she has been in America. To celebrate Hallows Eve, we will decorate the dining room with fall leaves and small pumpkins. Adele and I bundled Greta in her carriage, and we took a long walk to find the prettiest leaves of red and orange. It was Greta's job to hold them on her lap, and she laughed with glee each time we added another to her pile. We stopped at the market and bought two pumpkins, letting Greta pick out the ones she liked best. When we came home, we arranged them on the sideboard, which made the room look very festive, though I don't know if Jonas will approve of our display when he returns. Anna regards it as barbaric, but I do not care because Greta and I like it very much.

November 5, 1917

I received a letter from Mama today, with very sad news. Friedrich died in the war on September 20, but it has taken this long for me to know. I have cried so much because my dear Friedrich has gone to heaven. My heart breaks for Mama and Papa, too, since they are alone now. Adele has comforted me greatly, because she understands my sadness. She lost all of her family, so she has cried with me. War is so very terrible. When Jonas returns from his business, I will ask him if we can bring Mama and Papa to live with us. They should not be alone to suffer such heartbreak.

I felt great sadness for Hildegarde when I read about the devastating news of her only brother's death, and felt grateful that she had Adele to support her during such a difficult time. Perhaps because Adele had experienced an even greater tragedy, she found the words to comfort Hildegarde.

I put the diary back in its box and let Harvey out one more time. Beyond tired, and with a scratchy throat, I turned out the kitchen lights when Harvey came in, then checked on Charlie. To my relief, he slept soundly.

I knew I shouldn't sleep in the same bed, but I didn't care. I snuggled under the covers, and fell asleep in Charlie's embrace.

CHAPTER 8

*C*harlie's fever broke during the night but, unfortunately, mine started. In the morning, he brought me juice and Tylenol, and we both took some swigs of cough syrup. "What a pair we make," I muttered.

"I'm so sorry," Charlie said. "I must have given it to you."

"We probably caught it at the same time," I noted, "maybe last week at the mall, but you just happened to come down with it first."

Charlie nodded. "I'm glad you insisted we come home the other day. I hope no one else gets this bug."

"Me, too. I'm going to stay in bed today."

"Do you want me to bring you breakfast?" Charlie asked.

"No, I'm not hungry, but you're not totally better yet. We should both sleep."

I heard Charlie get up to answer his phone shortly after noon. He returned to tell me that Sister Cathy intended to come over, and she wouldn't take no for an answer. "She plans to stay a few days until we're both better," he said.

I couldn't muster the strength to reply. Charlie gave me some Tylenol, then went to the kitchen to let Harvey out and wait for Cathy. I didn't even stir when he returned to our bed. I remembered

Cathy bringing medication for both of us during the night, though I didn't realize until I awoke the next morning that Charlie had taken a shower and dressed. I thought about doing the same, but fell back to sleep.

When I woke up coughing sometime after noon, Sister Cathy brought me cough medicine and orange juice. "Thank you," I said, "but you shouldn't have come here."

"Nonsense," Cathy replied. "You both needed help. Can I bring you some soup?"

"I have to admit that I'm hungry," I replied, "but I'd like to take a shower first."

"Good," Cathy smiled. "I'm going to wash your sheets."

"Where's Charlie?" I asked.

"He's in the kitchen."

"OK," I said. "I'll be there shortly."

I felt a little better after my shower, so I put on jeans and a sweater, and padded to the kitchen in my slippers. Cathy had already dished out my soup.

"Are you sure that you feel OK?" Charlie queried when I bent down to give him a kiss.

"I could eat a horse," I chuckled, "so, I guess I am."

"The soup's good," Charlie said. "Amanda made it for us."

"She's a dear," I nodded.

"She wasn't such a dear yesterday afternoon when I told her that I planned to come over here," Sister Cathy said. "She had a major meltdown, and almost quit her job at the restaurant. Actually, she did quit, but Joe settled her down."

"Why?" I asked. "What caused the problem?"

"I did," Cathy replied. "Amanda told me that I interfered with her responsibility for taking care of her grandparents. She respected your wishes that she not come, then I blindsided her."

"We didn't want her to catch this bug," I said. "You either, for that matter."

"I'm not worried about me," Cathy stated. "I had a flu shot, and I'll stay until the incubation period is over so I don't bring it back to the monastery. It would be terrible if any of the Sisters in the infirmary came down with the flu, and we'd be at a great loss if Amanda got sick. That could still happen because she came here when you were most contagious."

"She didn't get it, did she?" Charlie asked.

"No, Amanda's fine. Leon mentioned that he felt a little under the weather for a while, but a cold night in his cabin under warm blankets cured him."

"Leave it to Leon to say something like that," Charlie said with a chesty chuckle. "What about Joe or the Holtzes?"

"So far, no one else is sick," Cathy replied.

"That's a relief," I sighed.

"Sister Julie went through the monastery spraying Lysol everywhere. She gave me a can of it, and insisted that I spray it here, too, so I squirted it around last night just to humor her."

"Probably a good idea," Charlie noted.

"Is Amanda still angry with you?" I asked.

"No," Cathy smiled. "She and I talked it through. Besides, her dad and Hannah will arrive at the B&B tonight, and they'll stay the weekend to do some wedding planning with her. Kate will also be there, so Amanda will have plenty of distractions."

Kate, Amanda's best friend, attended culinary school with Amanda, then worked part time at the monastery restaurant throughout last summer, and shared Amanda's room in the B&B on weekends. Kate announced at our wedding that she wanted to become a nun, and the Sisters accepted her into their aspirant program.

As an aspirant, which provided Kate the opportunity to discern if she had a vocation to religious life, Kate had her own room in the living quarters of the Sisters. She attended college to complete a business degree, and lived on campus, but returned to the monastery on weekends and school breaks.

Sister Cathy told us that the Sisters in administration had decided to use the Monastery at St. Carmella as their house of formation. Since I didn't know what that meant, Cathy defined formation as the time of training to become a nun. "Kate's in formation now," she explained, "and two other women have an expressed interest in joining her. The three of them can have all of their preparation here, and won't have to go to St. Louis."

"That makes sense," I remarked, "since you have plenty of room at the monastery. How long's the training?"

"If we accept an aspirant," Cathy replied, "she'll begin instruction as a postulant in the fall. Our community designates a period of about nine months in the postulate. If the woman wants to continue, she has to petition to be received as a novice, and the novitiate lasts about two years. Then, if approved, she can make temporary vows of poverty, chastity, and obedience."

"I thought they were permanent vows," Charlie said.

"Not at first. We want each woman to be certain about her decision. After she serves in ministry for five years, she has the opportunity to make her vows permanent. If the life as a Sister is not for her, she's free to leave."

"I didn't know all of that," I said. "Will Sister Marian need to take charge of the house of formation, in addition to her other responsibilities?"

"No, she'll still oversee everything for strategic planning, and the administration will send Sister Bridget to take charge of formation. You might know her because she made a retreat in a poustinia a little more than a year ago."

"We do," I nodded. "Charlie, do you remember her? She came here for Thanksgiving last year."

"Yes, she's nice. Kind of quiet, though."

"She might have been quiet because she was on retreat," Cathy said. "Bridget actually has a great sense of humor. I think she'll be perfect for the job and a nice addition to our community of Sisters at the monastery. She's arriving in just a few days."

"So many new things and new people," I commented. "It's exciting and overwhelming at the same time."

"That it is," Cathy agreed. "Now, both of you need some rest. Your bed has fresh sheets if you want to get under the covers, or you can take a snooze in the recliners in the den. I'm going to clean up the kitchen and let Harvey out."

Charlie and I both decided to opt for the bed. I hated to leave Cathy to fend for herself, but I just didn't have the stamina to continue conversing. Charlie apparently felt the same way, and we both fell into a somewhat restful sleep.

CHAPTER 9

$\mathcal{J}$ awoke to the sound of movement in the house, which startled me since I felt Charlie's presence next to me, especially whenever he hogged the blankets. It took me a few moments to remember that we had a guest or, rather, a caretaker bustling around the place. When Charlie also began to stir, I asked, "What day is it?"

"I think it's Saturday," Charlie said. "I guess we both slept through Friday afternoon and night."

"I feel better, except for this annoying cough," I muttered. "How about you?"

"Me, too." Charlie agreed. "I smell coffee brewing."

Charlie quickly dressed, though I went to the kitchen in my robe and slippers, where we found Sister Cathy preparing French toast. She handed me a steaming mug of tea when I sat at the table, then Charlie poured his coffee and joined me.

"It looks as if Mother Nature has started to clean up after herself," I remarked as I gazed out the picture window. "Some of the snow's melting."

Charlie followed my gaze before saying, "I should go out there and clear off the roof."

"Too late," Cathy smiled. "Leon did it yesterday afternoon."

"He doesn't have to take care of our place," Charlie said.

"Leon had all of the equipment in the back of the truck since he'd cleared the poustinia roofs. He said you'd do the same for him."

"I guess I would," Charlie admitted. "Did Steve arrive?"

"Yes," Cathy nodded. "I called Amanda last night to give her a progress report about the two of you. Steve and Hannah arrived in time for supper, as did Kate, and they all planned to watch a movie in the parlor."

"Was Amanda in a better frame of mind?" I questioned.

"I think so. She's relieved that you're both on the mend."

"Are they coming over here today?" Charlie asked.

"No," Cathy replied. "Amanda said that Steve and Hannah will stop by to see you on their way home tomorrow afternoon. Are you ready for breakfast?"

I had to admit that I enjoyed the royal treatment that Sister Cathy provided. After we ate, Charlie went to the den to work on a birdhouse, while I took a shower and dressed, and Cathy tidied up the kitchen.

Later, Sister Cathy and I decided to read Hildegarde's diary in the living room. I told her about the most recent turn of events for the Smithfields, and Cathy began reading aloud from where I'd left off.

November 14, 1917

When Jonas returned from his business trip, I told him about Friedrich. He agreed that Mama and Papa should come here. He showed me the letter he wrote to them, and told me that he will post it today. I must try to wait patiently for their response. Jonas understands my sadness, and he has been very kind. He is happy that Adele is with me because he sees that she encourages me to find things that lift my spirits. Adele and I take Greta for a walk every afternoon. Greta laughs when the breezes blow the brown leaves from their branches. Some days we go to the library and find a picture book to read to Greta. She likes stories about animals, especially kittens. Adele showed me the kinds of books she reads, and she picked Anne of Green Gables for me. She said it is one of her favorites, and reading it will be good practice for my English.

"I remember reading *Anne of Green Gables* as a child," I said. "It's a wonderful story about a young orphan girl adopted by an older couple. They wanted a boy to help on the farm, but Anne was sent in error."

"I don't think I ever read it," Cathy remarked.

"My grandmother gave it to me for Christmas one year, maybe when I was 10 or 11. I didn't like it at first because it was different from my favorite Nancy Drew or Cherry Ames books."

"My mother told me that she was a Cherry Ames fanatic," Cathy noted. "She said it's why she became a nurse."

"I'm not surprised," I said. "I'll bet plenty of girls wanted to follow in her footsteps, especially when they read about the various career options for nurses." I explained that Cherry Ames started out as a student nurse, and eventually became an Army nurse, a flight nurse, a visiting nurse, a cruise nurse, and many others. "I probably read all 27 books, and wanted to be a nurse, too," I chuckled. "Anyway, once I got into *Anne of Green Gables*, I loved the story. In fact, I read it over and over, just as I did with my other favorite books."

"Let's see if Hildegarde liked it as much as you," Cathy said as she returned to her place in the diary.

November 19, 1917
Today is Greta's birthday. I cannot believe she is now two years old. She is such a pretty child, and she makes me laugh with the things she says. Adele has been teaching her to sing nursery rhymes, and I think Greta is very smart because she remembers the words. Maybe she will be an actress when she grows up. She likes very much to sing and dance for Jonas, and I agree with Adele that Greta is the apple of his eye, though I think Jonas spoils her with too many gifts. After lunch, he came home with a kitten, and Greta was so very excited with the birthday surprise. She calls it Kitty, from the title of her favorite book at the library. I am not so sure that Kitty likes all of the attention, because poor Kitty runs away and hides.

November 29, 1917
It is Thanksgiving Day, and we will have a very festive dinner. Anna and

Adele have been busy in the kitchen for two days. I insisted that Greta and I help yesterday by snapping the peas from the pods. I want Greta to learn how we prepare food, even while she is young. Anna was upset, especially when she saw Greta eating some of the peas, but I was happy. Jonas read to me the special message from President Wilson in the newspaper this morning. We are to count our blessings, despite this time of war. I am praying for Mama and Papa, and I ask my dear Friedrich to watch over us from heaven.

December 5, 1917
Adele reminded me that we must return our books to the library today. I told her that I am not yet finished reading Anne of Green Gables. It is very difficult for me as I do not understand all of the words. Adele says that I should borrow it again, and she will help me with the reading. When I finish, I can get the next book called Anne of Avonlea. We will take Greta with us to the library, so she can look at her favorite book, My Kitty Cat. Greta's nanny will come, too. She can read to Greta while Adele and I are occupied. Jonas is away for two weeks, so I will have more time to focus on my book.

"Did you read *Anne of Avonlea*?" Cathy asked.

"I don't remember if I did," I replied. "In fact, I didn't even know there was a whole series of the Green Gables books until I worked at the publishing firm. Surprisingly, they're still popular today."

"One thing I've noticed," Cathy said, "is that Adele seems to get Hildegarde more involved with her daughter."

"I thought the same thing," I replied. "In fact, I wondered if Hildegarde might have had postpartum depression, but since Adele's been there, I'm not seeing the dark cloud that previously seemed to envelop her. Of course, she felt sad about the death of her brother, but that would be expected. Perhaps, she was just lonely before she met Adele."

Cathy nodded her agreement. "Imagine going to a foreign country, trying to understand a new language. Hildegarde must have found it difficult. A few years ago, I had the opportunity to present a paper at an international conference in Italy. Excited to visit places I'd never seen, I made plans to arrive a few days early, but finding my way around became a challenge. I didn't speak Italian, I couldn't read the signs, I didn't understand the currency, and I struggled with conversion to the metric system, so I could barely wait until my American colleagues arrived."

"That's a good analogy," I said. "I'm glad that JW finally realized that Hildegarde needed a companion, especially one who shared her language and culture."

Interrupted with the ring of my phone, and seeing the caller ID, I said, "Speaking of friends, it's Betty. Do you mind if I take the call?"

"Not at all," Sister Cathy replied. "I'm going to make some sandwiches for lunch, so tell Betty I send my regards."

CHAPTER 10

*B*etty Sweeney, a woman about my age whom I met on my first visit to the poustinias, worked as a public defender in the city, and often reserved a cabin at the monastery to unwind from her hectic pace. She told me that the place brought back memories of her deceased husband, John. She and John had no children of their own, but they'd invite city kids for weekends at their favorite campsite. "Are you busy?" Betty asked when I picked up the call.

"No," I replied, "I was just reading Hildegarde's diary."

"Where'd you find that?" Betty questioned.

I proceeded to tell Betty about the Holtzes, and how they'd discovered the diary in their attic during the big snowstorm. She knew the Holtzes since she'd helped with their apple harvest last fall. "Believe it or not," I noted, "Gunther's grandmother, Adele, was Hildegarde's servant."

"Trust you to unearth more intrigue at the monastery," Betty said. "I admit it's pretty amazing that there's a connection between the Holtzes and Smithfields."

"It is," I agreed. "I haven't discovered yet why Hildegarde gave her diary to Adele, but I know that Adele was with her before they built the mansion. Guess what else I learned."

"I haven't a clue," Betty chuckled.

"The Smithfields had a daughter, named Greta," I said.

"I thought they were childless," Betty remarked.

"So did I," I agreed, "but, apparently not."

"Well," Betty commented, "you've certainly been a busy girl. How'd you fare in the storm?"

I told Betty that I didn't ever remember getting so much snow at one time. "Luckily, Charlie hooked up our generator," I noted, "since most of the locals didn't have electricity for several days." I explained that the Sisters had a permanent generator, so they invited people to stay at the B&B during the power outage. "We had almost three feet of snow," I added, "so Charlie and Leon offered to bring the Holtzes to the monastery in the plow."

"And, they gave the Sisters the diary because they knew you'd be interested?" Betty questioned.

"No," I said. "Pauline Holtz thought the nuns should have it since it belonged to Hildegarde Smithfield."

"Then, how did it end up in your hands?" Betty asked.

"It's a long story. I told Charlie to bring the Holtzes to our place for dinner first because, initially, they closed the monastery restaurant, so Amanda came over here to pass the time, and we made a large pot of stew. Anyway, when Pauline told me about their attic discovery, and I expressed such an interest, she left it with me to read."

"That was nice of her," Betty replied. "I suppose you've had your nose in the diary all week."

"Not too much, since Charlie and I had the flu, and we've been really sick."

"I wondered why I hadn't heard from you," Betty said. "I thought for sure that you'd have called me to complain about winter in the boondocks. Do you feel any better?"

"Yes," I replied. "Today's my first day out of bed, and I'm already pooped. I think I'm going to need a nap."

"You'll tire easily," Betty noted, "so get plenty of rest. Is Amanda helping you?"

"No," I said. "We didn't want her to catch the flu and spread it around the monastery. Sister Cathy's here, and she'll stay until we get back on our feet. How'd you make out in the storm?"

"They closed all public offices," Betty replied, "so I just hunkered down in my apartment and relaxed. It was heavenly."

"You didn't lose power?" I asked.

"Some areas of the city did; but, luckily, not here, so I watched a couple of movies on TV, and made it an early night. Do you want me to come and give you a hand?"

"No, but thanks. We'll be fine now. Once we get all of the germs out of this house, Charlie and I would like you to plan a weekend visit."

"Definitely," Betty agreed. "In the meantime, I'll let you get back to Hildegarde's diary. Don't forget to take a nap."

AFTER LUNCH, Cathy and I returned to the living room. Despite the warmth from the fireplace, I felt chilled, so I took a blanket from the hall closet, and stretched out on the sofa. Cathy sat in the side chair, and began reading Hildegarde's next excerpts.

December 10, 1917
With Adele's help, I have been reading Anne of Green Gables every day. When I find a word that I don't understand, I write it on a note pad and Adele explains it. Sometimes, she even reads to me, which I like very much. The story is becoming more interesting, and I must tell Jonas about it. Anne is a young girl who comes from an orphan asylum to live with an older couple at Green Gables. It reminds me of the stories Jonas told me about his parents who were rather aged. He, too, was adopted and had lived in an orphanage until he was 11 years old. His new parents, kind and gentle people, didn't know how to handle a headstrong young man. He left their home when he was 18, and his mother and father both had passed before his 24th birthday. I think sometimes Jonas doesn't understand how to be part of a family, because he never really experienced it.

December 15, 1917
Jonas will come home in a few days, and he will be very surprised when he
sees that we have a Tannenbaum this year. Adele and I found a street vendor
who sold trees already cut and ready to be decorated. I used some of the
money that Mama and Papa sent to me in order to purchase it. Perhaps I will
tell Jonas that we found the tree in the gutter because I don't want him to
know that I have my own money. It is safely hidden in my jewelry box from
Germany. I showed Adele the beautiful glass ornaments I received last
Christmas, and she insisted that we use them to decorate the tree. We also
added candies and other decorations, so our Tannenbaum is very beautiful. I
hope Jonas is not angry.

The last entry caught my attention. "Read that part again about the jewelry box. Could it be the same one that Hildegarde gave to Adele with her diary? The one we have here?"

Cathy re-read the section, then added, "I don't know. I hadn't really looked closely at the box."

Curiosity roused, Sister Cathy retrieved the box from the coffee table and examined it carefully. As I had done a few nights ago, she moved her hands along the top and sides, feeling the beautifully carved wood.

"I don't see any kind of compartment," Cathy remarked. "Maybe Hildegarde meant that she just kept the money inside the box."

"Perhaps," I said, "but then it wouldn't be hidden."

I called to Charlie in the den. "Hey, Charlie. Can you come here a minute?"

When Charlie joined us, he queried, "What's up?"

"You work with wood when you make your birdhouses. Can you see if there's a hidden compartment in the diary box?"

Charlie lifted the lid and examined the lining of the box, declaring it firmly attached. He used his fingers to measure the depth from the inside, and then from the outside. "Let me get my ruler," he said, "because I see some variance here." Sure enough, the outer dimensions of the box measured 9 inches deep, but only 7 inches for the inside.

"My mother once had a jewelry box with a compartment you could remove," Cathy remarked. "She kept her necklaces in the bottom section, and earrings on the top."

"There's nothing to pull out in this one," Charlie noted, looking stymied.

Not to be outwitted, Charlie opened the lid again and felt along each of the side seams. When he tugged on a side piece, it slid up and out of its groove. A thin ribbon protruded.

We watched expectantly while Charlie gently pulled the ribbon to reveal a drawer, full of German currency.

CHAPTER 11

Sister Cathy and I gawked at the stash of money in Charlie's hand. Charlie rifled through the bills with an expression of total disbelief on his face. "These all have 100 Mark denominations," he remarked as he began counting them into piles of 10 on the coffee table. He ended up with 23 stacks and a few stragglers.

"The two of you certainly do like finding hidden things," Charlie grinned, staring at the money. I knew he referred to the fact that Cathy and I had discovered a hidden passage in the monastery basement that led to the camouflaged still used to make liquor in the lower level of the Smithfield's machine barn.

"How much do we have here?" I asked.

"It looks like 236 bank notes, each with a face value of 100 Marks," Sister Cathy replied. "If my math's correct, that's 23,600 Marks. Of course, it might be worthless now."

"Or, it could be quite valuable because of its age," I said. "We may have found a fortune for the nuns."

"Oh, no." Cathy shook her head. "Hildegarde gave the box to Adele, so the money belongs to the Holtzes."

"And, the Holtzes gave the box and diary to the Sisters," I contended.

"It doesn't matter," Cathy replied. "We have to give the money to Gunther and Pauline. It's the right thing to do."

"By all accounts," I said, "Hildegarde's parents must have sent her money quite often, and she apparently saved it for something, while hiding it from JW. Then, she gave the box with the diary to Adele, but Adele didn't use the money."

"We don't know that," Cathy said. "There could have been more cash in the box, or even some higher denominations."

"I'd guess that Adele didn't know about the hidden section," Charlie remarked. "I had to pull pretty hard on that side piece, and I only did that because you girls thought there was another compartment."

I nodded my agreement. "Maybe Hildegarde gave the box to Adele on her deathbed, but died before she could tell her about the money."

"I suppose that's possible," Cathy replied, "but, if she did, she couldn't have written about it in her diary, so we'll probably never know."

"Not unless Adele wrote her own memoirs," I mused. "I'd like to explore the Holtz's attic."

"Here we go again," Charlie laughed, "but let me ask you this. Why didn't Hildegarde give the box to her daughter?"

"Something must have happened to Greta," I said. "On the other hand, maybe they became estranged."

"It seems to me," Charlie said, "you need to keep reading the diary."

"We do," I agreed, "although I desperately need a nap. Can we continue after supper?"

"That sounds like a good idea," Cathy replied. "Let's put the money back in its drawer. Charlie can place the box in a safe location until we can get it to the Holtzes. In the meantime, I'll let Sister Marian know about our discovery, then make supper. I'll call you both when it's ready."

~

AFTER WE ATE, Sister Cathy insisted that Charlie and I relax in front of the fireplace while she cleaned up the kitchen. I felt a few pangs of guilt, but it didn't seem to bother Charlie at all.

We both took some cough medicine before settling in. I wrapped myself in the blanket on the recliner. Charlie flipped the switch to get a fire blazing in the hearth, then stretched out on the sofa. We could hear the wind whistling around the east corner of the house, but we felt warm and snug. When Cathy joined us, we cajoled her into serving as the designated diary reader, so she continued where she'd left off earlier.

December 24, 1917
Tonight is Christmas Eve, and I am excited for Greta. She understands that der Weihnachtsmann will arrive with gifts, and she wants to stay up late to greet him. I have explained many times that der Weihnachtsmann will not come if she is awake, but she does not believe me. All of our preparations are done, and the house looks very festive. That was not the case a few days before Jonas arrived home when Kitty discovered our Tannenbaum. We found it toppled to the floor, but she didn't destroy any of my precious glass ornaments, thank goodness. Adele helped me move the tree to the parlor, in front of the window, so now we keep the door closed, and do not permit Kitty to enter. Jonas saw our pretty Tannenbaum from the street, and he is happy with it.

December 26, 1917
This Christmas was the most wonderful since I have been in America. Jonas promised Adele that we would go with her to church. I dressed Greta in her new Christmas frock, a pretty red dress with puffy sleeves, while Adele fixed Greta's hair with a matching bow. I could see that Jonas approved, and he proudly held Greta's hand as she toddled up the aisle with him. All of the congregation laughed when she sang Silent Night with the choir. Adele served breakfast since the other servants went with their families for Christmas, and we asked her to join us. Then we all went to the parlor to open our gifts. Greta was so very excited, and loved her new picture books and baby doll the most. She told us that she saw der Weihnachtsmann when he visited

us, and we let her think that we believed her. Jonas gave me beautiful
diamond earrings and a pretty shawl. I gave Jonas a bottle of fine brandy
that I know he will enjoy. Our gift to Adele was a new hat she can wear to
church, as well as money to buy some dresses and whatever else she needs.
Our evening meal was very festive, and we had a lovely Christmas.

"Hildegarde didn't mention anything about her parents," Sister
Cathy remarked.

"I noticed that, too," I said. "I suppose she hadn't heard from them
since mail from Germany seemed rather slow during the war."

"Jonas, or JW as you two call him, must have come into some extra
cash to give his wife diamonds," Charlie said. "Either that, or he
kissed up to her big time."

"Well, you old rascal," I teased. "Maybe Hildegarde deserved them,
given all that she'd put up with him."

"It goes two ways, if you ask me," Charlie remarked.

"You wouldn't give me diamond earrings?" I asked.

"Not unless I came into a windfall," Charlie replied. "Even then,
I'm not so sure."

"On that note," Cathy chuckled, "Let's all call it a night."

"That sounds good to me," Charlie said. "I want to get a good
night's sleep so I can be up and about tomorrow."

"You still have your cough," I noted.

"So do you, but that'll probably linger. I don't think we're contagious anymore."

"Probably not," Cathy agreed. "In fact, I think it's safe for me to
return home tomorrow. I'd like to go to Sunday Mass at the
monastery."

"I'll drive you there in the morning," Charlie said. "Sweet dreams,
ladies."

Charlie stood and stretched, adding a loud yawn for good
measure. I watched him saunter down the hallway, with Harvey
following behind. I smiled at the touching scenario, and Cathy voiced
my thoughts, saying, "Charlie's a good man. Even your dog agrees."

"They've bonded, that's for sure," I grinned, "but Harvey will be back in a moment because he knows he's not allowed in the bedroom."

We both waited expectantly. When Harvey didn't return, Cathy giggled. "You may be relegated to the futon in the den."

I shook my head in wonder, then shrugged off the blanket. Cathy promised to turn off the fireplace and lock the doors before retiring after she said, "I just want to enjoy the peaceful coziness a little longer."

"That's fine," I smiled. "We really appreciate all that you've done for us." I padded to the bedroom and gasped. No wonder Harvey hadn't returned. He fell sound asleep, snuggled next to Charlie.

CHAPTER 12

*A*manda called after breakfast to say that she, her dad, and Hannah would come over later in the afternoon since Kate and Joe offered to take care of dinner service for the Sisters, as well as any guests who might show up at the restaurant. To my relief, Amanda insisted that I needn't make anything to eat as they'd bring soup and sandwiches. I didn't feel like preparing a meal, and with the cupboard almost bare, I needed to go to the grocery store on Monday.

Although Steve and Hannah had seen our place during the holidays, we hadn't yet become settled. Now, we could just relax and have a nice visit, so I looked forward to seeing them again. While we waited for their arrival, Charlie went to the den to work on his birdhouses. I joined him there, and sat in the recliner to continue reading Hildegarde's diary.

January 14, 1918
I received Mama's letter in today's post. She said that she did not send gifts for Christmas this year because she is very sad about Friedrich's death. Also, Papa has a problem with his heart, so he has a cough and is short of breath. They both would like to come to America for a visit, but Papa does not have the strength to travel. I asked Jonas if we might take Greta to Germany since

I want so much for Mama and Papa to see her, and for Greta to meet her grandparents. Jonas said it is not safe at this time, so we will plan a trip when the war is over. I was upset with Jonas, but Adele says that he is right. Now I pray that peace will soon return so that I can help Mama take care of Papa.

February 8, 1918
Greta was very happy to see that we have more snow today. She begged to go out and play, and Adele thought it was a good idea. I put on her winter leggings and coat, and Greta helped to tug on her boots and mittens. Adele wrapped a woolen scarf around Greta's neck, while I found her knitted hat, then Adele and I bundled warmly. First, we took a walk around the block, and Greta laughed as she tried to catch the snowflakes on her tongue. I thought she would be cold when we returned to the house, but Greta wanted to stay out. Adele showed her how to roll the snow into a big ball. I rolled another one, and put it on top of Adele's. Soon we had a snowman. We found pebbles to make eyes and a nose, and Adele wrapped her pretty red scarf around the snowman's neck. Greta thought our snowman was very lovely. It wasn't until we promised that she could watch her snowman from the parlor window that Greta would come in to get warm.

February 15, 1918
Jonas told Greta he is very proud of her for making such a beautiful snow-man. He laughed when she said that we must call the snowman "schnee boy" because he is German, and he is not big enough to be a man. Jonas knows that snow is called schnee in my country. Every evening before bedtime, Jonas makes up a story about schnee boy. Last night, the tale was about schnee boy going away to be a snow angel who would always watch over our family. Sure enough, when Greta was dressed this morning, she ran to the window to check on schnee boy. All that was left of him was Adele's red scarf on the ground. I thought that Greta would cry, but she told me not to worry because schnee boy will take care of us.

I chuckled out loud about Jonas' clever way of handling a melting snowman. For a man who didn't have much experience around children, he obviously felt great love for his daughter. "What's so funny?" Charlie asked.

"JW's been learning some parenting skills. He's now into story time with Greta."

"Stella used to read to Steve when he was little," Charlie replied, "but I never had much interest in doing that."

"What will you do once Amanda and Joe start having children?" I asked.

"You can do story time," Charlie said. "I'll teach the kids how to do manly things."

"Like what?" I countered.

"You know, like plant crops and build fences."

"Yeah, right," I teased.

We continued our banter until we heard the knock on the back door. Charlie and I went to the kitchen to greet our guests.

"ANYONE HOME?" Amanda called. She showed Steve and Hannah where to place their boots and hang their jackets, then began to unpack her bag of food items on the counter.

"Hi, everyone. Welcome!" I said with an inviting smile.

"You guys can all go into the living room and turn on the fireplace," Amanda said. "I'll bring in some snacks. Anyone want a ginger ale?"

I noticed how pretty Hannah looked in a stylish, though unpretentious, outfit. Her brown hair had an attractive cut, and she accentuated it with delicate silver filigree earrings. Steve also looked quite handsome in brown trousers and tweed jacket. Charlie says that Steve resembled his mother, but I could see a bit of Charlie in him, too. "Your new home looks lovely," Hannah commented as she joined Steve on the sofa. "How are you both feeling?"

"Much better," I said. "We still have a little cough and tire easily, but we're on the mend. I don't know where we got it from, but I'm glad it's gone."

"Sister Cathy told us at breakfast this morning that you were out of it for a few days," Hannah noted. "That was nice of her to come and help you."

As if on cue, Amanda arrived with a cheese plate and put it on the coffee table. After placing a basket of crackers next to it, she said, "I would've been here, but they wouldn't let me come." The hurt expression on Amanda's face spoke volumes, and it gave me a stark reminder that I needed to pay more attention to her feelings.

I tried to explain, saying, "We didn't want you to catch it, and the Sisters needed you."

"I know," Amanda replied, "but it wasn't right. I belonged here, not Sister Cathy."

"I'm sorry, Amanda," I stated contritely. "At the time, I didn't realize it meant so much to you, and I promise we'll let you help us in the future."

"You're both so darn stubborn," Amanda muttered.

"It seems to me that it runs in the family," Hannah teased. "Can I help you bring in the drinks?"

When Hannah and Amanda returned, I asked if they had finalized their wedding plans. Hannah confirmed that they'd made a number of decisions throughout the weekend. "We've decided to have a joint wedding at the monastery on May 19," Hannah said. "That's a Friday evening. We've booked the chapel, and Father Jim will be the minister."

"I guess you wanted to follow in our footsteps," Charlie grinned. Father Jim also officiated at our wedding in the monastery chapel.

"Yeah, but we'll do more planning than you did," Amanda quipped. "You just tied the knot, and were done with it, but our wedding will be awesome."

Where's the reception?" I asked.

"We reserved the *Monastery Restaurant and Inn* for the weekend," Hannah noted. "We'll have a catered dinner banquet on Friday evening, and our guests can stay until Sunday if they'd like."

"Joe and I will choose the band for our venue, or maybe a DJ," Amanda stated, "but we haven't made a final decision yet."

"As long as there's music that Hannah and I like, too," Steve reminded Amanda. "We don't want anything wild."

Amanda rolled her eyes. "Yeah, like we could have a wild bash at a monastery."

Ignoring Amanda's quip, I asked, "Do you have family, Hannah?"

"I do. My mom and dad live about an hour from here, and Mom's excited about staying at the B&B. My sister and her husband live in Cleveland, so they'll want to stay for the entire weekend, I'm sure."

"Joe and I will invite our culinary classmates," Amanda noted. "Of course, Kate has her own bedroom in the convent, so we don't need a room for her, and Dad wants to invite some of his friends from the university."

"It sounds as if you'll have a big celebration," I said.

Hannah nodded her agreement. "Amanda and I intend to arrange all of the details ourselves. We still have to decide on a color scheme for the bridesmaids, and choose our décor. Of course, we also need to send out our invitations soon."

"Have you selected them yet?" I asked.

"We can do that online," Amanda replied, "and we picked out a few designs we liked yesterday. Hannah wants to play around with the wording, then we'll place the order this week."

I could see that Charlie and Steve began to find all of our chit-chat boring, so I brought them into the conversation by asking Amanda, "What jobs will you give to your dad and Joe?"

"Dad's going to hire a bartender," Amanda said. "Right, Dad?"

"Right," Steve said.

"And, Joe has to work with me on the catering menu," Amanda added.

"Maybe your dad and Hannah would like some say in that," I suggested.

"Sure," Amanda replied. "It's not as if we can make any final decisions without their involvement. We'll just get it started. Right, Dad?"

"Right," Steve nodded emphatically.

Charlie started to laugh. "I'm just glad we didn't have to go through all of this folderol."

"You don't know what you missed," Steve said facetiously. "I figure we'll just let the girls go at it. You and I can watch football, and they can do whatever makes them happy."

"That's a plan," Charlie agreed. "Is anyone getting hungry? What happened to the soup and sandwiches?"

"The soup should be hot now," Amanda said. "I put it on the stove before I brought in the *hors d'oevres*. The sandwiches are ready to plate."

Charlie grinned. "What are we waiting for? Let's eat."

CHAPTER 13

*A*manda made the decision that we'd eat in the kitchen, and she'd already set the table, then encouraged Charlie and Steve to take their places. I helped Hannah arrange the variety of sandwiches on a platter, while Amanda ladled her vegetable beef soup into the bowls. "It smells delicious," I smiled as I put the sandwiches on the table, then took my seat.

Hannah and Amanda carried the bowls of soup to the table, then joined the rest of us as Amanda explained, "We had the soup and sliders for lunch at the B&B, and Sister Marian insisted that we bring the leftovers here for an easy dinner."

"She's so thoughtful," I said. "Everything's still fresh, and Charlie and I prefer a lighter meal until we're back on our feet." Charlie nodded his agreement while taking a bite of his ham and cheese roll.

"I never tire of eating your soup, Amanda," Hannah said. "You must give me your recipe."

"This one's really easy. I just used the stew we had last night, then added a can of diced tomatoes and some beef broth."

"You make it sound simple," Hannah smiled, "but I'll need a lesson."

The rest of us agreed that Amanda had a special talent, and she grinned when her father winked at her. Watching the interaction between the two of them made me think about Steve's comment that his daughter had never shown any interest in cooking until she met Kate, so I recognized that good friends can bring out the best in us.

Hannah offered second-helpings of soup before refilling her own bowl. Returning to her seat, she changed the subject, saying, "Sister Cathy mentioned that you've been reading an old diary that the neighbors found in their attic."

"It's fascinating," I said, nodding my head. "I feel as if I'm really getting to know Hildegarde."

"That's the wife of the guy who built the mansion? The one who made jellies and jams?" Hannah asked.

"Yes," I replied, "but I'm still reading the part of her diary when she was young and rather recently married to Jonas. She's just now adjusting to her role among the wealthy in American society."

"What's to adjust to?" Amanda asked. "I could easily get used to that lifestyle."

We all laughed, then I told Amanda how much I thought about her when I read the diary. "Hildegarde didn't like being told what her husband expected of her, or that she had no say in matters of the household," I explained. "She also missed her family in Germany.

"Hildegarde should have just told Mr. Smithfield what she wanted," Amanda replied.

"It didn't work that way back in the day," I noted. "Men didn't permit women to have much of a say in anything."

"Well, I'd give him a piece of my mind," Amanda retorted, "and, let me tell you, old JW, as you like to call him, wouldn't have entrance to the bedroom if he didn't soon learn how to behave."

"Apparently, Hildegarde hadn't learned that trick yet," I chuckled. "The Smithfields have a daughter named Greta."

"I thought they didn't have any kids," Amanda said.

"Me, too," I agreed, "but, they do. Greta's now a little more than two years old."

"Why didn't anyone know about her?" Amanda asked. "Do you

think she died? I hope not. It's a horrible experience, and it's something that Hildegarde would never get over."

Amanda didn't often talk about the death of her unborn baby that occurred during her last trimester of pregnancy. I knew she still grieved after that traumatic time last year and, without a doubt, she'd carry that memory in her heart through her entire lifetime. "I hope not, too," I said. "I do know that the Smithfields hired Mr. Holtz's grandmother, Adele, as a servant, and she became Hildegarde's best friend."

"Who's Mr. Holtz?" Hannah asked.

"The Holtzes have the apple orchard down the road," Charlie explained. "We've helped them with their harvest each fall, but we never knew they had any connection with the original owners of the estate until recently."

"They found Hildegarde's diary when they cleaned out their attic during the snowstorm," I added.

"Did you really find money hidden in the box with the diary?" Amanda asked. "That's what Cathy told us."

"GP found it," I nodded. "He discovered the secret compartment after Sister Cathy and I read about it in the diary."

"Way to go, GP," Amanda grinned. "Is it worth anything?"

"I don't know," I replied, "but the Sisters will present it to them at a meeting we've planned for next week. In fact, I intend to ask Mrs. Holtz if she'd like to be a tour guide at *Rock Creek Farm*."

"You have to be kidding," Amanda said. "She's a piece of work."

"You don't like her?" I asked.

"Sure, I do," Amanda replied. "She's nice enough, but she talks incessantly. Oh, I get it. She talks a lot, and she even has a family connection with the Smithfields. That's a pretty smart move, Vicki."

"On that note," Steve interjected, "I'm afraid we have to get going. Are you going to stay awhile, Amanda?"

"Not tonight. Joe and I want to watch a new series on TV. Can you bring me back to the monastery?"

"I never thought I'd hear you say those words," Steve said with a wink to the rest of us.

"Very funny, Dad."

Hannah wanted to help with the kitchen cleanup, but I insisted that we had nothing but the pot to wash, since the rest would go in the dishwasher. I did offer my services if she and Amanda needed any help with the wedding planning. "Maybe Amanda and I could come over here when we start addressing invitations," Hannah noted as she donned her boots and coat.

"That's a great idea," I replied, "and we have the guest bedroom if you want to stay over."

We said our farewells, and Charlie took Harvey out when he walked them to their car. I loaded the dishwasher, fixed Harvey's kibbles, and put away the leftovers. "I enjoyed their visit," Charlie remarked when he and Harvey returned, "but I'm pooped."

"Me, too," I smiled. "We could snuggle in bed on such a cold winter's night."

"It sounds good to me," Charlie grinned. The thump of Harvey's tail on the kitchen floor signaled that he agreed.

CHAPTER 14

The Sisters invited Charlie and me to their meeting with the Holtzes the following week. I'd already mentioned my interest to Sister Marian about asking Mrs. Holtz to be a tour guide. Marian seemed surprised, but gave her approval, and suggested that I present my proposal to Pauline when we met. I also prepared a report to provide an update on the grants I'd submitted, and Charlie planned to discuss the progress that he and Leon had made on the Smithfield's machine barn.

Charlie and I found the Holtzes chatting with Sister Marian and Sister Cathy when we arrived. As I took off my coat, I noticed Hildegarde's jewelry box on the side table, though I simply gave a cheerful greeting, saying "It's good to see you all."

"We're glad you're back on your feet," Pauline said. "Just yesterday, I told Gunther that we must invite you and Charlie over to our place. Didn't I, Gunther?"

"That you did," Gunther nodded.

"Charlie and I would enjoy that," I smiled.

Sister Marian expressed her welcome before calling the meeting to order. "We'd like to thank each of you for joining us today. I thought this might be an opportunity for Vicki and Sister Cathy to share with us what they discovered when they read Hildegarde's diary."

"I hope you can tell us about Gunther's grandmother," Pauline said. "I kicked myself for not reading the diary before I gave it to you though, frankly, I didn't have much interest since Adele didn't write it. Then, I realized that Hildegarde may have written about Adele."

"I haven't finished reading all of it," I said, "but there are a number of passages about Adele. I know that she made a huge difference in Hildegarde's life."

I shared with the Holtzes what I'd learned about the difficult time Hildegarde had adjusting to a new culture, and the loneliness she felt. "Without a doubt," I remarked, "Adele taught Hildegarde how to be a loving mother and wife. Did you know that Adele's whole family had been killed shortly after they sent her to America?"

"I didn't know that," Pauline replied, shaking her head. "Did you know that, Gunther?"

"Might be I heard something about it when I was a boy," Gunther said.

"When Hildegarde learned that her brother, Friedrich, died in the German army, Adele comforted her," I noted. "I think the grief they both experienced cemented their friendship."

"I told you they were friends," Pauline said emphatically. "How about that, Gunther? Your grandmother was a lovely lady. Well, I knew that she must have been, because she raised eight children, seven of them girls, and they all turned out good. Gunther's father was her only son, so that's why he inherited the homestead. Right, Gunther?"

"Right," Gunther nodded.

Sister Marian stood to retrieve the jewelry box from the side table, then handed it to Gunther, saying, "Hildegarde gave this box to your grandmother for a reason, and we think you should keep it."

"You haven't finished reading the diary," Pauline said to me. "Don't you want to find out more about Hildegarde?"

"I still have the diary," I said. "The box, however, belongs in your family."

"It's pretty, I have to admit," Pauline noted, "but I think it should go to the Sisters."

"Not after what we discovered," Cathy replied. She told Gunther to raise the lid and pull upward on the side piece, then showed him the secret compartment.

"What's in there?" Pauline asked. "Goodness gracious. It's currency. Look at that, Gunther."

"Hildegarde obviously wanted Adele to have the jewelry box," Sister Marian remarked, "because it contained the money she had hidden. That's why we believe it rightly belongs to you and your family."

Pauline wanted to know how we discovered the hidden drawer, so I explained that Sister Cathy and I had read a passage in Hildegarde's diary that made reference to the cash her parents had sent her. "She wrote that she hid it in her jewelry box," I said. "We weren't sure this was the same one, but Charlie helped us investigate, and he figured it out."

"Heavens to Betsy, Gunther," Pauline exclaimed while Gunther counted out the money. "Maybe there's enough there to get that new roof we need. This is very generous of the Sisters, and we don't know how to thank you."

"I'm not sure how much it's all worth," I said. "I did an internet search, and learned that the German Marks from that time period have no currency value now. However, you may be able to get some return from a collector's viewpoint."

I could see that the Holtzes felt very touched by the thoughtfulness of the Sisters. Gunther placed the pile of Marks back into the drawer and closed the compartment. Even Pauline seemed at a loss for words because she just shook her head in awe.

"The box was meant to be yours, not ours," Marian said, "but Vicki does have a favor to ask of you."

I spoke directly to Pauline. "Charlie and I told you about our plans to renovate the Smithfield's machine barn, and give tours of his boot-legging operation."

"Oh, yes," Pauline said. "I told Gunther we need to see if there's anything else in the attic you might be able to use. We just haven't had a chance to do that yet."

"That would be great," I replied, "though I'd also like you to serve as our tour guide. You have an interest in history, and I think you could best tell others about the Smithfields."

Once again, Pauline didn't seem to know what to say, at least for a few moments. Then, she stated, "I'm not a good choice. After all, I know nothing about the original owners of the estate."

"We're learning more about JW and Hildegarde every day, especially from the diary. I'd develop the script, and you'd just tell the story."

"Oh, I can tell a good story," Pauline grinned, "but being a tour guide is a horse of a different color, so I don't know. What do you think, Gunther?"

"It might be good for you," he replied. "I wouldn't mind lending a hand to restore the barn."

"I could use your help," Charlie said.

"When are we talking about?" Gunther asked.

"Pretty much any time now," Charlie noted. "I don't think we'll get much more snow. You can join Leon and me working in the barn's basement, where the still is located. When it warms up a bit, we'll move on up to the main level."

"I can't do much outside during these cold days anyway," Gunther said. "We might as well help our neighbors."

"Excellent," Sister Marian replied. "Vicki's the executive director, so you'll take direction from her. She'll meet with Cathy and me on a weekly basis until everything's up and running."

Sister Cathy asked if I'd had time to work on any grants, and I told her that I'd submitted two of them. One provided a stipend for my position; the other for educational programming, and that one included funding for the tour guide. "Now, I'm working on a grant to finance the barn renovation, and I hoped to have it completed by the weekend."

"I don't want any pay if I lead the tours," Pauline said. "It wouldn't seem right."

"It won't be big bucks," I replied. "Just think of it as a few extra coins in your pocket."

"And, you'd help the Sisters," Cathy added. "We really don't want to be in the business of giving tours, but we recognize that the estate has historical significance, so we think it would be wrong of us to keep it to ourselves."

"I guess it makes sense," Pauline said. "What do you think, Gunther?"

"It's OK by me," Gunther replied.

"Fabulous," Marian smiled. "That wraps up our meeting, and I'm sure Pauline and Gunther want to get going so they can show their children what was hidden in their attic all of these years. We'll see you next week, Vicki; same time and place."

CHAPTER 15

*C*harlie dropped me off at the house before heading into town to purchase wood to make a few more birdhouses, then ask one of his buddies at the firehouse to cut it to the dimensions he needed. I planned to start supper and read Hildegarde's diary. Without more details about the Smithfields, I couldn't write a script for the tours.

I made a cucumber salad, then prepped the chicken and two potatoes, which I'd put in the oven when Charlie returned home. I took the diary to the recliner in the den, and continued my reading.

March 31, 1918
Adele reminded me that we must move our clocks ahead by an hour today. I do not like this idea of Fast Time, though President Wilson said that Germany already has Daylight Savings Time. I suppose it will be good to have the sun longer in the day, but it will be more difficult for me to get Greta to go to sleep at her regular bedtime. It is now my responsibility since I told Jonas that we no longer needed a nanny for Greta. I explained to Jonas that I want Greta to love me as I do my Mama, and I will teach her the things Mama taught me. Jonas respected my wishes, so he found the nanny another position in the home of one of his friends.

May 18, 1918

Anna has decided to seek other employment because she felt angry that I brought Greta to the kitchen to make cookies. Jonas was upset with me when Anna came to him with her complaints, but I told him that the staff is my responsibility, and he must not take sides with Anna. In fact, I do not want to hire new kitchen staff since Adele is quite capable in the kitchen, and Greta and I will assist her when necessary. On the other hand, Adele will not have time for other housekeeping tasks, so we will hire a housekeeper to clean on Fridays. Our home is not so large as to need a full staff. Jonas may continue to employ the services of James, the butler. James helps Jonas with his businesses, and he often travels with him as manservant. I seem to have made my point with Jonas because he did not argue with me.

June 30, 1918

Jonas told me that he has learned about a large tract of land for sale in the countryside. Much of it is wooded, although there are several pasture areas and a lovely creek winds all around the property. He thinks we could easily have a vineyard, and build a large country house. I am excited about planting grape vines. Perhaps Papa can send me some clippings from his prized varieties. I agreed that Jonas should purchase the land for our estate, and I am very happy about it.

When I heard Charlie's truck as he pulled into the driveway, I went to the kitchen to preheat the oven for the potatoes and chicken. I opened the back door for him, and Charlie lugged in a carton filled with cut pieces of wood. "It looks as if you have plenty to keep you busy for a while," I commented, moving a chair out of his way.

"Yep, I dropped off a couple of the finished birdhouses at Flossie's Floral Shop. She paid me for the ones that sold since last month, so I had enough money to buy the lumber, pick up a dozen donuts at Jake's, and fill the truck with gas."

"I'm assuming you gave the donuts to your buddy for cutting the wood," I said.

"A couple of us guys at the firehouse ate some while he used the power saw, but he still had a few to take home. I guess I should've bought another dozen."

"Probably," I agreed. "Do you want a cup of tea before dinner?"

"How much time do we have?" Charlie asked.

"About an hour."

"I'll have it with my meal," Charlie replied, "since I want to lay out my wood in the den now."

"I'll keep you company, so I can continue reading the diary."

"Have you learned anything new?" Charlie questioned.

"Just the day-to-day stuff, although I have to admit that Hildegarde's now finding her voice."

"Is JW listening?" Charlie quipped.

"It seems so," I smiled. "He knows what's good for him."

"It goes two ways," Charlie reminded me.

"Sometimes," I chuckled. "Anyway, JW found the land, and intends to purchase it since Hildegarde gave her approval."

"And, here we are," Charlie said, "100 years later, and we own our own piece of the estate. Who'd have thought?"

"You're right, Charlie Munley. Who'd have thought?"

Charlie carried his carton to the den, while I finished the preparation for dinner. I set the timer on the oven, then joined him to continue my reading.

July 9, 1918

We have just returned from a week at the seashore, and we all had a wonderful time. James drove us, and Adele helped me with Greta. Jonas found a lovely inn, and reserved separate rooms for James and Adele. Our room had a perfect view of the ocean. On the days that Jonas conducted business, Adele and I took Greta to the beach. In the evenings, we walked the boardwalk, then let Greta ride the carousel. On the 4th of July, we went to the parade and watched the fireworks. Greta always slept soundly at night because of the sea breeze, which was very good for Jonas and me.

August 8, 1918

I received very sad news today. Papa died of congestive heart failure. I can barely breathe, and I cannot eat anything without getting sick. How could God be so cruel to take my brother, and now my father? What will Mama do? She is alone and I cannot go to her, nor can she travel because of the war. I have cried until I have no more tears. Adele and Jonas have tried to comfort me, but there is no solace.

August 20, 1918
Jonas has tried to find a way to bring Mama to America, but he says it is not possible for her to get a visa and passport at this time. Adele gives me comforting words, though we both wonder when this dreadful war will be over. I want to be brave for Greta, but she knows that I am not happy. I am sick every day, and Jonas said that I must see the doctor, so Adele will go with me in the morning.

August 21, 1918
I am pregnant. Mama always said that a new soul is born when a loved one dies. It gives me some comfort to know that Papa is with me in spirit. Jonas is very happy that Greta will have a brother or sister in the spring. Adele told me not to worry because she will help me. I pray that the war will soon end so that Mama can come to live with us. She will want to be with her grand-children.

"You're not going to believe this," I said, closing the diary. "Hildegarde's going to have another child."

"It wouldn't be unusual," Charlie replied.

"It is when we'd previously thought that the Smithfields had no children."

"Why don't you skip ahead and find out what happened to the kids?" Charlie suggested.

"That would be like reading the last chapter of a book. It ruins the suspense."

"Go at it, then," Charlie grinned. "Your timer went off, so I think we should go eat dinner."

∽

At the kitchen table, Charlie told me that he and Leon would begin organizing the basement of the Smithfield's machine barn in the morning since they wanted to determine the scope of work before Gunther joined them. I suggested that they ask Father Jim for some volunteers to help move all of the barrels on the lower level.

"We might need to do that," Charlie agreed, "but we want to check it out first. How do you want the barrels arranged? I guess you intend to keep all of them."

"I want it to look rustic, but realistic," I replied. The barn's basement had several stalls, including the compartment with the still, and those held numerous stacked barrels. "I'd like to salvage as many as we can, but we also need room for people to meander around, as well as space for Pauline to gather the group together to give her spiel. Perhaps we could use some of them for seating."

"What about the ramp leading to the still?" Charlie asked.

"Make sure it's sturdy enough for a group of 10 or so to walk on it at one time."

"Right," Charlie agreed, "though we might need to replace the wood. I also think we should install railings."

"That's a good idea," I nodded. "See if you can come up with some kind of estimate that I can add to the budget for the grant I'm writing."

"Yep," Charlie said. "We can do that. I'll feed Harvey and take him out, if you want to get back to the diary."

As I cleared the table, I told Charlie that I first had to do research on the internet since I didn't know the historical context that Hildegarde referenced in her writing. I had long forgotten facts about World War I from past history classes.

Charlie grinned when I placed a ramekin of egg custard in front of him. I considered his smile more a result of the surprise dessert than my fuzzy recollection of school subjects. "What are you investigating?" he asked, reaching for his spoon.

"I read that Hildegarde's father died during the summer of 1918. Hildegarde wrote that she tried to get her mother to America, but JW told her it wasn't possible."

"OK," Charlie nodded. "What's the problem? Do you think JW lied to her?"

"I'm not sure," I replied. "I know that WWI didn't end until November 11, 1918, but surely citizens could get a visa."

"We were at war with Germany," Charlie noted. "Do you think they'd let folks come to America? Would we even let them into our country?"

"That's what I want to find out," I said.

By the time we finished our dessert and Charlie returned with Harvey, I'd loaded the dishwasher and wiped the table. I booted up my laptop, then made a cursory visit to a couple of websites, bookmarking the ones that seemed to have the most reliable information.

I couldn't find any immigration statistics for Germans coming to the U.S. in 1918, though I learned that many people here feared German Americans during WWI, even those whose families had lived in this country for generations. "It's hard to believe," I told Charlie, "but they weren't permitted to speak their language. In fact, words of German origin had to be changed. For example, sauerkraut became known as liberty cabbage."

"It sounds like prejudice to me," Charlie noted.

"That's for sure," I agreed. "Hate crimes against German Americans became prevalent, to the point of destroying family businesses. Many people changed their names, such as Schmidt became Smith, so no one could identify them as German."

"I always thought that people of German descent were held in high regard for their work ethic and craftsmanship," Charlie remarked.

"Not during WWI," I said. "It's no wonder that JW made sure that Hildegarde learned to speak English fluently. I thought he merely wanted to wield his masculine authority, but he must have tried to protect her."

"That makes sense," Charlie nodded. "So, I suppose Hildegarde won't expect a visit from her mother."

"At least, not until the war ends," I replied.

CHAPTER 16

*L*eon arrived in time to join Charlie and me for breakfast. Between searching historical websites and reading the diary the previous night, I'd stayed up far too late, yet I felt energized and ready to work on the grant and, perhaps, even start the script for the tours. "Aren't you the early bird?" I teased as I handed Leon a cup of coffee.

"Not much to do around this place in the winter," Leon replied. "I guess I should get a hobby."

"You'll be plenty busy as we make the machine barn ready for tours in the spring," Charlie reminded him.

"It's still too cold to work on the upper level," Leon said. "Some of the wood's rotted and we should replace it, though I think our roof repair held up during the blizzard."

"Do you think we should put on a whole new roof and rebuild the outer walls?" I asked. "If so, I'll need an estimate for the budget."

"It wouldn't be a bad idea," Charlie noted. "The building's basically sound, and we could use it to store some of our farm equipment."

"I'm not sure about that," I said, "because I want to keep it as it might have been during the Smithfield era. Can we salvage the wagon? That has historical value."

Charlie shook his head. "It's in pretty bad shape. You could probably show it to folks, but I don't think it could be a working vehicle."

"I could fiddle with it in my spare time," Leon said. "My dad taught me a thing or two about axles."

"That would be good," I nodded. "I'll go ahead and add its repair to the budget."

While I jotted a note for myself, Charlie mentioned that he'd make a list of everything we'd need for the restoration. "How much money do you plan to ask for?"

"The grant I'm working on has a max budget of $25,000," I replied.

"Roof and siding will likely take up half of that," Charlie stated, "but we have to do those things, or the barn won't pass inspection."

"Right," I agreed. "I'll mention that in my narrative. Could you take a couple photos that I can add to my submission?"

"OK," Charlie nodded. "Don't worry about lunch because Leon and I have to go into town later. We might also stop to see when Gunther's available."

ONCE I HAD the house to myself, I returned to Hildegarde's diary. The night before, I'd read through to early fall of 1918, and learned that Hildegarde had finally adjusted to her pregnancy. Jonas had purchased the land for the estate, and she took a drive with him to see it. Together they picked out the location for their home, though Hildegarde voiced some disagreement on the expansive footprint that Jonas envisioned. In the end, Jonas insisted that they build a mansion that befitted a gentleman of his stature.

October 4, 1918
Jonas is very worried that some of his workers have the influenza. The newspaper has many articles advising citizens to avoid crowded areas. Streetcars must have open windows, despite the chilly weather, and many American soldiers have already died from this illness that they call the Spanish flu. I

feel very sorry for their families because their young sons are now with Friedrich and Papa.

October 8, 1918
Jonas told me that the school board has closed the public schools today because of the influenza. He says that thousands of students and hundreds of teachers were absent yesterday, and no one knows how long the schools will remain closed. Jonas wants Adele to buy a lot of food at the market so she does not need to go again this week, and James will assist her.

October 11, 1918
Churches and poolrooms are now closed. Businesses and shops must operate on restricted hours, though saloons may stay open. The hospitals are filled to capacity. Poor areas of the city have had many casualties, and there are not enough well people to dig graves. Greta wants to go outside to play, but Jonas insists that we stay in our home. I am getting very worried.

October 13, 1918
Jonas has a fever and a deep cough, so he drank some brandy before going to sleep in the guest room. He told me that we must protect Greta and our unborn baby, so only James is permitted to assist him. I understand why Adele and I must stay away from Jonas, because it would be dreadful if we also became sick. Dear God, please protect Jonas. I cannot bear to think that he could die.

Was it just three weeks ago that Charlie came down with the identical symptoms as Jonas? I remembered how helpless I felt as I tried to bring down Charlie's fever with cool compresses, then made a hot toddy for medicinal purposes. It made me wonder if that became the reason saloons could remain open for business during the virulent 1918 influenza.

We didn't know whether Charlie and I had both been infected at the same time, but I fell ill with the flu the very next day. With trepidation, I continued reading Hildegarde's diary because I had a strong sense of dread as to why the Smithfields became childless.

October 14, 1918
Adele and James are both very sick. I am trying to keep Greta in her
bedroom, but she is very fussy. Jonas coughs so hard that I feel his insides
will burst. Cool cloths do nothing to bring down the fevers that Adele and
James are experiencing. How can I care for all of them? I am so very tired,
and my head hurts.

October 28, 1918
Greta has gone to heaven, as well as our unborn baby. I cannot bear the
sadness in my heart. Jonas found the strength to get help when all of us
suffered from the influenza. Despite his prestige, the hospital had no
remaining beds, but two nuns from Adele's church came to care for us. Jonas
told me that Greta and I turned blue, and my cough was so intense that I had
a miscarriage. Jonas considers it a blessing that I didn't witness the foamy
blood that came from Greta's nose and mouth. She died within hours of
becoming sick. I have no more tears. I have no more strength.

With great sadness, I stopped reading Hildegarde's diary, even as I wondered how much suffering this woman could endure. I made a cup of tea and set up my laptop on the kitchen table, then found every reputable website that described the horror of the 1918 global influenza pandemic.

Estimated that more than 20 million people died from this particular strain of flu during 1918-1919, second only to the Black Plague, researchers continued to seek reasons for the viral mutation that killed its victims in a matter of hours. To this day, it remained an unsolved mystery.

I reached for my phone to call Sister Cathy, since I wanted to share with her what I'd learned about the Smithfields. More importantly, though, I just needed to talk through my emotions. "I know why the Smithfields were childless," I said.

"What happened to Greta?" Cathy asked.

"That's why I'm calling. Greta died in the 1918 influenza pandemic."

"Oh, no! How horrible!" Cathy exclaimed.

"I couldn't bear to read another word of the diary," I said. "Did I tell you that Hildegarde was pregnant?"

"No, I don't believe so," Cathy replied.

"Well," I said, "Hildegarde was probably at the end of her first trimester when she got the flu, but she had a miscarriage."

"Dear God," Cathy sighed. "How devastating that the Smithfields lost their two children. I totally forgot about the 1918 influenza. Didn't they call it the Spanish flu?"

"Yes, but it was misnamed," I said, then explained what I'd learned from my research. Originally, they identified Spain as the first country to experience the epidemic, particularly since it seemed to strike young soldiers heading to WWI. However, Spain didn't become involved in the war, so their health records remained uncensored, which made it seem as if Spain's high numbers indicated the source of the influenza, somewhat like a false positive. "The second wave of influenza went completely global in the fall of 1918," I noted, "and that's when the entire Smithfield household fell ill. Apparently, a third wave occurred in early 1919, presumably as nations returned to normal after WWI, but the second wave caused the most deaths."

"Gosh," Cathy muttered. "I know that some of our Sisters died from the 1918 influenza. Many of them volunteered to help in hospitals and make-shift clinics."

"Two nuns from Adele's church in the city came to care for the Smithfield family and their servants when they were so sick, and hospitals didn't have enough beds. Do you think they were from your community?"

"I'm not sure," Cathy replied. "Remember, I'm from the mid-west branch, but I recall reading that our Sisters served most of the parishes in the cities around here, so it wouldn't surprise me."

"Then, we've just solved another mystery," I said.

"What do you mean?" Cathy questioned.

"I imagine that the Smithfields bequeathed their estate to your Sisters because of the nuns who helped them during the epidemic."

"Wow," Cathy said. "I'd never thought of that."

"Do you know what's weird?" I asked.

"What? That a nun came to help you and Charlie when you both had the flu?"

"Yes," I replied.

"That's not strange at all, Vicki. We have a mission to help others, so it's just what we do."

CHAPTER 17

*G*unther and Pauline came to our place at their scheduled time on Monday morning. Charlie and I planned that Gunther would help Charlie and Leon in the lower level of the machine barn, while Pauline and I worked on the script for the tours. Charlie made a pot of his special hazelnut coffee, and I placed a plate of mini-Danish pastries on the kitchen table, though Charlie and Leon had already helped themselves to a few. "Come on in," I smiled as I welcomed the Holtzes.

"Oh, my. It's mighty windy out there today," Pauline said, trying to settle her hair into place, "but it sure does smell good in here."

"That's Charlie's brew," I replied. "Would either of you like the coffee or do you prefer tea?"

"We'll both have coffee," Pauline said. "Right, Gunther?"

"Yep," he nodded. "Don't mind if we do."

Once everyone settled around the table, we chatted for a few minutes, mostly about the weather, which seemed the usual topic of conversation when you lived in the sticks. Eventually, I drew us back to the purpose of our meeting. "Before we get to task," I stated, "I think we should all take a tour along the same route we'll set up for visitors to the Smithfield estate."

"I hoped we'd have a chance to see everything," Pauline nodded. "I told Gunther just this morning that I didn't know what I could say to folks when I've never even seen what all the hoopla's about."

"That's exactly what I thought," I said. "I've coordinated with Sister Cathy, and she's opened the monastery side of the passageway for us."

I explained that we'd go in from the machine barn, down the ramp to see JW's still, and enter the basement of the mansion to view the vintage bowling alley. From there, we would take the elevator to the B&B, pass by the restaurant, and finish our tour with a visit to the gift shop. Leon planned to meet us at the front entrance in my car, and drive us back to the house.

"I'm glad we don't have to walk all the way back," Pauline said, "but what will you do when you have visitors?"

"Pretty much the same thing," I replied. "For example, if an organization books a tour, they'll have a bus or van, and the driver can meet the guests at the B&B entrance. If individuals arrive, however, the tour will only include the machine barn."

"What if they want to see the bowling alley?" Pauline asked.

"I guess we could show it, though the Sisters don't want people traipsing through the monastery at any time of day or night. They prefer that we'd control the number of visitors by limiting the availability of tours."

"Are we giving tours every day?" Pauline questioned.

"No," I replied. "We'll start by having tours only on Fridays and Saturdays. We want to showcase the restaurant and B&B, so I thought we could schedule one in late morning, and another mid afternoon. That way, guests could have lunch or an early dinner at the restaurant."

"That sounds reasonable," Pauline said. "I have chores to do at home, so I can't spend all of my time over here."

"Of course not," I agreed. "We'll work it out to fit your routine. If you're tied up, I'll lead the tour."

"I feel better now," Pauline sighed. "I told Gunther that I didn't want to do this if I had to come every day."

"I understand," I nodded. "Remember, we've never done this

before, so we may have to tweak our plans several times before we figure out how to do everything most efficiently."

"Are you guys ready?" Charlie asked as he took the key for the barn from the hook by the back door. When we put on our jackets, Harvey thought that we'd invited him to join us.

"Sorry, boy," Leon said. "You stay here, and I'll take you out later."

THE WIND NIPPED at our feet and stung our cheeks as we walked across the driveway to the Smithfield's machine barn. Charlie unlocked the bolt and opened one side of the double doors. As he flipped on the light switch to his right, several sconces dimly lit up the room. "The barn's got electricity?" Gunther asked.

"Yes, the old knob and tube," Charlie said. "We'll have to hire an electrician to replace it in order to bring the place up to code."

"That's not going to be cheap," Gunther muttered.

"Vicki put it in her grant budget," Charlie said. "We might as well do it while we're renovating."

"What's this old wagon?" Pauline asked.

"We think they used it to move the booze," Charlie noted. "They probably had to roll the barrels up the ramp from where the still is located down below."

"They might have also needed the wagon to dump the used mash from the barrels into the creek," I added.

"What's mash?" Pauline asked.

"Mash provided the base for the production of whiskey or moonshine," I said. "Usually, the recipe called for some kind of grain, like corn or rye, then they needed to add sugar or, maybe, even grapes. Once they cooked it and drained the juice, they'd toss the mash."

Pauline nodded her understanding, while Gunther still eyed the wagon. "This might've been horse-drawn," he said. "It makes sense with two stalls along the side wall."

"Leon's going to try to restore the wagon," Charlie noted. "It's in bad shape."

"Will you repair the walls of the barn?" Gunther asked. "It looks as if plenty of wildlife made their home in here."

"It's in the budget," Charlie replied. "Let's head on down the ramp."

It pleased me that Charlie took ownership of his role in this endeavor for the Sisters. After he paused to make sure we followed behind him, he pushed the button to open the pocket door leading to the barn's lower level. The Holtzes looked amazed when they saw the stacks of barrels in several stalls and the old still ready to collect the next batch of moonshine. "Will you look at that?" Gunther exclaimed. "There's even a jug placed under the spigot. Do you think they used kerosene to cook the stuff?"

"That's what I figure," Charlie said. "Leon and I examined the vent the other day. It's held up pretty good over the years."

"This is unbelievable," Gunther said, shaking his head.

"Wait until you see this passageway," Charlie chuckled.

Charlie pushed the button on the pocket door, flipped on the lights, and invited us to follow him. "Are you sure this is safe?" Pauline asked.

"The Sisters had it examined by an engineer," I replied. "It passed with flying colors."

At the end of the passage, Charlie pushed the button to open the final pocket door. We emerged through the floor-to-ceiling wardrobe closet for entry into the monastery basement. Charlie showed the Holtzes how to close the door, using what I called the decoy bowling pin. Gunther examined the closet, saying, "They aligned the seams so well that you'd never know it had a door along its back wall."

I screwed the pole designed to hang clothing into place, and closed the closet door so that it became one of the many cabinets and wardrobes built along the entire front wall of the monastery base-ment. It didn't surprise me to see that the Holtzes looked shell-shocked. I'd felt the same way when Sister Cathy and I discovered the hidden portal during the summer.

"Cheese and crackers!" Gunther exclaimed. "How ever did you find this?"

I showed Gunther and Pauline the nodule embedded into the

basement floor near the bowling alley. When I pushed it, we all heard the faint click. "Sister Cathy and I didn't know what the sound meant, nor could we find anything in the closet. However, I noticed that the extra bowling pin stored in one of the cabinets had a hole drilled in the bottom of it, so we removed the pole from the closet and inserted the bowling pin over the pole screw. When Cathy turned the bowling pin toward the back wall, the pocket door opened."

"I'll never understand how you figured that out," Pauline commented.

"Frankly," I chuckled, "I don't know either, but I just put all of the pieces of the puzzle together. While the passage is open, Leon, do you want to go back and get my car? The keys are on the kitchen counter."

"OK," Leon agreed. "I'll meet you upstairs at the front entrance in about 15 minutes."

While I closed up the passageway, Charlie told the Holtzes what we knew about the construction of the bowling alley. He explained that they used pine for most of the length of the alley, though they needed a harder wood, like walnut, where the bowler would throw the ball. "Surprisingly, many of these old mansions had bowling alleys in the basement," he noted.

"Very interesting," Gunther stated.

When I put the decoy bowling pin back in its cabinet, I showed Gunther and Pauline the two bowling balls which had only two finger holes. "That's how they designed them back in the day," I said. "They're made from a very heavy tropical wood called *lignum vitae*."

"Who'd have thought?" Pauline mused. "I wonder if your grandmother ever came down here, Gunther. Maybe she and Hildegarde bowled a few times."

"Could be," Gunther nodded.

"Maybe she even helped make the moonshine," Pauline added. "Do you think she'd have done that? Was there anything in the diary about it, Vicki?"

"No, I had to stop reading for a while so I could finish up the grant proposal. Besides, it became too depressing."

"How so?" Pauline asked.

"The entire Smithfield household came down with the influenza in 1918, including your grandmother, Gunther. Hildegarde, pregnant at the time, lost the baby. Their daughter, Greta, also died."

"Oh, my goodness! How terrible," Pauline exclaimed. "I can't even imagine losing a child."

Charlie led us to the elevator, and turned out the lights before pressing the button for the first floor. As we passed by the restaurant, I mentioned that we'd invite guests to stay for a meal if they had made reservations, then we stopped by the gift shop. Sister Dolores, arranging some new items in the glass display, glanced up with a pleasant smile as she said, "How nice to see all of you. Did you enjoy your tour?"

"Absolutely," Pauline grinned, "and I think it's even more exciting since Gunther's grandmother was Hildegard's friend. Of course, we don't know if Adele took part in any illegal activity. I doubt it, though, because she wasn't that type."

"From what I've read in the diary," I said, "I can't imagine that Hildegarde was involved either. In fact, I wonder if she even knew about the passageway."

"You need to keep reading the diary," Pauline stated.

Dolores agreed, then told us that she'd decided to order some souvenirs with the *Monastery Restaurant and Inn* logo. Pauline suggested that she also buy some keychains and mugs, maybe even some post cards with pictures of the barn and still. I liked their ideas, and it pleased me that both Dolores and Pauline seemed to embrace this new venture.

"OK, folks. Leon's waiting for us," Charlie said. "Let's get a move on."

We bid farewell to Sister Dolores, then piled into my car as I mentioned that I'd prepared sandwiches for lunch. "After we eat," I said, "the men will work in the barn for an hour or so, while Pauline and I develop an outline for the tour script."

Charlie suggested that we wrap everything up by 3 o'clock, and we all considered that a good plan.

CHAPTER 18

$\mathcal{P}$redictions for another snowstorm had me scrambling to get to the grocery store before my weekly meeting with Sister Marian and Sister Cathy. Although the forecasters predicted only 4 to 6 inches, I considered the market a madhouse, and had barely enough time to put the perishables into the refrigerator and freezer before heading over to the monastery.

"I'm glad you could make it before the snow," Marian smiled.

"Me, too," I agreed as I took off my parka. "I have some good news and bad news."

"Uh-oh," Marian said. "Start with the good news."

"The grant application for the executive director position was partially funded. I'm invited to resubmit when we have data to show that *Rock Creek Farm* will benefit the disadvantaged in the city and surrounding counties."

"That's a great start," Cathy said.

"It was probably a long shot to get the whole amount I requested," I noted, "but at least the foundation saw the merit of our proposal. Unfortunately, the educational programming grant was rejected. Apparently, I didn't include enough detail about the types of activities we'd have."

"Not to worry," Cathy replied with a reassuring smile. "Maybe Cheryl can give you some ideas."

"What about the renovations to the barn?" Marian asked.

"I think we have a good chance with that grant because of the historical value of the still," I stated. "I could only ask for $25,000, and that won't cover all of the work that needs to be done, so I'll look for more funding sources."

"Are you getting frustrated?" Cathy asked.

"No, I figure this is what grant writing's all about. You put a lot of work into crafting the proposal, then you wait to see if the review committee thinks it matches their guidelines. I'm just not very experienced with it all."

"Every little bit of funding helps," Marian remarked. "We agreed to start slowly, and you've heard the old adage that 'Rome wasn't built in a day.'"

"I know," I nodded, "but patience isn't one of my strong suits. I'm worried that once spring arrives, I won't have much time to focus on grants."

"We'll have some income from the tours," Marian noted. "How much do you want to charge?"

"I'm not sure," I replied. "What do you think about $10 a person for adults?"

"Would people pay that much?" Cathy questioned.

I nodded. "A lot of historical places charge $15 to $20; a few less than $10."

"How about we start with $10, and offer a 20% group discount?" Cathy suggested.

"That's a good idea," I said. "Maybe we could also provide a voucher for 10% off the cost of a meal at the restaurant or items purchased at the gift shop."

"Definitely," Marian agreed. "What about kids?"

"I think we need to focus on cultural tours for adults as we get started. Let's see how that goes in the spring, and maybe we can expand our audience in the summer."

The Sisters thought that made a good objective. They also agreed to my suggestion that we'd offer the tours twice on two days of the week, and we'd require reservations for the tour, as well as for a meal at the restaurant.

"How was your work session with Pauline?" Cathy queried.

"We had a good start," I replied, "but we only played with the outline of a script. I want Pauline to tell the story in her own words, rather than have a stilted recitation, but she's not there yet."

"Have you thought about offering a brochure?" Marian asked.

"Charlie and I spoke about that. Unfortunately, there are just not enough hours in the day."

"I wonder if Sister Bridget could have the new aspirants design something. She told us she'd like to do creative things with the young women, and it would be good for them to know about the early days of the monastery."

"I didn't realize that the formation house is operational yet," I replied.

"Sister Bridget hit the ground running," Cathy said. "Kate, and two other women, are now in the aspirant program. Their names are Ellen and Marianne. They'll come to the monastery a weekend every month for prayer and reflection. Of course, that'll be interspersed with some fun time to get to know each other."

We all agreed that developing a brochure would make a superb activity for the young women. Relieved to have one thing off my plate, the Sisters encouraged me to go home since the flurries that started earlier in our conversation had changed to fluffy snowflakes, already sticking to the grass. I considered them the kind that prompted the joyful anticipation of a snow day during my childhood.

CHARLIE MUST HAVE PUT away the rest of the groceries when he came in from working in the barn. I found him in the den gluing pieces of wood for another birdhouse, and aromas of Elmer's glue tickled my nose. "I'm glad you made it back before the roads became too slick," Charlie said. "How'd your meeting go?"

"Good," I smiled. "We worked out more details, such as the cost of the tours and vouchers for meals. Marian plans to ask Sister Bridget if the aspirants could design some brochures."

"I thought it was just Kate," Charlie replied.

"Two others, too," I noted. "Their names are Ellen and Marianne, but I didn't meet them yet."

Charlie remarked that he had chatted briefly with Sister Bridget the other day when he dropped off a couple of birdhouses at the gift shop. "I think she and those aspirants will add more life to the place. Tony often spoke about the old days when they had a bunch of novices, though now it'll mean more mouths to feed."

"Right," I agreed, "but they'll have more income with the B&B and restaurant. Speaking of food, I bought a frozen lasagna, so we'll have an easy dinner. Hildegarde's diary is calling to me."

"That's fine with me," Charlie nodded. "You can keep me company while you read."

After making a quick salad, I put the lasagna in the oven and set the table, then returned to the den to continue reading.

November 12, 1918

The war is over, thanks be to God. Jonas showed me the newspaper headline that the armistice was signed yesterday, yet my homeland is in chaos. So many needless deaths. I have begged Jonas to process any paperwork needed to bring Mama to America, and he promised to do what he can. Adele is such a comfort to me. She says we must celebrate Thanksgiving, but I feel that Jonas and I are too sad. She says we should invite those who are less fortunate, so I will leave it in her hands.

November 19, 1918

Today would have been Greta's birthday. I will be glad when the day is done. Jonas, away on business, is lucky to have a diversion, but I must stay home to recuperate. All I have are reminders that Greta is no longer with us. Adele took Greta's toys and her precious Kitty to the orphanage, but her room is still there, empty of her laughter and joy. I remember last year when she

chose the pumpkins and leaves for our dining room, and she brought us such
delight. There is no more happiness. It is gone forever.

November 25, 1918
Adele told me that she met the Sisters who cared for us at church on Sunday.
The Sisters of St. Carmella did not escape the devastation of the influenza.
Many of them became very sick, and some of them died. The Sisters are
seeking families who will have a Thanksgiving dinner for those who are not
able. I have given permission for three couples to join us. All of them lost
children to the flu. Jonas may be angry with me, but I do not care because it
is the right thing to do.

November 28, 1918
Our Thanksgiving Day is done, and I am very tired. Jonas is having his
brandy in the parlor, but I have prepared for bed since he will sleep in the
guest room. I know that Jonas feels the pain of loss as I do. Perhaps more so
because Greta was so very special to him. Still, I learned that many families
in our neighborhood experienced the same grief that we bear. Adele says that
our Thanksgiving dinner was a tribute to our valiant attempt to recognize
that we must give thanks for our blessings. Many of our guests experienced
far greater losses than we have. None of us knows how we will continue
forward, but we all felt a kinship today.

December 12, 1918
I can barely believe that Mama will come for Christmas. Jonas helped
process the immigration paperwork, and booked her passage by ship. She will
arrive in New York on December 23, so James will drive us to the port to
meet her. I told Adele that we have so much to do to prepare for Mama. She
will have Greta's bedroom since Jonas still prefers to sleep in the guest room.
New furnishings for the room will come next week, then we will have only a
few days to prepare for Mama's arrival. I am so very excited.

If Charlie hadn't interrupted my reading to say that we should eat,
I'd probably have read through the night. Instead, I followed the

wafting scent of garlic to the kitchen, and observed the two lighted candles at our table and the dimmed overhead lights.

Charlie pulled out my chair, and gallantly invited me to sit. With the gusto of an Italian waiter, he uncorked a bottle of wine and filled our glasses. Before taking his seat, he served the lasagna, salad, and crusty bread. We had a delightful romantic evening watching the snow peacefully descend over the back pasture.

We both agreed that life couldn't get much better.

CHAPTER 19

$\mathcal{M}$arch arrived like the proverbial lion. Mother Nature brought a brief warm up with sunny days to melt all of our snow, but the wind howled as a reminder that we still had to wait for spring. Despite the gusts, Father Jim brought a couple of volunteers to help Charlie and Leon clean and organize the barn basement. Charlie wanted the barrels unstacked so they could determine which ones they might salvage then, once they swept the floor from the years of debris, they'd place the barrels as an appealing display.

I received good news in yesterday's mail. The foundation totally funded our renovation grant, and they'd electronically deposit the check in the non-profit's account. Charlie intended to start soliciting bids for the necessary work on the upper level of the barn and, if all went well, we hoped to offer tours by the middle of April.

I needed to complete the details for Pauline's narrative, which meant that I had to continue reading Hildegarde's diary. I threw in a load of wash, and ran the vacuum through the house, before I settled down with a cup of tea in the den.

December 24, 1918
I can hardly believe that Mama is here. It has been more than five years
since I have seen her. She is much too thin, and is tired from her journey. It
is evident that the deaths of Papa and Friedrich have had a toll on her spirit.
Though she never met Greta, she said that she shed many tears when she
received my post. Adele had a surprise for us when we returned from the
port. She bought a small fir tree at the market, and decorated it with my
beautiful glass ornaments. Mama thinks it is a lovely Tannenbaum, and we
will open gifts after church tomorrow.

December 25, 1918
Jonas did not go to church with us today since he cannot bear the memory of
last Christmas when Greta sang with the choir. He believes that God has
been very cruel to us, but Mama says we cannot blame God. We must pray
for strength to overcome our challenges, and ask for peace in the world. After
church, we opened our gifts. Though rather sparse this year, Adele had some-
thing for each of us. She bought Jonas a book she thought he might like, and
she gave me a pretty necklace. For James and Mama, she made a scarf.
Mama asked James to bring her steamer trunk to the parlor. It contained
many grape clippings, all wrapped snugly in burlap. She says we must keep
them moist until we are able to plant them in the spring. She brought a
carton of wine and brandy for Jonas, a box of glass ornaments for our
Tannenbaum, and a springerle rolling pin for the kitchen. Adele received a
jewelry box, similar to the one I have, but there is no hidden compartment.
Mama gave me a locket with Greta's picture, which made me cry. Adele
prepared a fine dinner that James served, and I insisted they join us at the
table because we are all family now.

January 1, 1919
It is a new year. Adele says that I must make a resolution since it is a custom
here, and I should choose something that will make me a better person. I have
decided that I will do charitable deeds for others. I want to help families who
are suffering. I told Mama my plan and she approved. Mama thinks we
should ask the Sisters who helped us where is the greatest need. Adele said I
need to do more than just acts of kindness. She reminded me that Jonas has

many friends of wealth. If I would socialize with them, I could ask them to share their resources, then we would assist more people. I will think about it.

January 10, 1919
Jonas is away on business. Mama and Adele are making springerle cookies in the kitchen. I have not tasted my favorite German cookie since coming to America, but I will have to wait until tomorrow to have one since they must set overnight before baking them. Mama noticed that Jonas has not been sleeping in my bed, so I told her that he is grieving, as am I. She says that we must comfort each other because suffering apart from one another will create a chasm that might never be resolved. I don't know how to fix the problem when Jonas doesn't want to sleep with me, but Mama says that I must make the effort.

Amanda's phone call interrupted my reading. Although we chatted often, I hadn't connected with her over the weekend. Since Hannah planned to arrive after lunch to work with her on the wedding invitations, Amanda thought I might want to help, and asked if they could use my kitchen table to spread out.

I wanted to decline because I hadn't planned for such an interruption as part of my schedule for the day. Nevertheless, I knew Amanda and Hannah considered it important to include me, so I gathered all of the enthusiasm I could muster, and told Amanda to come over when Hannah arrived.

While I had my phone in hand, I decided to call Pauline since we needed to set up a time to meet this week, probably later rather than sooner. I suggested that we get together on Friday afternoon to work on the script. Pauline readily agreed, but requested that we meet at her home. "We could take a gander at the attic," she said. "There's so much stuff up there, I just don't know where to look. Gunther doesn't have much interest, and I hate to pester him about it."

"That works for me," I replied. "I'll stop by around 2 o'clock. That'll give us time to do a little exploring, then we can talk about the story you'll tell on the tours."

"I still don't know what I'm going to say," Pauline said.

"That's what we'll figure out," I assured her.

"I noticed in the paper that the local Women's Guild is looking for venues," Pauline noted. "I wonder if they might be interested in the mansion. I don't know why I didn't think of that until just now. Of course, they would because the Smithfields put this town on the map."

"Do you know anyone we can contact?" I asked.

"Sure, I'm a member, so I'll give a few people a call."

I told Pauline the cost that we'd determined for the tours, and suggested that she also mention the group discount and meal vouchers. If they expressed any interest, she could go ahead and make the arrangements. I took a quick look at my calendar, and noted that we could make Friday, April 21, as the start date. "Do you think we'll be ready by then?" Pauline queried.

"Having a date to work toward is a great incentive," I said. "Yes, we'll have everything ready."

After we disconnected, I counted the time until start-up on the calendar. How would we ever meet our goal in only seven weeks? I decided not to overthink it. If Pauline could get a group together, I could certainly make sure that we'd covered all of the details.

AMANDA AND HANNAH lugged in their boxes of invitations shortly after 1 o'clock. I made sure that we had no crumbs on the kitchen table before we began, because we certainly couldn't send out anything soiled.

Amanda made stacks of the different components—the envelopes, the announcements, and the return cards, as Hannah spread out the guest list and addresses. "Here's the plan," Amanda announced. "I'll read the name and address to Hannah, and she'll write it on the outer envelope, since her handwriting's better than mine. Then, Vicki will put all of the pieces together, seal the envelope, and put a stamp on it. Got it?"

"Got it," I chuckled. "How many are on the guest list?"

"About 150," Hannah replied. "Do you think that's too many?"

"It's your wedding," I noted, "so you get to choose who you want to celebrate with you. Besides, you and Steve are paying for everything."

"We've tried to keep it manageable," Hannah sighed, "but you know how it goes. I think the list is as trimmed as it's going to get."

Within short measure, we had a good system, and each of us stayed focused and on task. Every so often, Amanda would declare how many names she hadn't checked off the list, until she came to the last one. "We're done," she grinned.

"Do you want to mail these out today?" I asked.

Amanda nodded. "Hannah's going to drop them off at the post office on her way home. You don't have to put a stamp on the one for you and GP."

"I figured that," I chuckled. "Anyone want a cup of tea?"

"I'm good," Amanda replied. "I need to get back to the monastery to start supper."

Hannah also wanted to get on the road. We boxed up all of the packets, separating the ones going in the mail from the extras that Amanda would hold in case they forgot someone. "We're going to bridal shops on Saturday if you'd like to join us," Hannah remarked.

"I'll take a rain check," I said, shaking my head. "Knowing Amanda, you'll probably be trying on wedding gowns all day."

"No doubt," Hannah chuckled, "since neither of us yet knows what style we want."

"Another reason you don't need my input," I grinned. "I'm sure you'll have fun shopping together." I couldn't help but think that I'd dodged a bullet on that one.

CHAPTER 20

*C*harlie spent the next morning soliciting bids for the barn renovations after he told me about the progress Leon and he had made with the help of the volunteers yesterday. He mentioned that they had to scrap five barrels, though they salvaged the others, then rearranged them to make the place look rustic, but realistic. He and Leon planned to buy lumber in the afternoon, so they could start rebuilding the ramp.

While Charlie made his calls for proposals, I set up my reservations binder. Feeling somewhat optimistic, I penciled in the Women's Guild as our first tour, then made a contact list for other potential groups that might have an interest in seeing the Smithfield estate.

To prepare for my meeting with Pauline, I outlined topics that she could discuss with an audience in the upper level of the barn. I wanted her introduction to start with JW and Hildegarde, from a human-interest perspective. She could tell a story about Hildegarde's friendship with Adele, then speak about why Hildegarde wanted a country estate, suitable for a vineyard. We had plenty of material from the diary that we could use to bring JW and Hildegarde to life.

I hadn't yet discovered how JW became involved in bootlegging, nor did I know if he'd told Hildegarde about his activities. She'd never identified what took him away on business so often, yet I wanted Pauline to paint a picture of them as husband and wife, breadwinner and supporter. I hoped to learn what they considered important when they developed the plans for their estate, and how the events of the stock market crash and Prohibition impacted them, so Pauline could include those in her talk.

From there, Pauline could discuss the enactment of the 18th Amendment and the difficulty enforcing it. From a business perspective, selling illegal booze became lucrative despite its risk. That would set the stage for bringing the group to the lower level of the barn to see the still, and through the secret passage to the basement of the monastery.

I figured that Pauline would find the first part of the tour an easy one since she had no trouble telling a story, but I didn't feel as sure about her confidence with the historical perspective of Prohibition, so I needed to find more fodder in the diary.

January 23, 1919
Mama and I visited the Sisters at the convent today. Adele reminded me that I should ask for the Mother Superior. I told the nun that I would like to provide assistance to families in need, but I didn't know what would be most beneficial. Without hesitation, she said that the orphan asylum was over-crowded, and there are not enough resources to provide proper nourishment for the children. For many of them, their parents had died from the influenza. I had never thought about that. We had lost our darling Greta, but what if Jonas and I had died, leaving Greta with no family. Before Mama and I departed, I promised to find a way to help the orphans. Jonas will be home in two days, so I will speak to him about their needs.

January 30, 1919
Today is Mama's birthday. She is only 67 years old, but she looks so frail. Adele made a lovely cake for dessert, and added a lot of butter to help make Mama plump. We have been teaching English to Mama every afternoon, but she is not making progress very quickly. She said she has many things to tell Jonas, but she cannot make good sentences in English. Mama must learn to

be patient. When Jonas returned home, I told him about my meeting with the
Sisters. He said we will send money to buy food for the children, but we will
not take any orphans into our home. I know he is thinking of his own childhood, and maybe Greta. I also told him that we should host a dinner for his
friends and their wives, which made him look very surprised, but pleased. I
did not tell him my motive.

February 16, 1919
Jonas has hired an architect for our home in the country. He showed me the
design, and I think it is much too grand. Mama told me not to argue with
Jonas about it because a man of his stature needs a visible sign of his success.
He wants to be lord of his castle, and have others admire his wealth. She said
that I should be his partner and support, but I may also insist on design
elements that will give me comfort, and afford me the opportunity to have
room to accommodate servants and guests. She suggested that we should have
a large kitchen and pantry, as well as plenty of storage, so I will heed
Mama's advice.

March 8, 1919
Adele looked flushed when she returned from the market today. I asked if she
felt sick, but she said that she had tarried too long, and hurried to get home.
Mama thinks Adele is seeing a young man since the grocer hired a German
immigrant to stock the shelves and help patrons with their purchases. I asked
Mama how she knows this. She told me that Adele spoke about him while
Mama helped in the kitchen. I do not understand why Adele has not
mentioned this to me. Mama told me not to feel slighted because Adele does
not realize that she is falling in love. She will tell me when she becomes
aware that their affection has progressed. How is it that Mama can be so
wise?

March 23, 1919
Jonas is very pleased that we have entertained guests for two dinner parties. I
believe he picked friends who I might also like because I found them quite
enjoyable. When the men retired to the parlor for their brandy and cigars, I
told the wives about the overcrowded orphan asylum, and they want to help.

We will go together to visit the children. Mama did not want to join us at table, so she ate in the kitchen with Adele. She and Adele are becoming very close. Adele says that she feels a kinship with Mama since she has missed her own mother so much. I am happy about many things now, but mostly because Jonas has returned to my bed.

When he finished all of his calls, Charlie came to the den to ask if I wanted to eat lunch. I joined him in the kitchen, and saw that he'd made two sandwiches, already plated at the table. I opened a jar of pickles, while he poured us both a root beer.

"Any luck with your bids?" I questioned.

"One of the electricians will be here later this afternoon to check out the barn. The other two will meet me tomorrow."

"That's good," I nodded. "What about construction on the outer walls of the barn?"

"All three builders will be here tomorrow," Charlie noted. "Most likely, we'll need to shore up the walls before they can do any of the electrical work."

"Do you think it can be ready by April 21?" I asked.

"We won't know until we get the estimates," Charlie said. "It'll also depend on how long it takes to receive the permits and inspections."

"How about the roof?" I queried.

"Roofers can't get out here until the end of the week. From what they told me, a number of folks had problems after the big January blizzard."

"Your patch job appears to have held up," I noted. "Maybe we can wait on the roof."

"Maybe," Charlie said, "but we'll let the professionals give us their opinion."

"That's fine," I nodded, feeling relieved that Charlie had everything under control. Certainly, we didn't know if we'd have any construction issues, although we could deal with those, as needed. I told Charlie that I thought we should place an ad for the tours in the newspaper, but he suggested that I wait until we received the projected timelines for the renovations.

When Charlie and I finished eating, he wanted to pick up Leon for their trip to the lumber yard. I knew he needed to return in time to meet the electrician, so I encouraged him to get on the road. In the meantime, I'd try to find more information I could add to Pauline's script.

CHAPTER 21

$\mathcal{I}$ found Sister Bridget chatting with Sister Marian and Sister Cathy when I arrived for our weekly meeting. As if they'd made me an honorary member of their community, I welcomed her to the monastery, and told her that I hoped she'd enjoy her new ministry. Sister Marian explained that Bridget wanted more information about the brochure, so she invited Bridget to join us.

"Do you think the aspirants can help to develop our brochure?" I asked.

"Not really," Bridget said apologetically as she shook her head. "They won't come here as a group until Holy Week. Even with an early Easter this year, we couldn't manage to have it ready for you in the timeframe that you need it." I supposed my disappointment showed because she quickly added, "I wouldn't mind playing around with it, since I like doing things like that."

"That would be wonderful," I said with relief. I told the Sisters about my outline and our plan for the tours, explaining that the leaflet could follow the same story line. We'd also add pictures to capture interest.

"Do you have enough detail for the script?" Cathy asked.

I nodded. "I have loads of it for setting the scene with the early days of JW and Hildegarde's marriage, but nothing yet for the boot-legging phase."

"Don't forget," Cathy noted. "We have the ledgers."

"We can't handle them," I reminded her. "They're falling apart."

"I wonder if we could get replicas made," Cathy said. "We should also try to preserve the originals."

"The historical society may be able to help," Marian said.

I agreed with Marian's idea, especially since I'd thought about making another visit there before the end of the month. Cathy offered to go with me. "Don't ask me why," she added, "but I still have a strong interest in the historical aspects of this place."

"Do you want to go next week?" I asked.

"Sure. How about we let Marian off the hook, and our trip could take the place of our regular meeting?"

"You can count me out, too," Bridget said. "Just tell me what you want to include in the brochure, and I'll design it."

I told Bridget that I'd send her some material by e-mail. In the meantime, I'd continue to read the diary. I also mentioned that Pauline had invited me to forage in the Holtz's attic.

"Are you looking for anything special?" Cathy asked.

"Not really," I replied, "though I wouldn't mind finding a jewelry box that Hildegarde's mother gave to Adele."

"Another secret compartment?" Marian chuckled.

"No," I said, "but perhaps Adele used it to keep mementos from Hildegarde. Regardless, we might find something useful from the Holtz's homestead."

We wrapped up our meeting with my progress report on our grants and the barn renovations. Marian agreed that Charlie could make the necessary decisions about the contractors, so I felt quite pleased with the headway we'd made.

Seeing Charlie still out in the barn when I arrived home, I put frozen meatballs into a pot of marinara sauce to heat on the stove, and made a quick salad. It didn't take long for me to settle in the den, and continue reading the diary.

April 25, 1919
We had a fine outing in the country today. Jonas wanted me to see that construction has begun on our new home, and he thought Mama could select the best location for our vineyards. I suggested that we bring the grape clippings, but Mama says it is still too early to plant them, and they will have a better chance to take hold if we wait another month. It was a lovely spring day, and Jonas asked Adele to make a picnic lunch. We all sat on a blanket that James placed near the creek, overlooking the area that will become our vineyard. After we ate, James stayed with Mama, while Jonas, Adele, and I explored the meandering creek. We didn't walk too far before we found a low-lying clearing where inlets seemed to merge. Jonas suggested that we might easily dam the creek to make a small lake, which I considered a lovely idea.

May 2, 1919
Adele told me that she has a beau, and his name is Dieter Holtz. I think she is quite smitten. Adele asked if Dieter might have permission to call on her. She said she can entertain in the kitchen so as not to disturb our family. I see no problem as Mama said she will chaperone. Jonas must feel that he has to protect Adele because he insisted that Dieter meet with him first. I told Adele that she may invite Dieter to join us for supper on Sunday evening.

May 6, 1919
I liked Dieter very much, so I can see why Adele finds herself attracted to him. Though he is not as fluent in language as Adele and I, Dieter spoke English at our table, and even Mama could follow some of the conversation. Dieter told us of his family in Germany. He, too, lost a brother in the war. Dieter plans to settle in America, find a wife, and own his own business. I noticed Adele's blush. When Jonas asked Dieter if he had any experience with tilling or planting, Dieter said that he worked on his family's farm as a boy. I knew that Dieter passed muster when Jonas offered him a job at our country estate. Initially, he will plant the grape vines and tend to the vine-

yard. When our home is completed, he will do all of the landscaping. Dieter
agreed immediately. Before Dieter departed, Jonas told him that he is
welcome to call on Adele.

May 30, 1919
Jonas told me that all of the concrete in the basement of our new home is
finished, and construction of the framework has begun. I had hoped to visit
the site, but Jonas said it would not be wise for us to interrupt the progress.
Instead, he and I will spend time to decide on elements for the interior. I
reminded Jonas that we must have a lot of storage space. In addition to large
closets in the bedrooms, Jonas suggested that we have a wall of built-in
wardrobes and cabinets in the basement. He will have the architect add the
design. Always I must be patient, though I am getting excited to soon live in
the country.

When we sat down to supper, Charlie looked exhausted. He accompanied his slow descent into the chair with a muffled grunt. Not only had he met with each of the contractors, but he and Leon had also torn out the old ramp to the barn basement. Charlie told me that he had expected to find rotted wood, but unfortunately, they'd discovered evidence of termites. "We'd better call an insect control specialist in case the place needs remediation," he stated.

"How long before we get any bids on the construction work?" I asked.

"I told each of them that I needed something in writing by Monday, but their verbal estimates are what I expected."

"I guess we can't do much but wait," I said.

"Right," Charlie nodded. "I'll find someone to check on the termite damage tomorrow. Once we get an all clear, Leon and I can put in the new ramp and railings. How'd your meeting go with the Sisters?"

I knew better than to remind Charlie that he should let someone younger assist Leon with the ramp. Tired or not, the man would do what he wanted to do. Instead, I recounted some of the things that the Sisters and I discussed, and updated him about the plan to visit the historical society next week.

Charlie didn't see the point in taking time away from our schedule, but I explained that one of their staff might preserve the ledgers that we'd found. Not only did we want to display authentic copies in the machine barn, but they also had great historical value.

After I sliced two pieces of apple pie, and made us each a cup of tea, we both sat quietly, gazing out the picture window. With the March days getting longer, the setting sun left hues of pinks and lavender as a stunning backdrop to the trees beyond the field. Eventually, Charlie asked if I'd learned anything new regarding Hildegarde.

"I don't think she knew about the bootleg operation," I replied. "Hildegarde wanted to visit the construction site for their mansion, but JW made up some flimsy excuse as to why she couldn't."

"He might have considered it dangerous," Charlie said.

"No," I stated with a shake of my head. "JW probably wanted to hide the passageway from Hildegarde. He placated her by saying that he'd have the architect design a whole wall of closets in the basement."

"Don't you think that's stretching it a bit? I don't really understand how you're making such a connection. Do you think he was planning ahead for Prohibition?"

"Yes, I do," I said. "The 18th amendment passed in 1919, but it didn't go into effect until January, 1920. Construction on the mansion began just about that time."

"I thought you found instructions for making moonshine among Hildegarde's jelly recipes," Charlie noted. "Wouldn't that indicate that she was involved in making his liquor?"

"Darn it," I frowned. "You're right, but why wouldn't JW take his wife to see the progress on their home? It doesn't make sense to me."

"I suppose you'll have to keep reading," Charlie chuckled.

CHAPTER 22

Friday morning dawned bright, though chilly. At breakfast, Charlie told me that he and Leon planned to spend the day in the barn, and Gunther would join them for the afternoon. After they met with the termite inspector, due to arrive shortly, they'd continue their work on the ramp. With that, Charlie put his plate on the floor so Harvey could lap up the residual scrambled eggs, making it quite clear why Harvey settled himself next to Charlie's chair at every meal.

While I loaded the dishwasher, Charlie donned his jacket to take Harvey out while he put our trash in the bin. As usual, an unsuspecting squirrel captured Harvey's attention, and Charlie patiently waited for his return from the woods. By the time Leon arrived, Harvey readily returned to his favorite spot under the kitchen table.

With the morning to myself, I cleared off the counter and organized the papers that always seemed to accumulate there. I reminded myself to create a file for the various reports, bills, and construction estimates because we'd need access to them when we filed the assessment documents for funding agencies.

After setting up my laptop on the kitchen table, I emailed more features for the brochure to Sister Bridget, as well as some of the pictures I'd uploaded the other day, then I put finishing touches on the first part of the script to give to Pauline.

I tried to imagine Pauline as she stood in front of a group to recount the story of JW and Hildegarde. Would she bring the narrative to life? Could she engage the visitors, then make them feel a part of the secret enterprise? Only time would tell.

I arrived at the Holtz's home just as Gunther got into his older model truck to head over to our place. When Gunther revved the engine, a poof of gray smoke emitted from the exhaust, and both the front and back fenders looked as if they'd come in contact with a few trees through the years. Gunther waved his welcome, then stuck his head out the window and called, "Pauline's ready for you. I hope you know what you're getting yourself into."

Putting up a good front, I laughed and said, "I'm prepared for anything." Of course, I didn't know what to expect. Since the doorbell didn't seem to work, I knocked on the front door.

Pauline greeted me, and invited me to take a seat in the front parlor. With its mishmash of antiques, modern furniture, and assortment of crocheted throws and doilies, the oblong room had a cozy feel. The stone fireplace on the left wall had a hewn wooden mantle that served as a display for various knickknacks, including Hildegarde's jewelry box. Lined with decades of black soot, the hearth paid tribute to its years of providing comfort and warmth.

Pauline joined me on the sofa, and we chatted for a while. Rather, she rambled on with stories about the old homestead. Eventually, Pauline wanted to know the details of anything I had learned about Gunther's grandmother, so I recounted the events in Hildegarde's diary about Adele falling in love with Dieter Holtz. I mentioned that both of the Smithfields approved of the young German immigrant, and JW offered him a job to plant and care for the vineyards.

"I don't think Gunther knew that his grandfather worked at the estate," Pauline said. She seemed fascinated by the idea that Dieter technically served as JW's groundskeeper. I had no doubt that Gunther would hear all about it when he returned.

I'd wanted to go over the script with Pauline, but she insisted that we first explore the attic. Expecting pull-down steps to a crawl space, the Holtzes had a door at the end of the upstairs hallway leading to a staircase. Another 13 steps led us to a massive area with beams and rafters, as well as a hardwood floor. Two small dormer windows dimly lit the large room until Pauline switched on the lights.

"Don't choke on the dust up here," Pauline said. "I keep the door to the stairs closed because I can't tell you how many times that we've had a bat flying around here." I had to admit that I felt some trepidation since bats gave me the heebie-jeebies.

"They designed the attic as an added bedroom to sleep several of Adele and Dieter Holtz's children, though we've used it as a storage room for the last 30 years or so," Pauline stated. I noticed that they'd packed all but the center of the room with boxes, old furniture, Christmas decorations, and clothing racks. "Now you see why Gunther and I never like to come up here," Pauline added. "We just don't know where to start."

"Where did you find Hildegarde's box with the diary?" I asked.

"Back in that corner by the windows," Pauline replied. "but there's no rhyme or reason for where things are located. That's the problem."

"It looks to me that the older things are buried behind the newer," I noted, "so let's start in the other corner."

Pauline and I moved a bunch of items to the center of the room in order to have easier access. We placed two rickety chairs in front of a stack of cartons, so we could sit while we went through a box. "Why don't we make a pile of things to donate while we're at it?" I suggested. "It might help you get rid of items you don't want."

Pauline foraged through the first three boxes, filled with old baby clothes. "Most of these have stains, so they're not worth saving," she stated. I tossed the boxes down the steps to put in the trash later.

Next, we opened four cartons containing vintage books with copyright dates from the 1920's to 1940's. "Some of these might be worth something," I said. "Adele liked to read, so I'll bet these were a part of her collection."

"I never knew they were back here," Pauline remarked. "Let's drag them over to the stairs, and I'll ask Gunther to lug them down."

We found a steamer trunk behind an old baby carriage and high chair, but couldn't open it. Instead, we went through several more boxes on an old dresser against the back wall, filled with hats and pocketbooks, with more in the bureau drawers.

"My goodness," Pauline sighed. "Who'd want all of these? No one wears hats anymore. This is a wild goose chase."

"Adele loved hats," I said. "She always wore one to church, and when she went out."

"Do you think we'd have any use for them on the tour?" she asked.

"Probably not," I said, "but we should go through all of the purses."

"Why?" Pauline pressed.

"I don't know. Maybe we'll find important documents, or even money."

Pauline had a skeptical expression as she said, "I don't think Adele and Dieter had two nickels to rub together."

Pauline and I went through each of the pocketbooks, one by one. As we completed our examination of them, we refilled the carton, and I dragged it over to the stairwell. We didn't find anything of value, just a penny at the bottom of every purse, so we made a pile of coins on top of the dresser. "My mother told me that you should always keep a penny in the bottom of your pocketbook for good luck," I remarked.

"I heard it was for prosperity," Pauline said. "No matter the meaning, Adele honored the old tradition. I'm sure Gunther will have lots of fun going through the coins with his magnifying glass. He has a whole collection."

"Hey, look at this," I said, rummaging through the last of the pocketbooks. "There's a key in the inside pocket."

"What of it? We changed all of our locks years ago."

Both of us stared at the skeleton key in my palm. It could have been a house key from a century ago, but I wondered why anyone would leave it forgotten in an old purse, unless it opened something in the attic.

The idea came to me suddenly. "It might fit the trunk," I grinned.

CHAPTER 23

*P*auline's eyes grew wide before she followed me to the vintage steamer trunk. We moved the baby carriage out of the way to make room for the two of us to examine the lock. Sure enough, the key fit perfectly. With one turn, the latch sprung open.

"I think we just found Adele's wedding gown," I said with awe as I gazed at the contents.

Pauline gently lifted it out of the chest, and held it up to the light, while I removed the long tulle veil from its storage place. "Adele must have been quite slender," Pauline noted. "It looks pretty good after all of these years. This gown is lovely."

I agreed, holding the veil next to the dress to admire the combination. We both commented on the beautiful artistry and craftsmanship. As we prepared to return it to the trunk, my eye caught sight of the handcrafted jewelry box in the bottom of the chest. Though smaller than the one that contained Hildegarde's diary, I noticed it even more intricately carved, and had no doubt that Hildegarde's mother had given this gift to Adele.

Pauline followed my gaze. "Would you look at that?" she exclaimed. "Maybe we've found some more money."

I told Pauline what I knew about the box from reading the diary, and explained that we would find no hidden compartment in this one. Still, I felt certain that we'd located something of importance. Pauline opened the clasp, and brought out a cluster of papers which she handed to me.

The first, an official copy of the transfer of 35 acres of land from Jonas Willard Smithfield to Dieter and Adele Holtz, had a stamp with the county seal. "There you go," Pauline smiled triumphantly. "I told you that the Smithfields gave Gunther's grandparents the land."

The next document, a handwritten letter, accompanied the transfer of land. "Read what it says out loud," Pauline urged.

March 16, 1920
To Dieter Holtz
Kind Sir,
In gratitude for your continued service in my employ. I trust that you recog-
nize the necessity of complete confidence in my private enterprise. No one
must know about the passageway or the still. Hildegarde believes that the
presentation of a parcel of our land is a deferred wedding gift for you and
Adele. While this is my public sentiment, I remind you of its actual meaning.
The property for your homestead is a testament to your continued loyalty
and utmost secrecy.
Sincerely yours,
Jonas W. Smithfield

"Oh, my," I said. "Do you understand what JW wrote?"

"I'm not sure," Pauline stated. "Did he give the land as a bribe?"

"That's what I think," I nodded. "It looks to me that Gunther's grandfather became involved in JW's bootlegging operation."

"I can't believe it," Pauline replied, shaking her head. "Do you think Gunther's grandmother knew anything about it?"

"We found the letter in Adele's jewelry box," I noted, "hidden under her wedding gown. Somehow, she had to know."

"There's another note," Pauline said. "What does it say?"

I carefully unfolded the paper, and my eyes focused on the signature line. "This one's written by Adele, and dated 1959."

"That's the year that Gunther's grandfather died," Pauline sighed.

June 5, 1959
To Whom It May Concern:
My darling Dieter is gone from this life. Our eldest child, Johan, will now
take over our orchards. I have given him the deed to my home, though I will
continue to live here until my passing. In preparation, I have donated
Dieter's clothing to charity. To my dismay, I found Mr. Smithfield's letter
and the transfer of property among Dieter's private papers. I do not fully
understand its significance, but it appears that my husband was involved in
nefarious activities during the time of Prohibition. I am certain that my dear
friend Hildegarde was also unaware of any unlawful actions that may have
transpired. I do not want Dieter's name sullied, since he was a good man,
and an edification to his children.
Sincerely,
Adele Holtz

"Geez," Pauline said in dismay. "I can only imagine how I'd feel if I ever found that Gunther hid something like this from me."

"I know what you mean," I agreed. "I wonder how long Dieter actually worked for the Smithfields. Obviously, he and Adele had an established orchard they bequeathed to Gunther's father. Is there anything else in the jewelry box?"

"Yes," Pauline nodded. "There's a little booklet."

Pauline leafed through it, then handed it to me. It looked like a ledger, but I wouldn't consider it secretive since Dieter kept track of all the work he had done for JW. I flipped to the end. "Here's the answer to my question," I remarked. "Dieter began working for the Smithfields in 1919. He recorded his monthly salary until 1926. From then, until 1931, JW paid him on a part-time basis, and he received remuneration based on the number of barrels he moved."

"When did Prohibition end?" Pauline asked.

"December, 1933. I guess he realized he could risk losing everything that he and Adele had built for themselves, so he got out of the business."

"By then, they had several children," Pauline said. "Johan would have been 9 or 10 years old. Old enough, maybe, to even wonder what his father did over at the Smithfield place."

"Probably," I agreed. "Is there anything else in the trunk?"

"Some packets of letters," Pauline noted. "They might be love letters between Dieter and Adele." Pauline wanted to take time to read those, so we put the other items, including Adele's wedding gown and veil, back in the trunk. I suggested that we return to the living room before I needed to head home.

Pauline offered me a cup of tea, but I declined when I saw the time. I gave Pauline her copy of the script. The ideas that had germinated in my mind while in the attic gave way to a fresh approach to our tours. "I'd like you to read what I've prepared," I said. "It contains much of the information I've gleaned from reading Hildegarde's diary, but I want you to consider a new angle."

"What's that?" Pauline questioned.

"This is now your family's story. Gunther's grandfather rolled those barrels up the ramp in the barn. He might have even delivered them to patrons using the old wagon. It's also possible that he made the moonshine and dumped the mash in the creek. Surely, Dieter walked through the secret passage, knowing that the decoy bowling pin was the key to open the hidden door."

"I don't know, Vicki. Gunther's going to be upset to hear that his grandfather was a bootlegger."

"You're not going to tell the tale in a manner that would bring shame to the Holtzes. Rather, you're going to emphasize the struggle of a German immigrant shortly after WWI who had to feed a growing family, while starting his own business. The folks who visit the machine barn probably don't know too much about the historical aspects of Prohibition, though you can put it into context for them."

"I'll think about it," Pauline said. "At least I have another six weeks or so to prepare."

"Is that for sure?" I asked.

"Yes," she nodded. "The Women's Guild has confirmed, so they're our first reservation."

CHAPTER 24

S ister Cathy and I both remarked about the decided feel of early spring in the air when I picked her up for our jaunt. She placed the box of JW's ledgers on the back seat of my car before belting herself into the front passenger side. Although I felt confident that I remembered my way to the historical society, I set up the GPS, just in case.

"How's progress on the barn?" Cathy asked.

"The ramp to the basement's almost done. Charlie, Leon, and Gunther are installing the railings today."

"What about the outer walls and the roof?" she queried.

"Charlie wants to hold off on the roof until we see how far the money goes for the critical items. He selected Matthews & Sons for the construction work, and they've already applied for the building permits, so they should start work on Monday."

"I honestly don't know how you're able to accomplish all of this," Cathy said. "I'd never be able to manage it."

"I couldn't do it without Charlie's help, because he thinks about the smallest details. We spend every evening hashing out what has to be done, and in what order it needs to be completed. For example, the electrician will start as soon as the outer walls have been shored, then they'll do the insulation and install the dry wall."

"You're adding insulation and dry wall in a barn?" Cathy exclaimed.

"Heating, too," I replied. "We can't have visitors shivering in the cold."

"That's amazing," Cathy said. "Will everything be finished by mid-April?"

"That's the plan," I nodded, "but you'd better have the Sisters say a few prayers, because any major glitch will delay our opening."

Our conversation switched to the subject of Pauline and Gunther. I'd called Sister Cathy on Friday evening to tell her what we had discovered in the Holtz's attic, so she wondered how Gunther handled the news about his grandfather's partnership in crime. "He seems fine about it," I said. "In fact, he told Charlie that his family's connection to the still made him want to be even more involved in the restoration work."

"That's good," Cathy nodded. "If Gunther's on board, then Pauline won't feel reluctant to lead the tours."

"Right," I agreed. "However, there's still a question about whether or not Hildegarde knew about the bootlegging activities, and I think visitors will want to know that fact."

"Didn't you say Adele's letter indicated that Hildegarde knew nothing about the still or passageway?" Cathy asked.

"Yes, but Charlie reminded me that the boxes Sister Julie found contained recipes for alcoholic beverages, as well as jellies and jam, all with the same handwriting. Why would Hildegarde have saved instructions for making booze?"

"Uh-oh," Cathy said. "She had to have known."

"Yep," I nodded as I pulled into a parking spot at the historical society. With closure to our conversation, Sister Cathy retrieved her box, and we walked to the front desk. I asked for Barbara, the staff member who had helped me the last time I visited.

Barbara welcomed us to her office, and I introduced Sister Cathy and me, though she obviously remembered both of us by the

comments she made about the photo shoot in the monastery basement. I informed her of the progress we'd made on the restoration of
the machine barn, and described our plan to offer tours to view the
Smithfield's still and bowling alley.

"I'm happy to hear that," Barbara smiled.

"We've asked Vicki to serve as the executive director for *Rock
Creek Farm*, our new non-profit organization that includes the historical aspects of the Smithfield Estate," Cathy explained, "so she'll
handle all inquiries, and set up any arrangements for tours."

I suddenly realized that I'd never thought to order business cards.
Kicking myself for appearing so inadequate, I rummaged through my
purse looking for something I could use to write my contact information, though Barbara didn't seem fazed. She retrieved a notepad and
pen from her desk, and handed them to me with a friendly smile.

"I hoped that you might include our tours in any cultural events
planned by the historical society," I stated after jotting my name and
phone number on the pad.

Barbara confirmed what I had already suspected. "I'm so sorry,"
she said. "We mailed our spring schedule two weeks ago." Seeing my
disappointed expression, Barbara added, "I'd like to discuss this at a
staff meeting because *Rock Creek Farm* holds such historical significance. I'll call you next week if we can add a tour to our calendar of
events."

"Thank you so much," I grinned.

While Barbara and I wrapped up that aspect of our visit, Cathy
opened her carton and began placing JW's ledgers on the desk. Eyes
widening, Barbara exclaimed, "Oh, my! What do you have here?"

"We believe these are accounting records that Jonas Smithfield
kept regarding his bootleg operation," Cathy replied. "They're in
fragile condition, but we'd like to preserve them."

Barbara carefully opened the cover of one of the ledgers, and I
could clearly see that she knew how to handle historical documents.
She commented on the use of initials in the first column, as well as
the prices indicated in column four. Just as we had conjectured, she
felt the anonymity and variety provided further evidence of JW's

illegal activities. "These ledgers are quite a find," Barbara smiled. "Do you plan to display them on the tour?"

"We think they're too brittle," Cathy replied. "We'd like to protect these, but use authentic copies as exhibits."

Barbara nodded as she stated, "One of our staff makes excellent reproductions, and we have the equipment on site. In fact, the cost is quite reasonable. Document restoration, on the other hand, is very expensive. Do you have a budget for that?"

"Not really," I said, "although it sounds as if we might be able to afford the replicas."

Barbara took time to reflect, then asked, "Do you really need the originals?"

Cathy and I looked at each other, neither of us quite sure what to say, until Cathy replied, "Frankly, we'd store the originals in a closet at the monastery since the ledgers are already falling apart. Before long, they'll have no value for posterity."

I agree," Barbara said. "However, we do have a line item for restoration in our budget. If you would donate these to the historical society, we can properly care for the originals. In return, I'll provide the reproductions at no cost to you."

Anything free sounded good to me, and Sister Cathy probably felt the same way. We both nodded our agreement. "You've got a deal," Cathy said, "as long as you promise that you won't sell the original ledgers."

"I can assure you they won't be sold," Barbara promised. "Despite Jonas' activities during Prohibition, the Smithfields did a lot for this county. We're planning an exhibit for the fall, and the ledgers will have a place of prominence."

"Perhaps we could combine forces by offering a discount on our tours for those who attend your cultural event," I noted.

"That's a fabulous idea," Barbara said. "In the meantime, we'll get you on our docket for the spring. I suppose you'll want the copies as soon as possible."

Nodding my agreement, I told Barbara that I'd need them by the first week of April since I had to get the replicas framed. That didn't seem to evoke any negative reaction on her part. "I'm sure we can manage that," she smiled. "I'll call you when they're ready."

"That's wonderful," I grinned. "Thank you so much!" With that, Cathy and I bid our farewells, and we both felt quite pleased with the outcome of our visit.

"Are you sure you won't get into trouble for giving away JW's ledgers?" I asked as we fastened our seatbelts in my car. I knew the Sisters had protocols for permission, and Cathy hadn't done that.

"Quite sure," Cathy chuckled. "Just this morning, Marian suggested that I try to get rid of them today. She'll be impressed with my negotiation skills."

CHAPTER 25

*C*athy and I encountered quite a commotion when we arrived back at the monastery. We saw the sheriff's car and a police van with lights flashing parked at the *porte couchère*, and Charlie's truck in front of them, with no one in any of the vehicles. "This doesn't bode well," Cathy muttered as I turned off my ignition. We scurried to the entrance just as a police officer led Leon out the front door.

"I didn't do it," Leon stated as a police officer ushered him into the back of the van. "I swear, I didn't do it."

The sheriff, Charlie, and Sister Marian, on her cell phone, followed quickly behind, and Cathy's facial expression confirmed my own sense of dread. As Charlie passed by me to get into his truck, he said, "I'm going to the police station with Leon."

Charlie pulled aside to give way to the sheriff and police van, then he trailed directly behind. Marian asked me to follow them as she positioned herself in the front seat of my car. Cathy hopped in back, and I settled behind the wheel. "Will you please tell us what's going on?" I asked.

"Some guy accused Leon of stealing his Bingo winnings from

Friday night," Marian explained. "I just got off the phone with Father Jim, and he'll meet us at the police station."

"That's ridiculous," I said. "Leon wouldn't take anything that's not his."

"The problem is," Marian noted, "the sheriff found $200 in Leon's cabin."

"No way," I said. "There has to be some explanation."

"Leon told us that he just cashed the $200 stipend check that Father Jim sent him," Marian replied.

"There you go," I sighed. "So, Father Jim can verify that he sent Leon the money. End of story."

"Hopefully," Marian said, "though the sheriff believes that Leon's the culprit."

"Whatever happened to 'innocent until proven guilty?'" I asked. "Do you think Leon will need a lawyer?" I didn't intend to take any chances since people didn't know Leon very well. Except for calling Bingo on Friday evenings at the firehouse, or working with Charlie, he stayed to himself. I reached into my purse and gave my phone to Sister Marian. "Search my phone contacts and see if you can find Betty's number. She'll know what to do."

Betty didn't answer, but Marian left a cryptic message for her to return the call as soon as possible. In response to Cathy's request for more details, Marian told us that the police arrived just after Charlie brought Leon back from working at the barn. They stopped at the monastery because Charlie wanted to give her an update on their progress. The three of them stood talking by the grand staircase until the doorbell rang. "Imagine my surprise to see the sheriff when I opened the door," Marian said. "His expression clearly indicated that he hadn't made a social call."

"Did Leon look guilty? I asked. "As if he intended to run or something?"

"Not at all," Marian replied. "Both Charlie and Leon went to the door to see if they could help. By then, the other officer had also arrived, and the sheriff began to question Leon. Leon looked shocked. Charlie did too, for that matter."

Marian told us that she invited everyone to the parlor so they could talk privately. The sheriff didn't seem to want her or Charlie present, but she told us that she insisted. Even before she closed the door, the sheriff asked Leon where he went on Friday night, and if he had taken any money. "Leon answered all of his questions without hesitation," Marian stated, "and insisted that he doesn't steal. Charlie and I both vouched for him, but neither officer seemed interested."

"Charlie knows the sheriff," I noted. "I can't imagine why the sheriff would ignore him."

"The sheriff seemed to have an axe to grind, for sure," Marian said. "Charlie offered to take him to Leon's cabin, so they left to do a search. Leon wanted to go, too, but the sheriff told him not to move, then he told the other officer to keep a close watch on him. I mean, really. It was like watching a prime-time crime show play out."

"It sounds a little extreme," I agreed, shaking my head. "So, apparently, the sheriff found cash in Leon's cabin?"

"Right on the kitchenette counter," Marian replied, "in plain sight, and the exact amount that the person accused Leon of stealing. As soon as he and Charlie returned, the sheriff placed Leon under arrest and read his rights. That's when you and Cathy arrived."

I pulled into the last remaining parking spot in front of the police station when my phone rang with a call from Betty. I quickly explained what had occurred, and asked her advice. She told me that she'd leave immediately, and meet us at the police station. "Tell the officers that I'm his lawyer," Betty stated, "and don't let them question him any further until I get there."

CHAPTER 26

$\mathcal{T}$he one-story brick police station, one of the oldest buildings in town, had a stark front entrance and thick wrought-iron bars to cover its few windows. I didn't consider it an inviting view from the outside.

The inside, not much better, consisted of a large main room with linoleum tile, fluorescent lights, and two large wooden desks in the center of the room, both strewn with papers and file folders. One wall boasted a table with a fax machine and coffee maker, while another had a row of straight-back wooden chairs. I assumed that the short hallway led to the cells and, maybe, an interrogation room.

We entered to find the sheriff and police officer at their desks, seemingly engrossed in their paperwork. Charlie sat sullenly on one of the side chairs, and muttered that they placed Leon in a cell. I walked up to the sheriff's desk, and introduced myself. "I'm Vicki Munley, and I'd like to see Leon, please."

Barely glancing at me, he replied, "and I'm Sheriff Jones. Lester Jones. You can all take a seat if you feel you need to stay, but Leon's not available." He provided an undertone of a snicker for good measure.

"Listen, Lester," I responded haughtily. "Don't you think you're carrying this charade too far? Leon's an honest man. Even if you think you have evidence of a crime, the money you found belonged to Leon. Besides, petty theft doesn't warrant putting someone in a jail cell."

"Do you think you're a lawyer or something, missy? You'd better think twice before you interfere with my investigation. And, by the way, it's Sheriff Jones to you."

"Leon's lawyer is on her way," I replied stiffly, "and she told me to remind you that you can't question Leon without her presence."

"Oh, now I'm really nervous. Leon has a lady lawyer," he sneered. "Go sit with your friends before I tell you to get out of here." Lester arose to pour himself a cup of coffee. He didn't offer us anything, not that I felt in the mood to socialize.

Charlie could see that Lester had made me angry, so he gently took my hand and suggested that we go outside for some fresh air. I waited until we'd walked far enough away from the doorway before I exploded. "Who does this guy think he is? I never met such a…"

"Calm down," Charlie said. "He's an elected official for the county. I can't imagine why he's acting like such a jerk, unless someone's pulling his strings."

"Yeah, well maybe his term is nearly up and he wants to get reelected. He won't get my vote, that's for sure."

"You're not registered," Charlie reminded me. "Better do that soon or you won't be able to cast a ballot. Anyway, Lester's not usually this rude and offensive. He says hello on occasion, but doesn't hang around chewing the fat with anyone in town. There must be more here than what meets the eye."

Before I could respond, Father Jim arrived, although he had to drive around the corner to find a parking spot. Charlie and I went to meet him as he exited his car, and it pleased me to see that he wore his black suit and priestly collar because it gave credence to official clergy business.

Charlie filled him in on what had already transpired, and gave Father Jim a heads-up as to the contrariness of the sheriff, then I mentioned that Betty would soon arrive, and she'd serve as Leon's lawyer. "Leon insisted that the money they found was from his stipend. Did you send him $200?" I asked.

"Yes, a month ago," Father Jim replied as we walked to the front door of the precinct. "Maybe he just cashed the check."

"At least there's a record of him having the exact amount," I stated. "It should be easy to clear up the confusion."

Charlie and I went to the side chairs as Father Jim walked over to the sheriff's desk. He introduced himself, and showed Lester his ID. "I'd like to see Leon," Father Jim said.

"What's with this guy who hangs around with priests and nuns?" Lester muttered. "Good cover. Sorry, no visitors."

"I'm his minister, not a visitor. I'd like to see Leon."

"You heard me. No visitors. Either take a seat or take your leave."

I grabbed my cell phone to Google who oversaw the sheriff. Evidently, the voters did. I didn't consider that a big help, but I learned that citizens could file complaints with the county commissioners. Unfortunately, the clock on the wall indicated the time as 6:40 p.m., so I felt certain that county offices had already closed.

While we all waited for Betty on the side chairs, Lester told the other officer, whom he called Stan, that he could clock out. Stan declined, saying, "I'll stay until the lawyer lady arrives." Shortly after, Betty walked in.

Although her glance indicated that she saw the rest of us sitting along the wall, she went straight to Lester's desk and placed her picture ID and bar license on top of an open file. "My name's Elizabeth Sweeney, and I'm Leon's attorney. Take me to see him, please."

"I don't see no paperwork filed," Lester snickered. "Read the announcement hanging by the door."

"Why don't you read it for me, Officer?" Betty replied.

"It says all visitors need clearance. It's a security thing."

"That's ridiculous," Betty said. "You have my credentials. How can I represent my client without meeting with him?"

"It's not my problem. Take it up at the county courthouse, which, by the way, is closed for the night."

"I insist on seeing Leon immediately," Betty contended.

"It's not going to happen, lady," Lester replied. "We've got rules in this county."

Betty sighed. "How much is bail? I'll post it now."

"No bail. The perp is wanted for murder."

"What?" Betty exclaimed. "You brought him in for petty larceny. Now, you say he's a suspect in a killing?"

"Guess she's not as dumb as she looks," he said to Stan.

Stan gave a half-hearted chuckle, but he didn't seem to embrace Lester's bullying tactics. In fact, I considered Stan, perhaps in his late 20's, as a new recruit, though he knew how to take orders.

"You're messing with the wrong woman, Sheriff Jones," Betty stated firmly. "I'll return in the morning with any clearance I need to see my client. In the meantime, you'd better have very strong evidence for detaining Leon, so I suggest that you put your paper-work in order."

"Honey, you don't scare me. You can take your pretty little butt back to the city. That's where I figure you're from, since I've never seen you at the courthouse."

"Darn right, Sheriff. We make mincemeat out of petty rural bigots like you. You couldn't get a job sweeping garbage out of the city gutters."

Lester's face turned an ugly shade of purple. "Get out! All of you. We're done here."

"You're right, Sheriff Jones," Betty replied smugly. "*You* are done here."

CHAPTER 27

Totally frustrated, the six of us decided to eat at Jake's Diner, two blocks down on the right. We all squeezed into one of the larger booths by the window and, in only a few moments, the waitress brought us menus and water. Like me, the others felt shell-shocked, though I said, "You were amazing, Betty. I guess I never saw you in action, but how did you keep your cool?"

"It's what I do," Betty replied. "Now you see why I come to the poustinias to relax as often as I can."

"I'm really worried about Leon," Father Jim commented. "He doesn't do well with any kind of stress. I wonder if he has his medication."

"Not unless he carries it around with him," Charlie said. "I can swing by his place and pick it up for Leon, then I'll bring it over there in the morning."

"Lester won't let you in," I noted, frowning. "He might not even give it to Leon, so we need to come up with a plan."

The waitress came by to take our orders. Most of us ate at Jake's often enough that we barely glanced at the menu. When she scurried off, Betty told us that she had already cancelled her appointments for tomorrow. "I'll get a room in the B&B tonight. That way I can be at the courthouse as soon as it opens in the morning."

Father Jim told us that he planned to do the same. They'd both get the required security clearances so they could obtain visitation rights. Betty remarked that she also intended to file a sexual harassment complaint against Sheriff Jones, and submit a statement about the sheriff's lack of due process to the county commissioners' office. By the time our meals arrived, I felt certain that Lester Jones would rue the day that he messed with Betty, or any of us, for that matter. I, too, planned to file a report.

One of Charlie's buddies from the firehouse stopped by our table on his way out. "I'm sorry to hear about Leon's arrest, Charlie. That guy who accused Leon of stealing his winnings is a seedy character, sly as a fox. Fact is, he did the same thing a few months back in the adjoining county. Believe it or not, the judge believed the jerk, and gave him restitution, which doubled his winnings, if you get my drift."

"I've never experienced anything like it in all of my years calling Bingo," Charlie said, shaking his head. "Folks in our town are pretty honest."

"I guess there's always a new scam," his buddy replied. "Just don't cross the sheriff, because he has an ornery streak."

"What's his problem?" Charlie asked.

"The way I hear it, he's been getting flak from the higher ups. Might be he's trying to show them that he's the reason for the low crime rate around here. The truth is, a lot of people are getting sick and tired of his way of handling things."

"I know what you mean," Charlie said. "Leon's still in jail."

"That's too bad. I wouldn't mind snooping at the sly guy's house, because I'll bet we'd find the money. Just mark my words. Keep your nose clean, and stay away from the sheriff."

Charlie's buddy departed, and our waitress came by with the check. Betty offered to give the Sisters a ride home, so I could just follow Charlie in his truck. Father Jim planned to tag after Betty. I invited Betty to stay at our place, but she thought she'd probably be up half the night working on Leon's case, so we'd touch base at some point the next day.

As we all walked to the parking lot together, Father Jim told Charlie not to bother getting Leon's medication. "I'll look for it tonight, as well as the stipend check stub, so we won't have any delay first thing in the morning."

"OK," Charlie nodded. "We'll see you tomorrow."

"Right," Father Jim said. "Don't worry, folks," he added. "We'll get this all worked out, and Leon will be fine."

CHAPTER 28

$\mathcal{I}$ put on the kettle and dished up Harvey's kibbles, while Charlie took him out. The poor boy didn't like that we'd left him alone for most of the day, but thank goodness, I didn't find any evidence of accidents in the house. When they returned, Harvey wolfed down his meal, and Charlie joined me at the table for a cup of decaf tea. Neither of us felt much like rehashing the day's events, yet we both found it difficult to shake off our anxiety.

"I hope Father Jim's right," Charlie said as he mindlessly stroked Harvey's back. "I just feel so helpless."

"We did all we could do," I said. "I feel certain that Leon could hear us from his cell, because I noticed the open hallway door at the police station. At least, I hope he knows that we stood up for him."

"Right," Charlie replied. "It's a good thing Betty's a public defender. I have no doubt that Leon's in capable hands."

"Have you heard anything about a murder investigation in the county?" I asked.

Charlie shook his head. "Not a thing, though the murder could have occurred in one of the other small towns around here. I'll ask about it tomorrow."

"I want to file a complaint in the morning," I stated. "Do you want to come to the courthouse with me?"

"Sure," Charlie nodded. We decided that we'd also apply for security clearances while there, then we'd stop at the police station to visit with Leon, not that I wanted to face another run-in with Sheriff Jones. I could only hope that he'd be out working on his criminal investigation.

After Charlie finished his tea, he decided to go to bed. As tired as I felt, I knew I wouldn't fall asleep, so I told him that I'd read Hildegarde's diary for a while, and join him later.

June 12, 1919
Mama and I now visit the orphan asylum every Friday while the house-keeper cleans our home. We bring fresh fruit and penny candy that Adele purchases for us at the market. Often, I read to the children, and sometimes Mama tells nursery rhymes that Adele has taught her. Mama says she is not so nervous speaking in front of the children, and they help by repeating the rhyme with her, so Mama can now make full sentences in English. Some of the children whose parents died of influenza have been adopted, but there are many who still need a home. I told Jonas about a little girl I have taken a fancy to. She reminds me in many ways of our Greta, but Jonas doesn't want to hear about her any more, and he refuses to entertain the idea that we are ready for another child, though Mama says to give him time.

June 22, 1919
Dieter requested Jonas' permission to ask Adele for her hand in marriage. Jonas is quite pleased with Dieter's work, and he thinks Dieter will make a suitable husband for Adele. Mama and I agree. We have promised not to tell Adele because the proposal will be a surprise. Jonas told me that Dieter will continue his employment at the market for the summer, and care for our vineyard during the evenings and on weekends. He expects to make the land-scaping work on the estate a full-time position come fall. Dieter will also oversee construction of our main drive and the development of our small lake.

June 29, 1919
Jonas, Mama, and I spent the afternoon reviewing the floor plan for our new
house. The west wing will be our grand entrance with a porte couchère to
protect our visitors from the elements. Jonas had the architect create a
massive office for him to the right of the front door, across from the grand
staircase. He will have a stone fireplace with a large hearth, and floor-to-
ceiling windows. I am pleased that he will do much of his work from home,
especially now that he is selling some of his steel mills. The east wing will be
a ballroom, with its own entrance, though it seems much too extravagant,
with the chandeliers and stained-glass windows. The central wing will be our
living quarters, with a large drawing room on the first floor. Upstairs, we
will have six large bedrooms, each with its own dressing room and bathroom,
while the third floor will be the servants' quarters, with a staircase to the
kitchen. The kitchen and dining room are grand. Jonas promises to include
the most modern appliances he can find, and he will bring me some cata-
logues, so Mama and I can select the ones we like.

July 8, 1919
We had a lovely 4ᵗʰ of July picnic at our estate. James served as our driver,
and Adele prepared a picnic lunch. We met Dieter at the vineyard, since he
was working there. The dirt driveway has many potholes from construction
vehicles, yet despite the bumpy road, it pleased me to see that great progress
has been made on the mansion. Stonemasons hope to complete the façade and
porte couchère within the next two months, while electricians and plumbers
have been occupied with the interior. Of course, no one labored on the holi-
day. Mama was very impressed with the layout of the vineyard. Dieter
showed us that the new plantings have taken hold. We ate our lunch at my
favorite spot by the creek. Mama sat on the fallen tree and thinks it is the
perfect peaceful place to dream, as she basked in the delight of nature. Dieter
agreed, telling us that he often rests there after tending to the grapes, and he
knew this was where he would propose to Adele. Suddenly, he went on
bended knee, and asked Adele to marry him. We cheered when she said yes.

July 27, 1919
I have been very busy the last few weeks because Jonas and I hosted several

dinner parties for business associates and a few visiting dignitaries. One
congressman is quite interested in helping to raise funds to add a wing to the
hospital. We told him how the lack of available beds might have contributed
to the devastating loss of life during the influenza outbreak. Mama and I
continue to visit the orphanage. Five more children have been adopted. When
I am occupied, Mama has been writing recipes for her favorite jams, jellies,
and spirits. She says that once the vines produce grapes, I will be able to
make delicious condiments and beverages, though Jonas is intent on having
instructions for wine and brandy. Mama told him to buy bottles and caps,
and she will help him perfect the process using Papa's techniques. Jonas does
like his brandy!

August 6, 1919
It has taken Adele and Dieter more than a month to decide when they will
marry. Adele would like it to coincide with our time to take residence at the
estate. She and Dieter cannot afford their own home at this time, and Adele
knows that I will need help to become established in the country. Since Dieter
will also be in our employ, it will be appropriate for them to share a room on
the third floor of the mansion once they marry. Jonas believes that we may be
able to move shortly after the New Year. For that reason, Adele and Dieter
will have their wedding at Christmas. They plan a short honeymoon, and
will return in time to assist with our relocation.

I found myself beginning to get very sleepy. As much as I wanted
to continue reading, I knew we had an early morning, and I needed a
good night's rest. I opened the back door for Harvey to go out, and
nibbled on a cookie while I awaited his return. I reminded myself that
I must remember to tell Charlie and Sister Cathy that the diary
provided the answer to another mystery. Hildegarde's mother wrote
all of the recipes in the box that Sister Julie found, and she had taught
JW how to make the alcoholic beverages.

CHAPTER 29

*C*harlie and I met up with Father Jim at the police station the next morning. He had already visited Leon, and made sure that he'd received his medication. The sheriff apparently left young officer, Stan, in charge. Stan, quite amenable when Charlie and I showed him our security clearances, suggested that we could meet with Leon in the interrogation room since it had a table and four chairs to accommodate all of us.

We took our places, then Stan led Leon into the room. I didn't like the fact that Stan turned the lock on the door, but he assured us that he'd stay at his desk until we wanted to leave. The same dingy tile and hard-back chairs made the room seem as stark as the station's waiting area, and a two-way mirror gave it the only decorative accent. It wouldn't have surprised me if Stan watched us through the glass, but I didn't care because we didn't plan any furtive moves.

Leon told us how much he appreciated our support. Despite his rumpled clothes and a day's stubble on his face, he didn't look as bad as I'd imagined after a night in the town's jail. He told us that Stan had given him dinner after the sheriff kicked us out the night before, then brought him coffee and donuts in the morning.

Despite Sheriff Jones' nasty and intolerant attitude, no one had mistreated Leon. Still, when all of this ended, Leon decided that he would take his leave. "I never had any trouble like this in the city," he told us.

"It could happen anywhere or any time," Father Jim said. "There are crooks in the city, just as well as in small towns. The sly ones know how to pin their crimes on innocent bystanders."

"I never had a police record before," Leon stated, looking forlorn. "Now the sheriff says I killed someone, besides taking that guy's winnings at Bingo. I don't know how to deal with it all."

"Betty will handle everything," I said, "so you don't have to worry about anything. Has she come to see you yet?"

"Yes," Leon nodded, "first thing after they gave her the authorization. I hadn't even finished drinking my coffee." Leon told us that Betty asked him a lot of questions. "She called it an official name like 'disposition,'" he said, "then she had to return to the courthouse to file the paperwork and schedule a court appearance with the judge. I'm sure glad she knows what she's doing."

"It sounds as if she had a deposition with you," Father Jim remarked. "I saw Betty at the courthouse and, let me tell you, she's on a mission."

Shortly after Father Jim's comment, we heard Stan unlock the door. I wondered if the sheriff had returned to cause trouble, though I didn't know why that became the first thought to cross my mind, but Stan stood in the doorway. "Your lady lawyer friend must know a lot of powerful people," he said. "Lester just called to tell me to escort Leon to the courthouse because Leon has to meet the judge in his chambers."

"I can't see any judge looking like this," Leon said.

"He's seen worse," Stan replied, and we assured Leon that he looked fine. We'd follow over in our cars in case the judge wanted our testimony.

After we went through the metal detectors, I asked where we might find the judge's chambers. As a private area, the guard didn't permit us to go there. Instead, he directed us to a waiting area adjacent to the courtroom where we found Stan, already present, checking out the vending machine in the corner.

"What's the story?" Father Jim asked him.

"I don't really know very much at this point," Stan said. "The judge is meeting with Leon, the sheriff, and the lady lawyer, so I'm supposed to wait here."

For some reason, my mind kept wandering to old Perry Mason re-runs on TV. I wondered about the need for a private meeting with the judge, and whether we'd actually have a hearing. Surely the docket of already-scheduled court cases would precipitate a delay for Leon. Still, we didn't have long to wait before Betty joined us.

Though smiling, Betty went right to business. "I had a feeling you'd all be here," she remarked. "The judge has agreed to an imme-diate arraignment, and you're welcome to attend."

Within minutes, a court officer opened the door to the courtroom, and directed us to the first row of blue upholstered stack chairs behind the two court tables. We saw four additional rows behind us, empty except for Stan in the last row. Sheriff Jones led Leon to sit next to Betty at the court table in front of us, then he took a seat next to Stan.

When everyone took their places, the court officer announced the presence of Judge Robert Lansing, and we all stood until he sat at the bench. The court stenographer, a middle-aged woman, transcribed on a shorthand machine to the right of the judge, and the judge invited Betty to present the case.

Betty gave a short speech about Leon's innocence. She told the judge that the $200 found in Leon's cabin came from the stipend that Father Jim's foundation sent to Leon for his living expenses. She presented the cancelled check and bank cashing statement from the morning of the alleged robbery at Bingo. She also mentioned the recent occasion of a similar scam in a nearby town by the same man who accused Leon.

Betty went on to say that "the other charge of murder was clearly a case of mistaken identity. Witnesses at the convenience store inci-dent indicated that the perpetrator was a young White man in his early twenties. In fact, he's already been arrested and in custody at a different jurisdiction."

With great dignity, Betty concluded with her summary statement. "Leon Johnston is an army veteran of the Gulf War. He not only received the Bronze Star for his meritorious service in a combat zone, but Leon's also an upright citizen who was improperly detained. I respectfully request that you drop all charges against my client."

Judge Lansing asked Leon to stand. "The court would like to recognize your service to our country," he said. "I served in the Vietnam war, so I personally know the struggles you face as you remember your band of brothers. I also have reviewed all of the documentation provided by Ms. Sweeney, and I agree with her counsel. All charges are dropped."

Charlie, Father Jim, and I cheered. Leon looked as if a weight had been lifted from his shoulders, and his lip quivered as he thanked the judge profusely. Betty arose to hug Leon, and she added her appreciation for Judge Lansing's swift, though thorough, review of the case.

The judge smiled about our obvious approval of the outcome for Leon, but his countenance soon turned serious. "The court would also like to make note about the unfortunate lack of due process that you experienced, Mr. Johnston. I believe Sheriff Jones has something to say."

Lester stood, appearing uncomfortable in the spotlight. We each turned our gaze to him.

"It seems as if I made a mistake," he muttered. "I'm sorry."

Leon nodded his acceptance of the apology, but didn't say anything.

"Court dismissed," Judge Lansing said, and we all stood as he departed the courtroom. I noticed the large clock on the wall indicated the time as after 3 o'clock. Stan and Sheriff Jones scooted out well before the rest of us, and we saw neither of them as we returned to our vehicles.

"I still have more paperwork to file," Betty told us, "but we could gather for supper at the monastery restaurant."

We all agreed to meet at 6 o'clock, though Father Jim said he'd take

Leon in his car, first to Leon's cabin for a shower and shave, then to the monastery. Charlie and I would go home to check on Harvey, and we'd join everyone for dinner.

In the meantime, I called for reservations and told Sister Julie to let the Sisters know that their prayers worked. The judge had declared Leon innocent.

CHAPTER 30

*E*ven with a shower and change of clothes, Leon looked drained when he and Father Jim joined us at the table. I had a feeling that Leon would have preferred the solitude of his poustinia to overcome his ordeal, but Father Jim may have thought otherwise, at least until Leon had a good meal. Although each of the Sisters expressed their heartfelt relief about Leon's return home, they respected his need for privacy, and didn't crowd around him. As Leon took his seat, I tried to lighten his spirits by saying, "Well, Mr. Johnston. You clean up very well."

Leon gave me a wan smile, then quipped, "The least you could do is call me Sergeant. I don't think anyone's ever addressed me as Mr. Johnston, except the judge, I guess."

"I never even knew your last name," I said, "or that you received a Bronze Star for your heroism. You'll always be just Leon to me."

"That'll do fine, Miss Vicki. Reckon I need to thank Miss Betty for what she did for me. I'll figure out some way to pay for her lawyer time and everything."

"That's not necessary, Leon," Betty reassured him. "The one thing I'd ask is that you stay here to help the Sisters because they really need you."

"They don't deserve trouble," Leon said.

"You won't have any more difficulty," Betty replied. "The judge has placed the sheriff on leave since other people also registered complaints. Judge Lansing is requiring Sheriff Jones to complete additional training, so the county's deputy sheriff will take over Lester's duties for the time being."

"That's a relief," Charlie said. "What about the guy who accused Leon in the first place?"

"The deputy sheriff searched the man's house yesterday, and found plenty of money stashed in his freezer, but had no way to know if the coffee can contained the specific $200 he accused Leon of taking. Regardless, he's banned from playing Bingo in the county, so he'll have to do some traveling if he intends to swindle anyone else."

When Amanda came by to take our dinner orders, she first spoke directly to Leon, saying, "I'm glad you're back, and I made your favorite cookies to take to your cabin."

"Thank you, Miss Amanda," Leon nodded. "I'll definitely enjoy those."

By the time our meals arrived, we'd all decided to make it an early night. Betty planned to leave first thing in the morning, but Father Jim intended to stay another day to spend time with Leon. Charlie invited them to stop over to see the progress on the barn in the morning.

"How's all that going?" Betty asked.

"Pretty good," Charlie replied. "I noticed when we got home today that they finished the wood siding on the outer walls, so the electrician will start tomorrow."

"I guess you can't do much more on the inside until that's done," Father Jim surmised.

"Not really," Charlie noted. "Not unless Leon wants to see if he can repair the barrel wagon."

"We can take a look at it," Leon said. "I have to figure out some way to shore up the axle."

"What about the fields?" Father Jim asked. "Will you start planting soon?"

"We decided on corn and oats for our field crops," Charlie replied. "I thought about hay, but it's probably better to let more experienced farmers handle alfalfa. We'll plant the last week of April."

"Do you need any volunteers?" Father Jim questioned.

"Not yet," Charlie replied. "Gunther has a neighbor who farms, so he has the big equipment, and offered to bring over his tiller and seed drill. We won't need any volunteers for that, but we will for the vegetable gardens. I guess we should have started seedlings."

"That could make a good activity for folks at the shelter," Father Jim nodded. "I can buy some seeds and potting soil, even those little planting cups. What kind of vegetables do you want?"

Amanda heard the tail-end of our conversation when she arrived with our desserts. She suggested so many options that we all began to laugh. I reminded Amanda that the farm would start small so, in the end, we decided to try two varieties of tomatoes, as well as carrots, lettuce, sweet peppers, hot peppers, beans, and green onions, and we could plant the seedlings by May 15.

"I have a feeling that the folks caring for their sprouts at the shelter will probably want to plant them," Father Jim noted.

"That's fine," Leon said. "I'll prepare the soil so it's ready for them." To my relief, it sounded as if Leon had decided to stay.

"What about the goats?" Betty asked as she gave Amanda her credit card. I knew she meant it as a joke, but just thinking about one more detail made my brain a frazzled mess. I tried to reply with a funny quip, but Amanda jumped ahead of me.

"We can't have goats eating all of our new plantings," she stated. "Sister Marian will have to be patient because our farm is starting small."

CHAPTER 31

*C*harlie, Father Jim, and Leon dragged the old barrel wagon to the backyard just before the electrician arrived. From the panoramic kitchen window, I watched Father Jim and Leon slide on their backs to reach the axle, and dirt already covered both of them. I figured that Charlie went in the barn with the electrician, which left Harvey, in his glory, chasing squirrels among the trees.

I had to nudge myself to start working instead of watching the goings-on. I set up my laptop on the kitchen table, and sat engrossed in reading the sample brochure that Sister Bridget had emailed me. The two designs she sent, a trifold and a single front and back page, had similar content, though I preferred the larger pictures on the full-page leaflet.

Harvey's incessant bark alerted me just before I heard a sharp rap at the back door, and my heart sank to see Officer Stan and another gentleman I'd never met. I couldn't help but wonder if all of the nonsense about Leon would ever end, yet I quickly opened the door to welcome the gentlemen. "How nice to see you again, Officer. Won't you both come in?"

"Sorry to bother you, Mrs. Munley" Stan said. "I don't know if you've met our mayor, Paul Webster."

"I've never had the honor," I smiled, "so I'm happy to meet you. Please call me Vicki. Can I offer you some coffee?"

Mayor Webster, a great deal shorter than Stan, and a lot older and more rotund, had white hair and a white mustache, which reminded me of the Monopoly mayor. If he had a goatee, I'd have considered him a dead-ringer for the Kentucky Fried Chicken colonel. "I could go for a cup," the mayor said as he took a seat. Stan didn't quite know what to do, but joined him at the kitchen table. "Sure, that'll be fine," Stan echoed.

I poured two mugs of Charlie's brew, and carried over a box of munchkins that Father Jim brought us this morning. The mayor's expression registered delight after he took his first sip of the hazelnut coffee. "I suppose you're not here for a social visit," I said. "What can I do for you?"

"Actually, we did stop by socially," Mayor Webster said. "Please call me Paul and, of course, you already know Stan. We both want you to know how sorry we are that you had such an unpleasant encounter at our police station the other day."

"That's very kind of you, Paul," I nodded, "but Leon was the person unjustly incarcerated. Anyway, you should know that Stan provided dinner and breakfast for Leon." I made sure to add that Leon greatly appreciated Stan's kindness.

Stan nodded his recognition of the compliment, and took another sip of coffee. Mayor Paul had a bite of his donut, then stated, "We first stopped at the monastery to see Leon, but the Sister told us that we'd find him over here. I suppose he's one of the guys under the wagon in the yard."

"He is," I replied. "Do you want me to ask him to join us?"

"We'll go out there," the mayor said. "No use traipsing all of that dirt inside, at least that's what my wife would tell me. I also want to welcome you to the neighborhood, such as it is. I've heard that you and Charlie are fixing up the old barn."

"We are," I said, then gave a brief rendition of what we needed to do in the barn to prepare it for tours of JW's still and the secret passage to the monastery basement. "Eventually, we plan to develop a working farm to provide fresh food for the Monastery Restaurant and learning opportunities for those who have never experienced life in the country."

"That's amazing," the mayor noted. "In a number of ways, the Smithfields built our town, and they certainly had influence in the county. I don't give a hoot that they produced whiskey, or whatever, during Prohibition, but this is a national historic site right here, and I'd like to be involved in some way."

Once again, with my brain reeling, I realized that I'd never thought to contact the town's mayor, though I didn't want him to know of my blunder. "How fortunate that you stopped by today," I smiled. "I've just started to work on setting up tours, and I thought we should have a ribbon-cutting event once they've completed all of the construction work in the Smithfield's machine barn. Of course, we'd like you to officiate."

Mayor Webster nodded. "My wife told me that she plans to join the Women's Guild for their tour. I think it's sometime next month, if I recall."

"Correct," I said. "The Women's Guild is our first, and only, tour so far, and they'll come on April 21st, though I also hope the county historical society can add us to their spring schedule."

"When do you plan to have the ribbon cutting?" he asked.

I pulled out my events calendar which, quite honestly, probably looked rather sparse to the mayor. "It all depends on when the work is finished," I said. "I think we should aim for the Sunday afternoon prior to our first tour. Would you be available on April 16th?"

The mayor took out his cell phone to check his schedule, and I realized that I, too, should set up my calendar on my phone. "Yes," the mayor said. "How about 3 p.m.? Maybe I'll take my wife to dinner at the monastery afterwards."

"Perfect," I said, jotting a notation in the events calendar while Paul added it to his schedule. As worried as I felt that we'd never have everything ready in just over a month, I really did consider it ideal that we'd receive free publicity with the mayor presiding over our grand opening. I doubted that Charlie would share my elation.

"I suppose we should go out there and meet with Leon," the mayor said. "You have a nice place here, by the way."

"Thanks, Paul," I smiled. "I'm glad you and Stan stopped by."

I led our guests out to the yard, where we found Charlie, Leon, and Father Jim chatting near the old wagon. I knew they didn't need my presence, but I wanted to hear what the mayor had to say to Leon. Charlie recognized the mayor right away, and reached out to shake his hand. "Good to see you, Paul," Charlie said. "I wondered whose car was in the driveway." He introduced the mayor to Leon and Father Jim, and they also shook hands with Stan.

"My grandfather had a vintage hay wagon like this," Paul noted. "Many a day he'd drive us kids around the field to pick up sticks for kindling. I don't remember how much work we accomplished, but we sure had fun."

"They're good memories," Charlie grinned. "You're finally stopping by to see the renovations?"

"Yes," Paul replied. "I've heard about what's keeping you busy since you returned from St. Louis. I guess you even found yourself a wife, and I'd say it's about time."

"I'm a lucky guy," Charlie nodded, putting his arm around my shoulder. That sweet gesture earned Charlie an extra piece of pie for dessert.

"We're also here to talk to Leon," the mayor said. "I want to personally apologize for the treatment he got the other day."

"I appreciate it, sir, but that's not necessary," Leon said. "Stan took care of me."

"Stan's still learning the ropes," the mayor remarked. "He followed orders, but didn't like what happened to you."

"Understood, sir," Leon said.

The mayor continued. "I've heard you received a bronze medal for your military service during the Gulf War. Have you ever thought about joining the police force?"

"No, sir. I had enough danger to last me a lifetime."

"We don't see a lot of crime around here," the mayor said in his most convincing voice. "The fact is, we rely on the county sheriff for any serious law enforcement. I initiated the town's police force last year, and received a grant for a good cop vehicle. Unfortunately, you already saw the inside of that. Anyway, Stan was our first recruit. He graduated at the top of his training class, so I'm mighty proud of him, but I wouldn't mind a guy like you also on the force."

"Thank you, sir, but I don't think I'd have much interest because the nuns need my help."

"I'm sure they do, Leon," the mayor said. "Still, I want you to think about it. I don't even have a budget for another full-time officer at this point, yet a couple of hours a day could give Stan some relief."

I wanted to add my two cents, but something in me told me to hold my tongue. Although I considered it a wonderful opportunity for Leon, I knew he had to make the decision. Father Jim and Charlie must have thought the same thing, because neither of them had anything to say.

"I'll think about it, sir," Leon said. "When do you need a final answer?"

"How about we say next month, when I'm here for the ribbon-cutting ceremony." I noticed Charlie's quizzical look, but I ignored it.

"All right, sir. I appreciate you thinking of me, and I'll let you know my decision."

CHAPTER 32

After lunch, I showed Charlie, Leon, and Father Jim the brochure samples, and they liked both designs, which didn't help my dilemma of choosing one. Father Jim suggested that I have the trifold printed professionally for display in the gift shop and to use in any mailings, and offer the full-page option as a handout for the tours, but both needed to include our hours of operation and contact information.

"Good observation," I nodded. "I'll ask Bridget to make those changes so I can have copies made."

"What's the deal about a ribbon-cutting event?" Charlie asked. "The mayor's comment caught me off guard."

"I had to think fast on that one," I said. "The mayor told me that he wanted to be involved in some way, and I don't know why I'd never thought to include him. I figured we can have some kind of opening ceremony, and he can say a few words. Do you think we'll have everything ready by April 16th?"

"I hope so," Charlie replied. "Obviously, it depends on the construction timeline. I'll keep on top of it, but we don't know if they'll have any delays."

"I think it's a fabulous idea," Father Jim added. "Having the support of the mayor is good business practice, and it might even bring some free publicity."

"That's what I thought at the time, though a little late," I nodded. "Still, it's just one more thing I have to worry about, and I'm starting to feel overwhelmed."

"You and Charlie don't have to do everything," Father Jim said. "I know the nuns put you in charge, Vicki, but a good leader knows how to delegate. I'm sure you did that as a VP."

"Sure," I stated, "because I had a full staff. It's not as if we have any employees to rely on."

"You said yourself that you'd need a lot of volunteers to get all of this going," Father Jim remarked. "Look at what you've accomplished with Sister Bridget's help on the brochures. It wouldn't surprise me if the other Sisters might offer to lend a hand. In addition, think outside the box. How about people in town? The mayor's wife probably has a lot of connections, and she might even want to offer her assistance."

The more I thought about it, I agreed with Father Jim. I'd never even thought to tap his experience of putting together a soup kitchen and homeless shelter. He didn't do it on his own. Obviously, he had the bishop's support, but he figured out ways to find others' strengths, then put them to use. I considered his suggestion a good one, and it reminded me that I didn't always need to take control.

"I can see that you're mulling," Charlie said to me. To the others he added, "That's what she does when you've struck a chord."

"You're right, smarty pants," I chuckled. "Now, you boys get out of here so I can think in peace. I thought you planned to go to the hardware store."

Charlie, Leon, and Father Jim went off to seek the things they needed to repair the barrel wagon, while I quickly loaded the dishwasher, then began putting ideas to paper. Rather than providing a summary of my activities at the weekly meeting with the Sisters, I made a list of items that needed completion within the next month.

On a whim, I Googled the website of the Women's Guild, and searched the membership roster to find someone with the last name of Webster. Sure enough, I found a Rose Webster listed, along with her phone number.

Rose answered after only two rings. I introduced myself, and told her that I'd had the pleasure of meeting her husband that morning. "His visit was a good reminder that you might help me connect with local resources," I said. I suggested that we meet for coffee at her convenience, but never expected to find her available that very day. Rose had a few errands to run, then she wouldn't mind stopping at Jake's Diner around 3:30 p.m., which worked for me.

After emailing my suggested changes for the brochure to Sister Bridget, I downloaded a grant application for additional renovation funding. I considered this one another long shot, but we had enough bills to indicate that the $25,000 we had already received would not suffice. Besides, the foundation's website noted that they had money available before their June 30 fiscal year ending.

Next, I called Pauline to set up a meeting to review her script. It didn't surprise me when she admitted that she hadn't done too much work on it, and needed some help, because I couldn't expect her to draft a speech with little to go on except my brief outline. We agreed to get together at my place after lunch on Friday.

With another hour at my disposal before my meeting with Rose, I headed to the den to continue reading Hildegarde's diary. As I found the place where I'd left off, I noticed that the excerpts had become fewer and farther apart.

September 10, 1919
Adele purchased a bushel of grapes at the farmers' market this week. Our vines did not produce this year, but Mama says that is typical. With Dieter's care, there will be a harvest next year. We will also add several new rows of cuttings in the spring, so our vineyard will grow each year. Mama showed Adele and me how to prepare the grapes to make fine jelly and jam. She told us that grapes are the perfect fruit for preserving because they have plenty of pectin to help the juice gel. After a good washing, Mama put the grapes into a large pot with a cup of water and let them boil for about five minutes. Occasionally, she mashed the grapes, then she poured the cooked fruit into cheese-

cloth in a sieve over a deep bowl. After the mash drained overnight, Mama measured the juice. We had four cups, which she considered perfect. She told Adele to add three cups of sugar, and cook the juice until it was 220 degrees Fahrenheit. In the meantime, Mama had me prepare the glass jars and lids by simmering them in water. When the juice was ready, Mama helped Adele pour it into the hot jars and cap them. We put the jars into a pot of boiling water, then carefully removed them to the counter. Within minutes, each of the jars made a funny ping sound, and Mama told us that meant the jars had sealed. Our jelly will be ready to eat tomorrow.

October 12, 1919
Jonas took Mama and me to see the progress on our new home in the country. The trees in the woods surrounding our home were vibrant reds and oranges, and I don't think I have ever seen so much beauty. The stone façade is completed, as is the beautiful grand staircase. The hardwood floor has not yet been laid, but the subfloor is sturdy and level. The plumbers worked upstairs, so we spent most of our time in the kitchen and dining room. Mama and I planned the arrangement of equipment, while Jonas talked with the construction manager. When he returned, we walked the main floor all the way to the ballroom. It is so grand, with its lovely windows and entrance. Electricians were hanging the stunning chandeliers from Italy, as are the ones they will install in the dining room. On our drive home, Mama and I spoke about all we must do to prepare for our move. Thank heavens, she is here with me.

November 3, 1919
Mama has been busy making Adele's wedding gown with the sewing machine that Jonas purchased. Though Mama had an old treadle sewing machine in Germany, she says this new electric Singer machine is much easier to work, and she will teach me to use it when we move to our estate. Now, she must finish the gown, and I must pack cartons. Adele wants a simple dress, without a lot of beads, and Mama found a Butterick pattern that Adele likes very much. The gown is made of white bias-cut satin, ankle length, and sleeveless with a V-neck. It is loosely fitted, with a dropped waist, snaps up the left side, and is adorned with a beautiful satin flower at the hip.

The long tulle veil is Venetia style with two lovely rhinestone clips above the ear. Adele had a first fitting yesterday, and already I can see that she will make a beautiful bride on her wedding day.

I would never have imagined that Hildegarde's mother hand-crafted the gown I saw in the Holtz's attic. It also surprised me to read that ladies had sewing patterns available that long ago, and I thought Pauline might want to add that tidbit to her speech.

I didn't have time to think about that, since I needed to get myself to Jake's Diner.

CHAPTER 33

$\mathcal{I}$ had no idea what Rose Webster looked like, but I felt sure that everyone in town must have known her. The hostess at the diner led me to the booth by the window where Rose waited for me. Rose, a woman about my age in her mid-60's, had white hair, with a short, attractively-styled cut. Casually dressed in slacks and a sweater, and like her husband, having a few extra pounds around the waist, she welcomed me with an engaging smile.

I introduced myself and sat across from her. Our waitress brought the steaming mug of hot chocolate with a large dollop of whipped cream that she had already ordered, and I asked for a cup of hot tea. "I've wanted to meet you," Rose said. "I hope you didn't think it was too presumptuous of me to suggest that we get together today."

"Not at all," I smiled. "Actually, I'm really grateful. As you probably know, we plan to showcase the Smithfield's still and hidden passage to the monastery basement."

"I've heard," Rose nodded. "Pauline Holtz hasn't stopped talking about it, so I'm looking forward to the Women's Guild tour."

"I guess she's told you she's the tour guide," I remarked.

Rose gave a hearty chuckle. "Of course. I thought that was a pretty smart move on your part. Pauline knows a lot about this town. In fact, we attended the same schools, though she's older. Still, we go back a long time since one of her younger sisters was in my class."

"You both grew up here?" I asked as the waitress brought my tea.

"Just about everyone has," Rose replied. "Well, I suppose some folks made their way to the city when they thought the grass was greener. Most decided to come back here to raise their children. It's a healthier environment, if you know what I mean."

I nodded my agreement while adding a packet of sugar substitute to my tea and giving it a little swirl. "I never thought I'd want to live in a rural area, but I've changed my mind. For the most part, people are a lot friendlier and more laid back."

"Definitely," Rose stated, "and more trusting, too. We don't even need to keep our doors locked during the day. Kids can play outside after school until moms call them in for dinner. Paul's actually been on a mission to remind us that the world is changing. That's why he wants to bring back a police presence in town."

"I figured the town must have had a force at some time. The jail looks as if it's been there for years."

"Yes," Rose said. "They took the staffing out of the budget 20 or so years ago, once the state beefed up the county sheriff's office. Paul didn't agree with that approach, so he'll get our local law agency up and running, no doubt about it."

I brought our conversation back on track by asking Rose what she knew about the monastery. She told me that she didn't know much, except for occasionally seeing some of the nuns in town. A few girls she knew had joined, but one left and married a few years later. "I suppose many of us were curious," Rose noted, "since the monastery was a pretty private place. The Sisters didn't open it up until a few years back when they built those cabins with a strange name."

"That's how I learned about the monastery," I said. "I rented a poustinia for a week's stay the summer before last."

"I suppose that's how you met Charlie, because he worked for the nuns. I heard the cabins were his idea."

"You're right," I replied with a giggle. "I never thought I'd end up as Mrs. Munley."

Rose asked how I became involved with the renovations on the old Smithfield barn, so I told her my story. I gave her a snapshot summary since I thought we'd have time to fill in the details on another occasion, and I needed to ask her assistance before both of us had to go home.

"Being new to the area," I explained, "I'm really at a loss for finding vendors who can help me get ready for our opening day. I need someone who does printing, and another who frames pictures, all on a shoestring budget, and that's just a start."

"It sounds as if you need an assistant," Rose said. "You can't do everything yourself."

"I know, but we don't have the money to hire anyone at this point."

"OK," Rose said. "This is what I think. I'll get the contact information for a printer from Paul's secretary, then I'll deliver the items and pick them up for you. I know a good framer in a nearby town, so I can also take care of that for you. What about someone to book the reservations? I can help with that, too."

I looked at Rose in amazement, since I never expected such a response from the mayor's wife. "Are you serious?" I questioned.

"We found each other at the right time," Rose said. "I've been so bored lately. Paul is often tied up at work, and our two girls both moved out of state with their husbands. Paula's in California, and Stephanie's in Tennessee, and I don't even get to see the grandkids but once a year. It's driving me crazy."

"Oh, my gosh," I exclaimed. "I can't tell you how much I need you."

"It goes two ways," Rose said. "Besides, I can already see that we'll get along well. I'll stop out to your place tomorrow morning, and you can show me your office."

I laughed and said, "Right now, that's the kitchen table, but tomorrow's perfect."

"You don't know how happy I am that we met up today," Rose smiled as she signaled the waitress for our check. She paid the tab and I left the tip.

I could hardly wait to get home and tell Charlie that I now had an assistant. He wouldn't begin to guess who I'd found.

CHAPTER 34

$\mathcal{T}$he next day, Gunther Holtz came over after breakfast, and went out to the yard to help Charlie and Leon get the wagon in working order. I checked on Harvey, and saw him lying in the grass to watch the men, seemingly tuckered out after his morning run, then made the kitchen presentable and ran a duster around the house in preparation for Rose Webster's visit. She arrived shortly after 10 o'clock.

"What a great location you have," Rose exclaimed when I invited her in.

"I feel as if we live in the shadows of the monastery," I said before giving her a brief tour of our home.

Obviously impressed, Rose loved the living room with the gas fireplace, but she could see why I enjoyed working at the kitchen table. "With that expansive window, you have wonderful natural light here," she noted, "and the scenery's breathtaking."

"I know," I smiled. "I'll never tire of the view. Would you like coffee or tea?"

"No, thanks. Let's get down to business."

I showed Rose the copies I'd printed of the latest editions of the brochure, as well as a design for my business cards. "Take a look at these," I said, "because I'd like them to go to the printer today."

Rose read through each, expressing positive comments about their clarity and attractive arrangement. As always, when another pair of eyes took a look, something struck a chord. In my previous position, I'd say, "The ink is never dry before we find a mistake." In this case, Rose wondered if I'd reserved the phone number that I included in the samples for just the enterprise.

"No," I replied. "It's my cell phone number."

"You might want to think that through," she said. "You don't want your personal number on all of the advertisements, nor do you want to share your own phone when I'm assisting with reservations."

"I hadn't thought about that," I said, shaking my head. "I mean, I knew I didn't want to use our land-line because I may be out in the barn or fields when I receive a business call."

"That's wise," Rose nodded, "but I'd suggest that you add another cell phone line. Most carriers offer good deals on an extra line, as well as another phone. Who do you have for your service?"

I gave her the company's name, and noted that Charlie and I had a dual contract. We'd set up that account back at my previous home, and I had no idea where to find a store nearby. "Paul and I use the same carrier," Rose stated. "I'll show you the closest location, and we'll return before your afternoon meeting. There's no use taking the brochures to the printer before you have a separate number."

I agreed with Rose, and we headed out to her car. When we passed the men, I told Charlie our plans, and he waved me off after saying that they needed to go into town for a few more items from the hardware store. "We'll probably stop for lunch while we're there," Charlie added, "so don't worry about us."

While she drove, I updated Rose on the tasks I'd recently worked on. I told her about Hildegarde's diary, which I needed to finish reading in order to finalize Pauline's script. I also mentioned that I hadn't heard from the county historical society as to when I could pick up the replicas of JW's ledgers that needed frames. "I don't know when I'll find the time to work on the grant for additional renovation funding," I added, "but I have to do that sooner, rather than later."

Rose's ears picked up on the last item. "Did I tell you that I wrote the grant for Paul's police van? I did a pretty good job, if I may say so myself."

"You like writing grants?" I asked, still astonished that I may have found a gold mine with Rose Webster.

"I may be nuts," Rose chuckled, "but I do. I'm kind of a detail freak. You know, make sure to dot the i's and cross the t's."

"That's definitely not my strength," I replied. "I've done all right because I had one grant fully funded, and two partially funded, but I lost the fourth. Maybe you can help me with this next one."

"I'm your gal," Rose said as she pulled into a parking spot at the phone store. "Just give me the information, and I can work on it from home."

We had a successful trip, and made it back to my place before noon with a new business line and two cell phones. I immediately updated the brochure and business card templates, then copied them to a flash drive for Rose to take to the printer. Rose reminded me to send her a copy of the grant application, preferably by email, so I'd have her address in my contacts. While I did that, Rose created our voicemail introduction, added a few apps, and built the schedule on both new phones.

Before she departed, Rose informed me that she'd work for me on Thursday mornings, and run errands when needed, but she'd focus on the grant during her spare time. Otherwise, we'd keep in touch by phone and email. I felt as if she'd lifted a weight from my shoulders.

WHEN I ARRIVED for my meeting with the Sisters, I could barely wait to tell them my news that the mayor's wife now served as my office assistant. Their surprised reactions delighted me, and I explained, "Father Jim suggested that I could accomplish more if I involved people in my projects who have connections."

"You couldn't find a better person than Rose Webster," Marian said. "I've met her several times. She's smart, and knows just about everyone around here, so you made a good choice."

I told the nuns what we'd accomplished that morning, and what we still needed to do. "Believe it or not, Rose likes to write grants, and she offered to work on the next one."

"That's great," Cathy smiled. "I can create the budget for the new application." She also mentioned that Sister Cheryl had developed lesson plans for various educational programming, which we'd need in our next grant-writing venture.

"Do we have any more reservations for tours?" Marian asked.

"Not yet," I replied. "I haven't done much marketing, but I'll turn my focus on it as soon as I know when they'll finish all of the construction work."

"I think it needs attention now," Cathy said. "You already know when you'll have the first tour, and it will take time to create a social media presence."

"I thought I'd just write a newspaper ad and make some flyers," I stated. "That worked when Sister Tony advertised the poustinias."

"This is different," Cathy noted. "The monastery's now on the National Historic Register, so we need a website and links to accounts like Facebook and Twitter. Probably others, too."

"Do any of the Sisters know how to design a website?" I queried.

"I doubt it," Marian said. "We might have to outsource it, but Cheryl and Cathy have Facebook accounts."

To my relief, Cheryl offered to set up a Facebook page for the non-profit, though she thought we'd need someone to update posts periodically. "I don't think I could manage to do that along with my other responsibilities here," she stated.

"I understand," I nodded. "As for the website, I'll ask the guy who runs the technology department at the publishing firm I worked for if he could create it for us, but again, we'll need someone to keep it active and current." As had been the case so often lately, I needed to tackle things I didn't know how to do.

I told the nuns about the mayor's visit yesterday, and my decision to invite him to an opening ceremony with a ribbon cutting. I didn't think we needed anything too elaborate, but suggested that Sister Marian should also say a few words.

She liked the idea, and remarked that all of the Sisters would attend. To my delight, she lifted another burden from my shoulders when she said, "I can take charge of that for you."

Before our meeting concluded, Marian reminded me that next week, Holy Week, the Sisters would spend more time in prayer to prepare for Easter, so our little group wouldn't convene until the following week. "Father Jim plans to make a retreat in one of the poustinias," she added, "and he'll officiate at church services on Good Friday and Easter Sunday. You and Charlie are welcome to attend."

"Thanks, I'll let him know," I said. "Will you close the B&B and restaurant?"

"No," Marian replied. "Amanda feels that she and Joe can handle everything. We don't expect a large crowd during the week, but we may have people who want to join us in prayer. I imagine the restaurant will be busy on Easter Sunday, especially with the full brunch they've planned. Bridget intends to have the aspirants help out, so I think we'll be fine."

"I'll check in on Amanda to see if she needs any help," I said. "In the meantime, I'll start working on the marketing."

CHAPTER 35

*B*y the time I left the monastery, I noticed a distinct change in the air, as well as a blustery wind. We'd had several lovely spring days, but I definitely felt something wintery brewing. The trees had begun to bud, though the leaves stayed in their little cocoons, perhaps realizing that the time to embrace new life had not yet come.

I walked across the parking lot and along the path through the woods to our place. Previously an impenetrable route, Leon and the volunteers had cleared out all the brambles, though the shrubbery and tall firs afforded a buffer from the gusts. The chill in the air made me consider it a good evening for Charlie and me to snuggle together in front of the fireplace.

I noticed that we no longer had the old wagon in our yard, no open door to the barn, and no utility vehicles parked in the drive, just my car and Charlie's pickup, which signaled the end of work for the day. Unfortunately, I still had to decide what we'd have for dinner.

As I took off my jacket to hang on the hook, the pleasant aroma of pepperoni and mushrooms wafted through the kitchen, and drew my eyes to the pizza box on the counter. I found Charlie in the den, working on a new birdhouse. "You must have read my mind," I grinned, then gave him a peck on the cheek.

"How's that?" Charlie chuckled. "The pizza?"

"Yes, it's perfect, because I really didn't feel like making anything. We should eat in the living room, cozy by the fire."

"That sounds good to me," Charlie nodded. "How'd your meeting go with the nuns?"

"Good," I replied. "No, not really. My brain is whirling, but the walk home helped. I have to say, though, it's getting darn chilly out there."

Charlie nodded. "A cold front's coming in, and we might have a couple inches of nuisance snow."

"Enough already," I sighed, plopping into the recliner. I told Charlie about the Sisters' suggestion that we create a social media presence for marketing. "I don't disagree, but it's just one more headache."

"I don't even know what social media means," Charlie noted as he glued a perch to the front of his creation.

"We need a website, and a Facebook page, and a Twitter account," I remarked, shaking my head in frustration.

"You mean like tweeting?" Charlie asked. "I've heard of that."

"Yes," I nodded. "I'll put you in charge of the tweets. It goes with the birdhouse theme."

"Forget it. I'll stick with what I do best."

When Charlie came to a stopping point, he went to flip on the switch for the fireplace in the living room. In the kitchen, we each put two slices of pizza on our plates, took bottles of beer from the refrigerator, then settled ourselves on the sofa. The flickering flames gave a warm glow to the room, and neither of us wanted to ruin the ambiance by turning on a light.

As we ate, I told Charlie how much I appreciated Rose Webster's help. "She made the brilliant suggestion to set up a separate phone line for the non-profit, and even took the time to deliver everything to the printer. On top of that, she offered to complete the renovation grant for additional funding."

"You can't beat that," Charlie smiled. "The Websters are good people, and I probably should have thought to introduce you to them."

"That's OK," I said. "Anyway, it was nice of Paul to stop by yesterday. I'm sure Leon appreciated it."

"I'm sure he did," Charlie replied, "but Leon doesn't know what to do about the job offer. It took him by surprise."

"Do you think he might ever want to be a cop? It sounds like a wonderful opportunity for him."

"I don't know," Charlie shrugged. "He didn't really talk to us about it, but he still has nightmares about his war experience. He feels that he didn't deserve the Bronze Star because he could only pull three soldiers of his unit to safety before the tanker exploded."

"It must be horrible for Leon to live with what he's been through," I nodded. "I have no doubt those memories will affect him for many years, but he had training in military tactics. He could easily transfer his skills to law enforcement."

"Maybe," Charlie stated, "though Leon likes his privacy. Anyway, it's his decision. Do you want another slice of pizza?"

I knew Charlie's comment brought an end to our topic of conversation, but I could see why the mayor had considered Leon for the force. In addition to Leon's military background, he handled the past week's unfortunate experiences with dignity, diplomacy, and respect; characteristics that Mayor Webster would certainly want to engender in the people entrusted with our welfare.

Charlie returned with the rest of the pizza and two more bottles of beer. I popped an old Nat King Cole CD into the player, then returned to the sofa. In my rusty voice, I sang along with *"Unforgettable, that's what you are; unforgettable, though near or far..."*

Before I knew it, Charlie took my hand and pulled me to my feet. We slow-danced to the music, cozy as love birds nestled together. At the end of the refrain, we both crooned, *"That's why darling, it's incredible, that someone so unforgettable, thinks that I am unforgettable too."*

There we stood by the flickering flames, locked in an embrace that reinforced the love we shared.

CHAPTER 36

On Thursday, Rose called just as Charlie and I finished eating breakfast. Although she'd stopped by the day before, we had designated Thursdays as her work day, so she wanted to know if I had anything on my agenda that warranted her presence. If not, she'd spend time working on the grant.

"Frankly," I said, "that would be the biggest help today." I explained that I wanted to finish reading Hildegarde's diary, then work on the script for Pauline. "If I can manage it," I added, "I'd like to also craft a newspaper ad."

"Email it to me when you have it ready," Rose stated, "and I'll submit it to our local paper."

"The Sisters think we need a webpage," I remarked. "Do you know anyone who does that sort of thing?"

"Not offhand, but Paul does, I'm sure. I'll check with him later. When do you plan to meet with Pauline?"

"She's coming here tomorrow," I noted. "I should be fine, unless you want to join us."

Rose chuckled. "Too many cooks spoil the broth. I'd just be in the way, so I'll come next Thursday, as we'd planned."

When I disconnected our call, Charlie mentioned that the electrician had finished his work yesterday, so the builders would install the dry wall today. "Leon and I planned to spend the day spackling," he added.

"Isn't it too chilly to work in the barn?" I asked.

"The wind has died down," Charlie noted, "and the inch of snow last night has already melted on the paved driveway." He didn't want any delay in our progress.

"Have at it," I smiled. "I forgot to tell you that I stopped to see Amanda after my meeting with the Sisters yesterday. She seemed pleased that Hannah had success on their wedding gown shopping trip, but she couldn't find anything she liked." Charlie's expression led me to believe that it didn't surprise him.

I explained that Amanda wanted a retro type of dress, one reminiscent of the historical aspects of the mansion. "For some reason, a thought came to me in the middle of the night, and I wondered if Pauline might let her wear the wedding gown that we'd found in her attic. It would certainly be vintage."

"Amanda's picky," Charlie said. "I can't imagine that she'd want to wear someone else's dress."

"Hildegarde's mother handcrafted Adele's gown," I noted, "and it's in really good condition. I didn't think of it when I spoke to Amanda, but I'll ask Pauline if we might show it to her."

"It can't hurt," Charlie remarked, "but you might want to ask Amanda first."

"Good idea. I guess we should figure out what we'll give as our wedding gifts. Have you thought about it?"

"Money's always appreciated," Charlie said.

"I guess so," I nodded, "though the couples are at different stages in life. Steve and Hannah both have good paying jobs, and Hannah's going to move into Steve's house, then sell hers. In other words, they're already established. Still, they're paying for the wedding, so I'm sure they'd welcome cash."

Charlie agreed, saying, "Amanda and Joe probably need more since they don't even have a place to live."

"That's what I'd thought. Amanda once told me that she and Joe would like to buy land from the Sisters and put a house on it, like we did. I'd love to help them with that."

"How much are you talking about?" Charlie asked.

"I don't know, maybe enough for a down payment. We could tap into our savings."

"It wouldn't hurt to check with the nuns to see if they'd be willing to sell off another piece of land," Charlie noted as he took his jacket off the hook. "We'd better not make any decisions until we know our options."

"OK," I agreed, "I'll ask Sister Marian." With that, Charlie took Harvey out while I tidied the kitchen. Before I did anything else, I intended to finish reading the diary.

~

November 28, 1919
We celebrated Thanksgiving Day yesterday. This was Mama's first Thanksgiving in America. She helped Adele prepare the roasted turkey and made the pies, while I peeled the potatoes and cut up the vegetables for the stuffing. Dieter joined the table for our meal, as did Adele and James. Jonas was in good spirits, and Mama says she has never enjoyed such a fine time. Dieter told us that the long driveway at our estate is now completely paved, and lamp posts have been installed. I am grateful that we had an extended autumn so the outside work could be finished before winter.

December 18, 1919
Adele, Mama, and I have conducted interviews for additions to our staff at the country estate. We selected a young woman named Louise, who Adele will train to assist her in the kitchen, and a more experienced widow, Ella, as housekeeper. They will begin employment when we move to our new home. In the meantime, Ella has offered to assist with packing one day each week. Preparations are complete for Adele and Dieter's wedding, and they plan a simple church ceremony on December 26, with a luncheon reception immediately following. Jonas has reserved an inn at the seashore for their honey-

*moon as our wedding gift. I am very happy for my dear friend, but I worry
that I will not have Adele with me for much longer.*

January 8, 1920
*Adele and Dieter have returned from their honeymoon. They are so much in
love, and they both have a glow about them. Mama says she remembers
when I had the same smitten look whenever Jonas was nearby. It seems long
ago, though it is only seven years. I told Jonas about my fear of losing Adele
once she and Dieter are ready to start a family. I asked him if we might give
them a gift of some of our land to build a home near ours, and Jonas will
think about it. We will begin to move our furnishings to the mansion in less
than two weeks. Already he and James have brought cartons each time Jonas
checks on the final work being done. I am excited, but full of anxiety.*

February 15, 1920
*Our move is complete, though it has taken a toll on all of us. Mama looks
frail, more than ever, yet she spends many hours in the kitchen with Adele
and Louise each day. Adele reminds me not to worry so much. Mama's
spirits are good, and she is happy to help with Louise's training. Ella assists
me with the unpacking, and she handles all of the housekeeping. She also has
a keen eye for design. Dieter and James have helped Jonas in the basement.
Why Jonas insisted on a bowling alley, I do not understand, but they spend
many hours there. Occasionally, I can hear the ruckus from the ball hitting
the pins. I believe the men are playing, though they tell me they are setting
up Jonas' game room. Our furnishings upstairs are sparse, so Jonas and I
will shop for more décor in the city. Still, I am pleased with the progress we
have made.*

March 20, 1920
*Adele is pregnant. She and Dieter are so very happy. Mama laughs when I
tell her I am surprised that already a little baby is on the way, yet it has been
more than a year that Jonas and I have tried to conceive. Always I must be
patient. Jonas is very pleased with Dieter's work, and has agreed to give a
large parcel of land to Dieter and Adele as a deferred wedding gift. He will
build a home for them, not far from us, and Dieter will continue to work on*

our estate as groundskeeper. Adele shed tears of joy when I told her the news. She and Dieter could never have afforded a house of their own, nor enough land to operate a business. Dieter will plant apple trees, and one day it will be known as Holtz's Orchard, though they will continue to live with us until their own residence is constructed.

June 28, 1920
Mama has not been well, though she tries to hide her illness from me. She continues to lose weight, and she is ghostly pale. Mama refuses to let me call a doctor or take her to a clinic, though Jonas says it won't do much good because the closest hospital is in the city. We have decided that we will have a soiree to raise funds to build a hospital in our county. It will provide a superb opportunity to christen our ballroom, and we can meet other nearby residents, as well as many of Jonas' wealthy acquaintances and business partners.

August 1, 1920
We have hired a nursemaid for Mama. She is now bedridden, and sleeps many hours because of the medication for her pain. When she is awake, I sit with her. Sometimes I just hold her hand. Other times she tells me stories of when I was a child in Germany. Every day she wants to see Adele. Mama rubs Adele's big belly, and says she will not go to heaven until she can hold the baby in her arms. Adele's baby is not due until the end of September. I want Mama to get well, but I fear that is not possible.

October 3, 1920
Adele and Dieter's son, Johan, was born in our home on September 30. Mama insisted that Adele be brought to the bedroom next to hers when the labor began, so that Mama's nurse might assist her. Adele was very brave, and cried out only at the end. Dieter paced the hallway for hours, until the nurse finally let him in to see his newborn. The next morning, I told Mama about the baby's birth. She smiled softly and said she was there, praying for a short labor and an easy delivery. When Mama asked to hold Johan. I helped her sit in the bed, cushioned in Adele's arms. The nurse carefully placed Johan in Mama's lap, and Mama cradled him, rubbing his belly and arms.

*Tears streamed down her cheeks, as she leaned to kiss his little forehead.
Mama received her dying wish. She passed away the following day, on
October 1, so she is now at peace with Papa, Friedrich, and our Greta.*

October 18, 1920
*We have buried Mama across the creek from her favorite perch on the fallen
tree. She will watch over our vineyards, breathing her life-giving spirit,
basking in the eternal peace of heaven. I can feel that she is giving me
strength, and Adele says she knows that Mama is watching over both of us.
We sense her presence in every room, but especially the kitchen. Adele and
Dieter will soon move to their home with little Johan. I will visit with Adele
every day because she is my friend. I also think of her as my sister, since we
shared my mother's deep affection. I will not continue to write in my diary as
I no longer feel the need to express my sentiments on paper. I have my love
for Jonas to sustain me, and that is the gift that Mama bequeathed to me.*

WHAT A BEAUTIFUL STORY, I thought. What a lovely legacy. I, too,
considered myself a friend to Hildegarde. She shared with me her
transition to womanhood, and I recognized that her trials and fears
led to the development of her courage and fortitude. I could identify
with Hildegarde sensing her mother's presence, because I had the
same experience. Although my mother died nearly 20 years ago, her
spirit has remained with me, which I counted as a very special
blessing.

CHAPTER 37

*W*anting to savor what I'd read in Hildegarde's diary while reflecting about the elements that would bring the Smithfields to life for the tours, I decided to take a walk to the monastery. I hadn't remembered seeing a grave marker near the fallen tree by the creek that I'd so often visited, so I made that my first stop.

I followed the pathway past the barn through the woods to the parking lot. Though aware that the trees had buffered me from yesterday's wind, I took a good look at them today. Among the majestic oaks and maple trees, I counted numerous pines. Hildegarde mentioned in her diary that she would plant fir trees on the estate, reminiscent of the type of Tannenbaums of her home in Germany.

I had no doubt that these firs had become a part of the Smithfield legacy. I picked one of the cones that grew upright from the branches, and noticed its difference from ordinary pine cones. Much less woody and decorative, the fir branches looked sturdy enough to hold heavy ornaments at Christmas.

I strolled along the drive toward the vineyard, noticing for the first time the old-fashioned lamp posts. Certainly, the Sisters had updated the electrical work, but I considered these as the ones originally installed. Approaching the cabins, I saw newer lamp posts, closely matched, but somewhat different. Perhaps the Smithfields added those later, or the nuns modernized the driveway after they took ownership.

Reaching the fallen tree by the creek, I sat and gazed at my surroundings. Usually, I focused on the stream, but now I scrutinized the embankment on the other side. Lush with underbrush, I saw nothing to indicate a burial site.

Tempted to try to cross the creek by balancing on the old log, I considered it too risky. Instead, I took off my socks and sneakers, rolled up my pants legs, and slowly made my way in the frigid water. Not deep, it didn't even reach my knees, but the bottom felt slimy, and squished between my toes.

When I climbed the bank, I grabbed a stick to push aside the brambles and shrubs. I didn't have far to travel because, in less than 20 feet, I found a small marker, engraved with the name *Elsa Krug*, dated October 1, 1920.

Ecstatic, I returned to the other side, and put on my shoes and socks. My feet felt so cold that I couldn't feel my toes, so I decided to warm up in the monastery, and let the Sisters know about my discovery. I had no doubt they'd want to learn about the gravesite.

I met Sister Marian as she left the gift shop, and pulled her into the parlor to tell her that I'd just found the burial site for Hildegarde's mother. I gave her all of the details, even to crossing the creek to determine the truth of the reference in the diary. She must have thought me crazy, although she listened intently to my story, then suggested that we wait until later in the spring when we had volunteers to clear out that area of the bank.

I accepted Marian's invitation to join her for lunch, since my toes burned, I felt hungry, and I thought it would give me an opportunity to ask about the availability of land for our wedding gift to Amanda and Joe. Marian and I each made a sandwich from the fixings on the sideboard, then took a table by the window where I told her that Charlie and I wanted to help Amanda and Joe become settled here by the monastery after they married.

Marian chuckled and said, "I don't know how you're always on our airwave, because we've had similar discussions."

"Would you consider selling another plot of land, perhaps adjoining the acreage that Charlie and I purchased?" I asked.

"No," Marian replied. "The Sisters have decided to *give* Amanda and Joe an acre as a wedding gift."

"Are you kidding? You can't be serious."

Practically in a whisper, Marian said, "Amanda has made the restaurant a success by working on a shoestring budget, and receiving little more than room and board. Joe volunteers his time, and even pays to stay in a poustinia. They deserve far more than an acre of land. In fact, we plan to offer both Joe and Amanda a full-time salaried position starting in June."

"Oh, my goodness," I exclaimed. "That's wonderful! Have you told them yet?"

"No, we won't tell them about the gift of land until their wedding day, though I've recently received permission from our administration. On the other hand, the chef positions are a local decision. Sister Cathy has assured me that our income from the restaurant will support their two salaries, so we'll tell them on Easter Sunday."

"That's fabulous," I grinned, "and they'll be really excited. I promise that you'll have more guests by the time the tours are up and running."

"Cathy factored that into the equation. Thanks to you and Charlie for coming up with these ventures, we're actually doing quite well. So, now that we've taken your brainstorm for Joe and Amanda's wedding gift, what will you give them?"

"No question about it," I said in an undertone. "We'll give them a house or, at least, the down payment for one. It'll fulfill Amanda's wish that we'll be neighbors on the farm."

"More like free babysitting when the time comes," Sister Marian chuckled.

"I'm not sure I'm ready for that," I said as Amanda arrived to take our empty plates to the kitchen.

"What aren't you ready for?" Amanda asked.

"Babies," I grinned.

"Aren't you and GP a little old to be thinking along those lines? I mean, really, Vicki. Don't even go there."

Marian and I broke into laughter, then I invited Amanda to have a seat since I wanted to tell her about finding Adele's wedding gown in the Holtz's attic. I explained that Hildegarde's mother had fitted it to Adele's petite size, and the satin gown remained in fine condition. "Would you be interested in seeing it?" I asked.

"Sure," Amanda nodded. "It wouldn't hurt to take a look. Do you want me to call Mrs. Holtz?"

"No, she's coming over tomorrow to work on the script, so I'll ask her to bring it. Can you stop by after lunch?"

"Definitely," Amanda smiled.

CHAPTER 38

Gunther brought Pauline to our place just after lunch on Friday, and I knew they'd arrived by the sound of a backfire from his rattletrap pickup. I opened the back door to invite them in, and Gunther lugged a large carton to the kitchen, while Pauline continually reminded him not to drop it. After he placed it on the table, Gunther responded to my greeting, then hastily left to join Charlie and Leon in the barn.

I'd called Pauline the night before to ask if she might bring Adele's wedding gown to our meeting, since Amanda wanted to take a look at it. Pauline immediately expressed her delight that Amanda would consider wearing Adele's gown for her own wedding, which I truly appreciated, and it made me even happier that she remembered to bring it.

"Thanks so much for coming," I said with a welcoming smile. "I'm excited about our meeting today."

"Good to see you, Vicki. I put a couple of padded hangers in the box, and we should hang the gown right away so it doesn't have too many wrinkles."

"That's a good idea," I said. "Amanda will be here soon."

I held the hanger, while Pauline deftly draped the dress and adjusted the folds. She hung it on the door frame to the den where the light made a good backdrop, then we did the same with the tulle veil. I had to admit that the outfit looked stunning.

Before long, I heard Amanda's typical announcement of "Anyone home?" when she arrived at the back door.

"In the den," I called.

Amanda stopped at the hall entrance, and gazed in awe at Adele's gown. "Wow," she exclaimed. "Wow," she said again as she looked at the intricacies of the design. "This is exactly what I've been looking for! Do you think it will fit?"

"We won't know until you try it on," I smiled.

Amanda removed her sweater and jeans in a flash. She lifted her arms for Pauline to raise the dress over her head, then let it flow to her ankles. I fastened the side snaps, adjusting the satin flower, and Pauline fussed with the drape of the fabric. We stood back to admire its arrangement, while Amanda looked at herself from all angles in the bathroom mirror.

"Obviously, Gunther's grandmother was a little mite of a thing, just like you," Pauline said. "The gown fits perfectly. Let's try on the veil."

It took us a few minutes to figure out how to position the two rhinestone clips, but when we finally had the tulle folds arranged, I stepped back to see the full image. With misty eyes, I pictured Adele long ago having a final fitting with Hildegarde and her mother. Even Pauline had no words to say.

"You look beautiful," I grinned. "Absolutely stunning."

"This is so awesome," Amanda declared, still eyeing the mirror. "Take my picture, because I need to see the whole effect."

Amanda stood in front of the fireplace in the living room, and I snapped at least ten different views of her using my cell phone. It didn't surprise me that she teared up when she saw the photos. "The gown is perfect for you," Pauline stated. "If you like it, you can have it."

Amanda hugged Pauline in response. Finally, she said in a quivering voice, "I love it, and would be so honored to wear it."

"Well, don't cry about it," Pauline replied. "Tears will stain the satin."

We all laughed, then Amanda danced around the room, while I took a few more pictures for good measure. Finally, we helped Amanda pull the gown over her head, and told her to meet us in the kitchen. When she joined us, I showed her the passage in Hildegarde's diary, where she wrote the description of Adele's gown and the pattern that her mother used to design it. Neither Pauline nor Amanda could believe that a professional seamstress hadn't made such an amazing creation.

Amanda took my phone and texted each of the pictures to herself. Once she made sure that they'd all transmitted, Amanda turned to Pauline, asking, "May I pay you for the gown?"

"Not a penny," Pauline stated. "In fact, I intend to have it expertly cleaned and pressed for you. It will be our wedding gift to you and Joe."

"This is so awesome," Amanda grinned. "Joe's going to be blown away when he sees the pictures."

"I guess you've never heard of the old superstition that the groom shouldn't see the bride in her gown before the wedding," Pauline commented.

"Not really," Amanda said. "What'll happen?"

"I don't know," Pauline replied, "but I wouldn't want to find out."

"Well, I don't believe it," Amanda quipped. "It's probably an old wives' tale. On that note, I'm going to let the two of you get to work since I have to do some prepping for supper. I just want you to know how grateful I am."

Amanda practically bounced off the back stoop.

PAULINE TOOK OUT HER NOTES, as well as the outline of the script that I'd given her, and spread them on the kitchen table. She shook her head in dismay, saying, "I don't think I can do this, Vicki. I told

Gunther last night that I'm not good at speeches. Every time I write down something I could say, I forget my lines."

"You're good at telling stories," I reminded her.

"I am," Pauline nodded, "but this is different."

I suddenly realized that the thought of relying on a script caused the problem for Pauline, so a scripted story wouldn't work for her. I decided to take another approach. "Let's try something different," I said, gathering the notes and putting them on the counter. "We'll imagine that I'm on the tour, and you'll lead me through the barn to the monastery. How will you greet me?"

"I don't know," Pauline said. "I guess I'd just be myself. I think I'm pretty hospitable."

"Yes, you are. So, welcome me."

"Hi, I'm Pauline Holtz, and I'm glad you could join me today." She stopped, and looked at me for affirmation.

"That's a good start," I nodded. "Now, you can introduce the topic. Why have people come for a tour?"

Pauline took a deep breath, then added, "Have you ever wondered what it must have been like to live on a massive estate back in the 1920's, or wealthy enough to own almost 400 acres of land and build a mansion fit for a king? Let me tell you about Jonas Willard Smithfield and his wife, Hildegarde."

"Do you have any personal connection?" I asked. "Tell me about it."

Pauline nodded, pausing a moment to gather her words. "I have a special interest in this place. When I married Gunther Holtz, I learned that his grandmother, Adele, had been a servant to Hildegarde Smithfield. Actually, she was more than a servant. They were best friends. Recently, we discovered that Gunther's grandfather, Dieter, also worked here as a landscaper. We didn't know much else, except that Mr. Smithfield gave 35 acres of land to Adele and Dieter, then built them a home across the road. Of course, we didn't have a road then, but the county eventually put one in."

Pauline came to a stop, so I prompted, "How do you know so much about the Smithfield's? Did Gunther's grandparents tell the story?"

"Well," Pauline continued, "that day we had the blizzard, Gunther and I decided to clean out the attic. Oh, my goodness, you can only imagine how much stuff we have up there. Anyway, we came across an ornate wooden box that Hildegarde must have given to Adele, and it contained Hildegarde's diary."

"Excellent," I said. "By the way, I've finished-reading the diary, and I want you to take it home and read it. It'll help you add more details to your story. How do you feel so far?"

"Good," Pauline replied, "but what if I forget something?"

"It doesn't matter, because you're just telling your story. Besides, I think folks will interrupt with questions, just as I did now."

"How long do I talk before I lead the group to the lower level?" Pauline asked.

"There's no time limit," I said, knowing it would add one more thing for her to worry about. I suggested that she explain the purpose of the old wagon, and talk about how Dieter used it to transport barrels from the still on the lower level. While I felt certain that Pauline could imagine Dieter moving the kegs, I knew that she'd falter when it came time to discuss Prohibition. I had a sudden brainstorm.

"A lot of historical places show videos," I said. "If Charlie rigged up a monitor on the wall of the barn, we could have a DVD about Prohibition, then you wouldn't need to talk about it. Just click on the remote."

"That's a great idea," Pauline remarked, "and I could show it before I lead folks to the lower level. After that, people on the tour can just stroll around and explore."

"Exactly," I replied. "We'll also have some replicas of JW's ledgers hanging on the walls of the upper and lower levels, so visitors can take time to read about his extensive bootlegging business."

"You don't know how relieved I feel that I don't have to memorize anything," Pauline stated. "I can just talk about what I know, answer questions, and the rest is easy. I'll lead the group through the passage, let them see the bowling alley, then take them upstairs to the gift shop and restaurant."

"I think you have it," I smiled. "We'll do a practice run the week before the Women's Guild tour. In the meantime, I'll find an appropriate DVD, but one not too long. Maybe, 10 minutes, at best."

Pauline nodded her agreement, then said, "Are you sure you don't mind if I take the diary home to read it? After all, I did give it to the nuns."

"You absolutely need to absorb it," I replied. "Adele and Dieter will come alive for you, as well as Hildegarde and JW."

Pauline boxed up Adele's wedding gown, and added the diary on top. She retrieved her notes from the counter, folded them, and put them into her coat pocket. Before long, Gunther returned to take her home. She handed him the carton to carry to the truck, talking all the while.

I had no doubt Gunther would get an earful that night.

CHAPTER 39

*E*aster, early this year, literally ushered in the month of April. I didn't consider the weather entirely spring-like, though we'd had some sunny days, but I thought it a tad too chilly for my liking. Despite that, crocuses and daffodils popped up in places I didn't expect. Even Harvey turned his attention from the squirrels to the robins pecking the ground, and I knew he'd soon realize that birds had the advantage. They just flew away.

Charlie and I decided to go to the church service at the monastery on Easter Sunday, and also made reservations for the full-service buffet brunch afterwards at the restaurant. Charlie looked decidedly handsome in his black suit, and I wore the new spring outfit I'd purchased the week before at the outlet mall. The sleeveless dress with a floral design had a matching bolero jacket, and it looked very nice on me, according to Charlie.

When I finished applying my makeup, I reminded Charlie that Amanda and Joe would celebrate their birthdays during the week, and we'd give them each a card and some cash after Mass. Other than that, we didn't plan anything special, although I'd ask if they wanted to come over for ice cream and cake some evening after work.

Charlie and I slipped into the side door of chapel just as everyone stood for the entrance hymn. Kate and two other young women, perhaps the aspirants, moved over so we could join them in the pew. As usual, Father Jim gave an uplifting homily that reinforced his theme of the change of seasons that brought new life and new beginnings. My spirit felt revitalized as the chapel resonated with our songs of triumphant Alleluias.

A few of the Sisters, and all of the young folks, scurried to the kitchen immediately after Mass. The rest of us chatted in the vestibule, knowing we still had some time before the restaurant opened for service. I had just told Leon about needing volunteers to help clear the overgrown gravesite of Hildegarde's mother when Father Jim joined us. "Where's this burial site?" he asked.

"Across the creek, near the fallen tree, just beyond the vineyard," I replied. "I found the marker last week."

"How did you get over there?" Father Jim queried. "From what I remember, the other side of the bank is quite overgrown. There's not even a path."

"I rolled up my pants legs and waded across the creek. It wasn't bad, just cold and slimy." I scrunched my nose as I recalled the squishy feeling between my toes.

Father Jim stared at me in amazement. Charlie chuckled and said, "Do you expect anything different from this gal? Once Vicki read about it in the diary, she had to go looking for the gravesite."

"Of course," I grinned. "We'll need volunteers for setting up the gardens soon, so we might as well have them also clear the area across the creek."

"How about next Saturday?" Father Jim suggested. "If it's a nice day, I can rent a van and bring some folks out here. Does that work for you, Leon?"

"Yes, sir. I can take charge."

"You're a good man," Father Jim said. "By the way, we have hundreds of little sprouts growing. One of the ladies at the shelter, Althea Davis, calls them her babies. Do you remember her, Leon? I know she'll want to help with the planting."

"The name sounds familiar, sir, but I can't exactly recall."

"It's a sad story," Father Jim noted. "She lost her whole family in a fire a couple of years back. She tried to get them out, to no avail. Althea pretty much lives at the shelter nowadays, and she's a big help, mostly in the kitchen. I'm just saying, so you'll know when you meet her."

"I appreciate the heads-up, sir, and I'll look out for her."

Charlie encouraged us to move along to the dining room, so we could find a table. Luckily, we arrived when we did, since we saw a steady stream of guests walking in from the parking lot. I noticed that the cooking crew set up buffet tables in each corner of the room, as well as along the entire side wall.

The menu offered a fine-dining smorgasbord. Breakfast items included scrambled eggs, bacon, sausage, ham, and home fried pota-toes. Another station had a variety of salads, crudités, and mixed toppings, while another offered a steamship round of beef, leg of lamb, and roasted turkey, all hand carved by Joe. Side dishes included rice pilaf, mashed potatoes, steamed corn, and green beans amandine. Assorted desserts, breads, and pastries finished out the meal. Initially, I considered the buffet pricey; but, when I saw all that it included, it seemed like a good value for a very special occasion.

Father Jim and Leon shared a table with Charlie and me. Once we each filled our plates and returned to our table, servers arrived with beverages of our choice. I selected the mimosa since it seemed rather fitting for an Easter celebration. "By the way, Father, I took your advice," I remarked after my first sip.

"How's that? Have you requested some help?"

"Yes," I nodded. "I met with the mayor's wife, and she volunteered to be my office assistant. She's wonderful."

"That's how you do it," Father Jim said with a chuckle. "Go right to the top."

"Honestly, I only intended to ask for names and locations of vendors. Instead, she wanted to help in a more tangible way, probably due to a combination of empty nest syndrome and her husband's busy schedule."

"Do you feel better now?" Father Jim queried.

"As you can see, I'm totally relaxed and sipping mimosas," I grinned. "Rose finished one grant, and has started working on another. She also found someone to set up our website, and Sister Cathy has our Facebook page up and running. Our newspaper ad has brought in three more reservations for tours, and that's just a start."

"That's wonderful," Father Jim smiled. "Sister Marian asked me to give the invocation for your ribbon-cutting ceremony on the 16th. Will your barn be ready, Charlie?"

"It's just about done, thanks to Leon and Gunther Holtz. The electrician's coming back this week to install a few monitors on a couple of walls so visitors can watch a video about Prohibition, then we'll finish up the painting and trim work."

All four of us went back to the stations to select the next course of our meal, and I picked up another mimosa. When we returned, Father Jim asked Leon if he'd considered the mayor's part-time police position.

Leon nodded. "I've thought about it, sir, but I don't know the answer."

"What's holding you back?" Father Jim asked.

"I like working for the Sisters, and they're good people," Leon replied. "I suppose I don't want to let them down."

Charlie must have thought I'd add my two cents, because he kicked my foot under the table to remind me to let the scene unfold. Instead of opening my big mouth, I forked some mashed potatoes over my turkey as Father Jim continued, "That's a good reason, and I see your point. After all, they gave you a new start, with a place to live and food to eat."

"Yes, they've been good to me, sir. This place suits me fine, and there's plenty of work for me to do here, especially with our busy season starting soon."

"Definitely," Father Jim agreed. "You have to till the land and plant the crops. Of course, once all that's done, you'll have volunteers to do the weeding or tending the vegetable gardens. Still, someone has to keep them all on task."

"That's right, sir."

"Perhaps you have something else on your mind," Father Jim said. "Otherwise, your decision would be an easy one."

"I guess I've thought that I wouldn't want anyone else to have an experience like I had, sir, locked up in the jail for no good reason. That young officer just followed orders, but he knew I shouldn't have been there, so I could help him. You know, like show him the right way to enforce the law."

Father Jim nodded as he buttered his roll, then he said, "That's probably what the mayor had in mind. The problem is, you'd need police certification. When would you have time to take the courses?"

"Well, sir, like you mentioned, we'll have volunteers to work the farm. It's possible that I could do the program little by little. Besides, the town doesn't have a budget for another full-time officer. A couple hours a week working as a cop might not be a problem for the nuns."

"I can see your dilemma," Father Jim remarked. "It seems to me that you're leaning towards not taking the mayor up on his offer. After all, you're happy with what you're doing here. Why rock the boat?"

"Problem is, sir, there's not a lot to do here in the winter. We stayed busy this year because we renovated the barn, but next year, I could help out in town by protecting the citizens. Do you know what I mean?"

"I sure do," Father Jim nodded. "I suppose if I was in your shoes, I'd look into what's entailed in joining the mayor's police force. In other words, how do you get certified? Who pays for it? What hours would you have to work? Those kinds of things."

"Yes, sir. That's what I want to do, because you can't make a good decision if you don't know the facts."

"Like I told you, Leon," Father Jim smiled. "You're smart, and you have good instincts, so I trust your judgment. Does anyone want dessert?"

As I walked to the pastry table, I recognized that I had just learned an important lesson. Counseling didn't mean telling people what we thought they should do. Rather, it involved presenting options that a person may not have considered so, in the end, he or she could make better decisions. My former neighbor, Myra, used to tell me that I needed to use psychology when I spoke to Amanda. I didn't always understand what she meant, but Father Jim definitely put it into context for me.

Amanda stopped by our table to see if we needed a refill on our beverages. Tempted to order another mimosa, I decided that I'd had enough, and requested a cup of hot tea instead. Reaching into my purse, I retrieved the birthday cards and gave them to her. "Charlie and I wish you and Joe a happy birthday. Do the two of you have any time this week to come over for cake and ice cream?" I asked.

"I'll check with Joe and get back to you," Amanda said. "I don't have time to talk right now, but I have the most amazing news. The Sisters have decided to hire Joe full-time, and they'll pay both of us a real salary."

"Congratulations!" I grinned, even as Amanda practically skipped away to check on the other patrons. While I sipped my tea and gazed around the crowded room, I knew that the dream Charlie and I once held for the Sisters had become a reality.

We could now declare the *Monastery Restaurant* a success.

CHAPTER 40

he following Saturday dawned clear and bright, with no "red sky, sailors' warning" for us. We had a perfect day for removing brush and tilling the fields, and Father Jim planned to arrive with his team of volunteers by mid-morning. Mayor Paul Webster gathered a group of townspeople, and we expected them around the same time. To top it off, Rose organized a service outing for local high school students. It delighted me to have so much help, though I hoped we wouldn't have chaos.

Leon arrived early, joining Charlie and me for breakfast. Harvey, in his glory, didn't know which spot would reap the greatest reward, so he went from Charlie to Leon in search of morsels. I ignored Harvey's antics while I poured another cup of coffee for everyone, then asked, "Are you boys ready for the day?"

"We have everything planned out," Charlie nodded. "Leon will work on the vegetable gardens with Father Jim and his volunteers, while Gunther and the mayor will have the people from town prepare the fields for tilling. I'll supervise the high school kids as they clear out the gravesite by the vineyard. What about you? I figured you'd take care of things here."

"Right," I agreed. "Rose and I will make sandwiches and set up the food. She procured donations from vendors all over town, so she'll bring the rolls, lunchmeat, condiments, cheese, donuts, and even cases of soda."

"Very nice," Charlie smiled. "Do you need me to lug out the folding table and chairs?"

"I'd appreciate it," I nodded. "Rose will lend us hers, too, then we'll just make it a gigantic picnic. I figure folks can sit on the ground, if necessary, or find themselves a restful spot."

"Will you call a time for lunch?" Charlie asked.

"No, we can let everyone take a break when they feel they need it. Do you think that's OK?"

"It works for me," Charlie nodded.

While I cleaned up the kitchen, Charlie brought out the folding table from the den, then he and Leon went outside to unload the pickup. They'd purchased extra shovels, hoes, rakes, garden soil, and whatever else they thought the workers might need for the day. Harvey jumped at the chance to go out with his two buddies.

I barely had the dishwasher loaded when Sister Cathy called, and I thought she may have wanted to know if we needed her help. "Are you coming over today?" I asked.

"I don't know if I can make it," she replied. "We have an incident going on, as we speak."

"What's happening?" I questioned.

"A major meltdown," Cathy said. "Can you hear Amanda yelling at Joe?"

"Not really," I replied.

"I'm by the elevator, and they're in the kitchen. It's bad. I heard Amanda say the wedding's off."

"That's crazy," I muttered. "Put her on the phone."

"That's not a good idea right now," Cathy sighed. "Besides, I don't want her to know I called you. Could you try to reach her on her cell phone? Tell her you need something like pickles, or whatever."

I agreed, and we disconnected our call. I wondered why all hell broke loose at the most inopportune time. Still, I dialed Amanda's number, and it rang until her voicemail picked up the call. I texted

Amanda that I needed mayonnaise, if she had any to spare, and offered to pick it up, but I received no response.

I put the phone in my pocket, and thought I could help Charlie with our folding chairs. As I began to carry two of them outside, my phone rang again. Thinking that Amanda returned my call, I said, "Can I borrow some mayonnaise?"

To my dismay, Steve Angeli replied that he had some in the refrigerator, but I could probably get it faster if I made a trip to the store. I explained the mistaken identity, and told him that I'd tried to reach Amanda. He chuckled as he remarked, "This might not be a good time, because Amanda just called to say that we won't have a double wedding. She's pretty upset."

"I can't imagine what could have happened to set her off like this," I said. "She and Joe just celebrated their birthdays, and she was as happy as a lark last week."

"Apparently, the birthday's the issue," Steve said. "Well, let's just say Joe's gift is the problem. He gave her a spatula."

"Amanda's calling off their wedding because of a kitchen utensil?" I asked incredulously.

"That's what she said," Steve replied. "I'm not sure what to do. That's why I'm calling you."

I had no idea what to tell Steve, but I felt pretty sure that I knew what Amanda would do. She'd lock herself in her room and cry it out. Trying to talk to her right now wouldn't work.

I suggested to Steve that he might want to give Joe a call to hear his side of it. "Maybe there's an underlying issue, and Joe can clarify it for you," I said.

"I'll give it a try, and get back to you later," Steve said. Once again, I put the phone in my pocket and turned my attention to the chairs.

By the time I had my measly seating arranged, Father Jim pulled into our driveway. I enthusiastically welcomed him and the volunteers, although I knew that I'd never remember each of their names, except for Althea, the woman Father Jim told Leon about. Though she wore a long-sleeved sweatshirt, I could see the severe burn scars on her hands. Dark skinned with a pretty face, maybe in her 40's, she wore a scarf on her head, but I noticed that she had salt and pepper hair, similar to Leon.

Father Jim and his gang helped Charlie and Leon finish unloading the truck, then carried the equipment to the areas they would need the tools. Other cars began to arrive in caravan format, and volunteers poured out of the vehicles.

Delighted to see Rose among the mix, she instructed the teens to unload her car. Food could come into the house, while they should place beverage coolers, tables, and chairs in the yard. She and I went into the kitchen as Charlie gathered the others around him and gave them their duties.

Rose and I made room for the perishables in my fridge, then she suggested that we put a few boxes of donuts on the table outside for anyone who hadn't had breakfast, or who needed a snack. After that, we went to work on building sandwiches. "I can't believe you got all of this food donated," I said. "We could feed an army."

"People like to help," Rose replied. "Besides, I offered free publicity at the ribbon-cutting ceremony. I'll make an ad page to insert in the program, something as simple as 'please patronize these businesses.'"

"Brilliant," I smiled, just as my phone rang with a call from Amanda.

Between Amanda's sniffles and stuffy nose, obviously still crying, she murmured, "I have mayonnaise if you want to come over to get it."

I made up some story that I didn't need it after all, since Rose brought all of the fixings for the sandwiches we needed to make for the volunteers. I added, "You're welcome to help us, if you'd like."

"I can't," she said, her voice quivering. "I'm really upset, because I just broke up with Joe."

"Uh-oh," I said, not quite sure how to proceed. "Do you want to talk about it?"

"No, but Joe's such a jerk, and I can't believe he'd do what he did. I mean, really. He gave me a spatula for my birthday. What kind of scumbag would do that? It's so condescending, as if I'm the little wife in the kitchen or something. Is that how he thinks of me? Well, I'll tell you, he can find himself some bozo who'll do his cooking for him, because it won't be me."

I looked at Rose and shook my head. I had no idea what to say, so I just let Amanda rant. When she finally ran out of steam, I asked if she wanted me to come over there. Again, she said no, but that led to another tirade.

I knew Amanda well enough to realize she needed time alone. I suggested that she ask Sister Cheryl to cover for her, and she could have a good cry in her room. "I'll call you later to see how you're doing," I promised.

"What was that all about?" Rose asked when I returned the phone to my pocket.

"Amanda's upset because her fiancé gave her a spatula for her birthday, so she just called off her wedding. Who ever heard of anything so ridiculous?"

Rose burst into laughter. "Me," she sputtered. "I did the same thing. You can ask Paul. I called off our wedding because he gave me an electric mixer."

"I guess you eventually got over it," I noted, "because you and Paul have been married a long time."

"It took me a while," Rose giggled. "You have to realize, the problem's not the spatula or the mixer. It's what those things symbolize. Paul didn't understand my reaction, and Amanda's fiancé probably doesn't either."

"So, it's not as simple as telling Amanda she has to let it go. Joe has to make amends?"

"Definitely," Rose nodded. "It might be a good idea if I get Paul to talk to Joe. Not right now, of course, but maybe before we head home. Is Joe planning to lend a hand this afternoon?"

"He was going to," I said, "but I don't know now."

"If Joe doesn't show up on his own later, give him a call. I promise, Paul can offer him good advice."

∾

JUST AFTER 12:30, Charlie came in to wash up when he and the student volunteers finished their task of clearing the gravesite. "We only found one snake," Charlie grinned. When he saw my expression, he laughed, saying, "Don't worry, it was just a little old garden variety." Still, I hadn't thought about encountering snakes when I'd explored the creek bank.

From the picture window, I saw the teens straggling in through the wooded path. Most of them, engrossed with their cell phones, barely watched where they tread. Rose offered to take a tray of sandwiches out to them, while I started preparing the next batch.

Charlie went outside to sign their service vouchers and tell them they could have lunch, then leave whenever they wanted. I noticed Rose going to each of them, shaking his or her grimy hand, while offering thanks for the help. The students obviously appreciated her gesture, and I considered her a very classy lady for taking the time to do that.

When Charlie returned to the kitchen, I told him about Amanda's meltdown, all over a silly thing like Joe's gift of a spatula. Charlie shook his head, saying, "Oh, no. I should have warned Joe."

I stopped short, still holding a piece of cheese in my hand. "What? You've experienced this sort of thing?"

"I sure have," Charlie grinned. "On our first anniversary, I gave Stella a really nice butcher knife, but she went ballistic. I even thought she might throw it at me."

"What is it with you men? You can't think of flowers, or jewelry, or something?"

"That's what you have to do to fix it," Charlie noted. "You have to be careful, though. It can't be too soon after the incident, and you can't be patronizing. Let me tell you, we men have it rough."

"Yeah, right," I quipped. "In the meantime, Amanda has called off her wedding."

"Don't worry," Charlie assured me. "I'll talk to Joe, and everything will be fine. Trust me."

Rose returned at the tail end of the conversation. She chuckled and said to Charlie, "I guess you and Paul have had a similar experience. Maybe, it's a rite of passage."

"I don't know about that," Charlie replied, "but I'll tell you one thing. It's a lesson you don't forget. I'm going to check on the folks in the field. Do you have enough sandwiches made if I tell them to take a break?"

"Enough to get started, and more to come," I said. "We'll have plenty ready." I handed him a container of hand wipes to place on the picnic table.

As the work crews returned, Rose and I brought out the remaining food. We all enjoyed lunch, and I had an opportunity to chat with each of the volunteers, mostly because they didn't all return to the backyard at the same time. I didn't say anything, but I noticed Leon and Althea sitting, deep in conversation, on the tailgate of Charlie's pickup. It made me happy to think that Leon might have discovered a lady friend.

Charlie had done a great job organizing the workers, which didn't surprise me since I'd seen him in action at the grape harvests, but I considered this time more challenging because of the number of people who came to help, as well as the extent of their tasks. All in all, we had a very productive day, with the fields and garden beds ready for planting as soon as we had little chance for a deep frost.

Eventually, Rose and I began to carry empty trays into the kitchen, while others collected trash or folded tables and chairs. Father Jim gathered his volunteers for their departure, and they promised Charlie to return for the planting. I knew many of them had never experienced farming endeavors.

Joe didn't show up, so Rose and Paul took their leave with the rest of the townspeople. Leon waved as he departed on the path to his cabin. Charlie and I said our last farewell, then he took my hand, and we trudged into the house.

We decided to definitely make it an early night, or so we thought.

CHAPTER 41

After such a busy day, Charlie and I both decided to take a nap before I needed to think about preparing supper. I sprawled out on the sofa in the living room, while he took the recliner in the den. Even Harvey snoozed. It seemed as if I'd barely closed my eyes before I heard a light tap on the back door. I padded to the kitchen in my stocking feet, and found Joe on our stoop. "May I come in?" he asked, looking quite morose. "I need to talk."

"Of course, you can," I said as I led him to the table. "Do you want anything to drink?"

Joe shook his head while he cracked his knuckles, which I couldn't do, but the sound drove me crazy. Finally, he looked up at me with misty eyes and murmured, "Amanda broke up with me today, and she gave me back her ring."

"I heard," I nodded. "I guess you've had a pretty upsetting day."

"I don't even know what happened, Vicki. It was like she was laughing one minute, then she went off her rocker when she opened her present."

"Do you think, maybe, it was the spatula?" I asked. I felt Charlie's presence behind me, and figured our talking must have awakened him.

"It probably was," Joe replied, "but I don't get it because it was a really nice spatula, and it didn't come cheap. In fact, I'd told Amanda that her gift would be late since I ordered it online, and it didn't arrive on time. She didn't seem upset about it the other day. I mean, we've both been really busy and all."

"Maybe she anticipated something somewhat personal," I said. "Something you wouldn't find in a regular store."

Joe shook his head with a forlorn expression. "I honestly don't know, and just don't get it."

"Let me tell you, Joe," Charlie explained. "You won't ever really figure out women, but you need to learn how to determine what they want. Once you pay attention to their clues, you'll have a better understanding of how they think."

I sensed that Joe and Charlie needed some man-to-man time since Joe grew up without his dad. Surely his mother gave him pointers on how to treat a lady, but perhaps she didn't tell him anything specific. "Why don't the two of you go into town and get a beer or something?" I suggested, because I thought a little male bonding with Charlie might do Joe some good.

"Are you sure you don't mind?" Charlie asked. "What are you going to do?"

"Maybe I'll check on Amanda to see if she needs any help," I replied. "Without Joe, she'll be short-handed."

"I'd appreciate that," Joe said. "I didn't want to go and set Amanda off again."

Charlie agreed that Joe made a wise decision to stay away, and let Amanda cool off a bit. "That's the first step to resolving the issue," Charlie stated. "I'll teach you more tricks when we go out on the town." Charlie told me not to wait up.

I tried not to worry when they departed, but I had no idea what advice Charlie would give to Joe.

∽

BEFORE SETTING off to help Amanda, I changed into a pair of my black slacks and Charlie's powder blue golf shirt with the logo of the *Monastery Restaurant and Inn.* I didn't want to walk alone in the woods after dark, so I drove over, and parked on the grass near the kitchen entrance. Amanda looked surprised to see me, especially since I hadn't called to give her a heads-up.

"What are you doing here?" she asked as she put the finishing touches on an order of the seafood combo. Her eyes still looked puffy, but she'd managed to pull herself together.

"I had a feeling you might need some help. Joe and your grandfather are having a boys' night out, and before you get all riled up about it, Joe's pretty upset. He came over to ask GP's advice."

"So, you're taking his side?" Amanda questioned.

"Of course not," I sighed. "I'm here to help, and I can wait tables for you or, at least, bus them."

"Thanks, Vicki. I appreciate it. Kate's on her way, though it'll take her an hour to get here. Sister Cheryl's taking orders now, but Saturday nights get really busy."

"That's what I figured," I replied. "Is there anything ready for me to bring to the dining room?"

It took me a while to get the hang of everything, and I'd mixed up several orders. Sister Cheryl suggested that I seat the guests, fill their water glasses, and bus tables, while she did the running back and forth to the kitchen. Once Kate arrived, we had a pretty good routine.

By the time the last patron departed, Cheryl, Amanda, Kate, and I each made ourselves a plate of leftovers, and sat at a table in the dining room. "You need more help," I remarked as I forked a cherry tomato from my salad. "My feet are killing me."

"We just hired a dishwasher and a waitress, both part-time," Cheryl said. "Of all days, they each called out sick."

"They're not right for the job if they aren't reliable," I said. "If Kate and I hadn't arrived, you'd never have made it."

"I know," Cheryl replied, nodding her head in agreement. "Can you help me interview? At least, teach me the kind of questions I should ask."

"I'll be happy to guide you with that," I stated. "Honestly, in addition to reliability, you need a pool of workers who can substitute when anyone can't make it in."

"Well, Joe should have been here," Amanda grumbled. "I mean, he didn't even call to say he wasn't coming."

We looked at Amanda as if we couldn't believe the words she'd uttered. Each of us knew that, no matter what we said, Amanda would hold it against us, at least for the short term. Amanda eventually got over whatever upset her, but she just needed time. Still, I decided to take a stab at responding, so I asked, "What would you have done if Joe had arrived?"

"I don't know," Amanda shrugged. "I certainly wouldn't have talked to him, but he could have done his job."

"It's not his job," Cheryl said gently. "Not yet, anyway. Joe volunteers his time, because he wants to be with you. After what happened today, I'm not so sure it's a good idea to offer him a full-time position."

"Well, you already did," Amanda retorted, "and you can't take it back. I mean, that wouldn't be right."

I realized that Cheryl and I made a good team, because she actually played right into my hand. "You obviously can't work together," I stated, "so, perhaps, Cheryl should split your hours. You'd work one day, then Joe would work another. Something like that could resolve the situation."

Amanda shook her head. "I don't think that's such a good idea. If Joe hadn't given me that stupid spatula for my birthday, we wouldn't even have this discussion."

"Probably not," I agreed. "What did you expect as a gift from him?"

"I don't know," Amanda said. "I mean, all last week I gave him hints. I even showed him a bracelet I liked on the internet. When Joe told me that he'd bought my gift online, I thought he must have ordered the one I wanted."

"It doesn't really matter if you formed a wrong assumption, or he made a mistake," I remarked. "You've already decided to call off the wedding, and your dad confirmed that."

"Right," Amanda grumbled, "so let it go, because I don't want to talk about it anymore."

"Agreed," I said. "Let's begin the cleanup so you can close the restaurant."

Cheryl suggested that she and I finish bussing the tables, while Kate and Amanda ran the dishwasher and wrapped up in the kitchen. As soon as the girls left us, Cheryl whispered that she suspected Amanda would make up with Joe by tomorrow.

"I have a feeling that Charlie will advise Joe to let Amanda stew for a few days," I grinned. "Regardless, let's not worry. We'll have a double wedding, as scheduled."

Of that, I had no doubt.

CHAPTER 42

*A*fter breakfast the next day, Charlie and I sat reading the Sunday paper at the kitchen table. He told me that he and Joe had first gone to the firehouse last evening, just to chat with the guys. Then, they went to a bar across town that served a menu of pub food with a reasonably priced assortment of beer. "We had a late night," Charlie added, "but I think Joe felt better by the end of it."

"So, what's the plan?" I asked.

"I don't know what you mean," Charlie said nonchalantly.

"Charlie Munley, you knew exactly what I meant. How long did you tell Joe to stay away from Amanda?"

"I never told him anything of the sort," Charlie replied. "He's the one who figured that he should just let Amanda chill for a few days."

"Did you tell Joe he should bring Amanda flowers when he wants to apologize?" I queried.

"Nope, I don't think he has anything to be sorry about. He's not the one who made such a big stink about the birthday gift. Amanda got her nose out of joint, so she needs to deal with it."

"I thought you said yesterday that Joe would have to fix the problem by giving Amanda something nice."

"I did, but not as an apology. It's all in the timing."

Charlie buried himself with the sports stats, so I knew he wouldn't tell me what advice he gave to Joe. That would only divulge the secret male-brotherhood rite. I immersed myself in the coupon circulars when Amanda called. "Do you know where Joe is?" she asked.

"I haven't seen him," I said. Charlie looked up from the paper and winked at me.

Amanda sighed, then stated, "I just wondered if he plans to work today. We have Sunday brunch, and it can get hectic."

"Let me ask GP," I replied. "Charlie, do you know if Joe intends to work at the restaurant today?"

"I don't think so," Charlie said, loudly enough for Amanda to hear his response. "I think he told me that he's getting together with some friends from the diner, and they're going to a rally in the city."

"I guess you heard that," I said. "Do you need any help?"

Amanda seemed distracted, but muttered, "No. Kate's staying for the day, so we'll be all right. I just wanted to know."

"Well, call if you need anything," I stated. "I'll be here."

Though Charlie again pretended to review the latest game statistics, I noticed the grin on his face. Whatever tactic he had recommended to Joe, it worked. As for me, I thought it better to let Amanda face her own challenges, rather than interfere. I felt no need to solve Amanda's problem, since she could figure out the solution herself.

With the ribbon-cutting ceremony only a week away, I had a few last-minute details to arrange. I didn't have to focus on the program, since Sister Marian spearheaded that aspect. The DVDs I ordered about Prohibition had arrived on Friday, and I intended to watch them during the afternoon, then select the segments that we could showcase on the tours.

Charlie also promised to hang our framed prints of JW's ledgers on the walls, so he and I had planned to work in the barn later today. In the meantime, I decided to call Betty. We hadn't really found a chance to catch up since she came to defend Leon. Even then, we didn't have any personal time. "Are you busy?" I asked. Betty chuckled as she noted that she'd thought of touching base with me, too.

"Before I forget about it," I noted, "I wanted to invite you to our ribbon-cutting ceremony for JW's barn and still, next Sunday afternoon. Would you be able to come?"

"I think so," Betty replied. "Do you mind if I bring a guest? Mike's really interested in history, and I'd like to show him the monastery."

It made me happy to hear that Mike, also a lawyer in the city, remained in the picture. Last summer, Betty felt uncertain about continuing to date him, since she didn't know if she could ever love someone else after the special relationship she had with her deceased husband. Mike's wife died several years ago, and it seemed that they both decided to give romance a chance.

"Definitely bring Mike," I said. "I'm not sure if we'll have a large crowd, but the opportunity might give us some news coverage."

"How many people do you expect?" Betty asked.

"I have no idea," I sighed, "nor do we know if the weather will cooperate." I explained that we rented 100 folding chairs. If we had a nice day, we'd set them up outside the barn. If it rained, we'd have to use the upper level of the barn. "I'm not going to worry about it," I said. "It'll all work out in the end."

"Will you offer tours?" Betty questioned.

"Not on Sunday," I replied. "We'll let visitors walk through the barn, if they want, but we require reservations for the guided tours, and they won't start until the following Friday. Also, we'll have an entrance fee for those."

"It sounds as if you have everything ready," Betty stated. "How have you managed to stay so calm?"

"Believe me, I felt frazzled a month ago," I chuckled, "but all of the pieces have now fallen into place. Charlie did a wonderful job overseeing the restoration, and Rose Webster has been a godsend." Betty didn't know about Rose, so I explained how we'd met, and what she did as my volunteer office assistant.

"I'll look forward to meeting her," Betty replied. "What time should we arrive?"

"The program begins at 2 o'clock. Come early, so we'll have time to chat."

CHAPTER 43

*O*n Wednesday afternoon, I walked over to the monastery for my meeting with Marian and Cathy. On such a beautiful spring day, sunny and warm, it surprised me to see that all of the leaves on the trees had popped out overnight. As I meandered across the parking lot, I couldn't help but notice the numerous flowering dogwoods and cherry blossoms that embraced the mansion. The blooms sparkled in the sunlight, leading me forward.

I'd told Charlie that I planned to visit Amanda after I met with the Sisters. Neither of us had heard a thing from Amanda or Joe, and we both decided that we wouldn't permit them to drag us into their drama. We'd make ourselves available if either of them wanted to talk but, otherwise, they had to work out their own difficulties. Still, Amanda didn't usually sulk for more than a day.

Sister Marian began by saying that we wouldn't need to meet every week any longer, since we could update each other on an as-needed basis. Besides, the Board of Trustees for the non-profit would meet quarterly, and Sister Tony, who agreed to serve as Chair of the Board, designated Marian, Cathy, and me as members. Although currently assigned to the Sisters' administration team in St. Louis, Tony had always held a special place in her heart for the Monastery of

St. Carmella. She didn't intend to travel for each board gathering, but she planned to connect through Skype or a phone conference.

After her announcement, Marian asked Sister Cathy and me to review the copy of Sunday's program for the ribbon-cutting event. She pointed out that Father Jim would provide the invocation, followed by her opening words of welcome, then she'd introduce me, and ask me to give a brief rendition of how we discovered JW's barn and still. I noticed that she emphasized *brief*. Finally, she'd invite Mayor Webster to come to the podium.

"Podium?" I asked. "We don't have one."

"How about a barrel?" Cathy suggested. "That'd be cool." Marian and I liked that idea, and we agreed that Charlie could easily place one outside, near the barn door, weather permitting.

"After the mayor finishes his speech," Marian continued, "I'll ask him to cut the ribbon draped across the front of the barn. Mayor Webster offered to bring the town's ceremonial scissors for that."

"Nice," I smiled. "Do you plan to invite folks in to see the still?"

"Yes," Marian nodded. "I'll do that in my closing remarks after I thank the mayor. I've also ordered a canopy that we can set up on the grass, and we'll have iced tea and small pastries available there for the guests. What do you think?"

"It sounds great," I said. "I sure hope it doesn't rain."

"We're watching the forecast," Cathy said, "and the Sisters have been praying, so I think we'll have a nice day."

"Good," I replied. "Do you want me to take the program to the printer?"

"No," Marian said. "Sister Bridget's going to make copies in-house. How many do you want?"

"I have no idea," I sighed. "She'd better make 100."

Marian nodded. "I told her 150, just in case."

Cathy and I laughed, more because we enjoyed Marian's optimism, rather than our doubt. Still, I didn't think we'd attract so many visitors, though I tried to stay positive. It amazed me that we accomplished as much as we had.

Before Marian concluded our meeting, I mentioned that Rose had finished two grants. "We've mailed both of them," I said. "Now, we just have to wait for their responses. In addition, we've confirmed reservations for eight tours in the next month, and we've set up the videos about Prohibition. They're good to go with the push of a button."

"Do you think Pauline's ready?" Marian asked.

"I'm keeping my fingers crossed," I replied, "and we have a rehearsal next Tuesday."

"That sounds good," Marian smiled. "Thank you, Vicki. We couldn't have accomplished all of this without you."

"It took everyone working together," I said. "Now, we can enjoy the ride. I just hope we don't meet any potholes along the way."

"Did you plan to visit with Amanda?" Cathy asked. "She's been like the proverbial cat on a hot tin roof."

"No sign of Joe yet?" I questioned.

"Not that we're aware of," Marian said. "Amanda just says she doesn't want to talk about it."

"Do you think she's in the kitchen?" I asked.

"Probably," Cathy said. "Go see her, because we think she needs your advice."

I FOUND Amanda working on dinner service for the Sisters, as well as preparing the trays for the infirmary. Even before I offered to help her spoon vanilla pudding into ramekins, she handed me a jar of maraschino cherries and asked me to place one on top of each dish. The simple garnish made the trays attractive, which I considered a signature trait of Amanda's. Despite her mood, she tried to bring cheer to the older nuns, and they loved her for it.

"What did you make for supper?" I asked, glancing at my watch. I hoped Charlie didn't expect a full-course meal when I returned home.

"Meatloaf, mashed potatoes, and green beans," Amanda replied. "It's not too original, but the girls like it."

"Can I help you plate it for the trays?" I questioned.

"Sure," Amanda nodded. "I'd like that."

Amanda showed me the card on each tray with a Sister's name and her diet order. Some had "no added salt;" others had "sugar-free." I let Amanda handle the special orders, while I took care of the regular meals. When she gave her approval, I placed the lid on each plate and slid the tray into the warming carrier.

"Do you have to deliver these now?" I asked.

"No, Cheryl will do that after Vespers. I just need to set up the serving stations for those of us eating in the dining room, so I'm good now."

"I guess I should get going," I said. "GP will wonder if he has to fend for himself."

Amanda smiled, knowing that Charlie would worry if I didn't make it home before dark. I took her advice, and sent him a text to remind him that I'd stopped to visit his granddaughter, and intended to leave in a few minutes. I didn't give Amanda any guidance about her personal dilemma, though I did drop a hint that she might want to take a walk after supper. "It wouldn't hurt to stop by Joe's cabin," I suggested.

Amanda didn't argue or become defensive, so I had a feeling that she'd already decided to do that.

CHAPTER 44

The weather cooperated on Sunday for our ribbon-cutting ceremony, as the Sisters predicted it would. A cobalt blue sky, with just a few wisps of clouds, brought a sense of relief that we wouldn't need to move the seating into the barn. Rose Webster had offered to assist with any last-minute details, and she arrived before noon while Charlie busied himself sprucing up the yard, making sure it would show nicely as a backdrop in any photos. He also planned to direct parking, since we had no lot, and no idea how many vehicles we'd have on the grassy areas.

I greeted Rose enthusiastically, although I had a feeling that she sensed my nervousness. Before she even exited her car, Charlie showed her where he wanted her to park, then she and I walked together toward the barn. "I don't anticipate any glitches today," I said, "but I know all about Murphy's Law. 'Whatever can go wrong, will go wrong.'"

Rose laughed, then calmly stated, "We've covered all of the bases, so we have nothing to worry about. Just relax and have fun."

"I'm trying," I nodded, "though I wish we knew how many people to expect. Charlie set up the chairs this morning, and we might have too many. What if only a few visitors come today?"

"It doesn't matter," Rose replied. "I have to say, you made Paul very happy by inviting him to participate, and I know that whoever arrives will enjoy the experience. However, I do think we should rearrange the chairs to provide better visibility to the speakers."

I took a good look from Rose's perspective. After all, she had certainly participated in numerous public speaking events. "I agree," I said, then called Charlie to help make the change. We placed the chairs on a diagonal, so we had clear sight lines to the barrel podium from every vantage point. "That's much better," I nodded. "What's next?"

Rose scanned the area, and nodded her approval of the open barn doors, the microphone by the podium, and the canopy under which we'd serve refreshments, then said, "Everything looks good out here. I brought the vender appreciation flyers, so let's insert them into the programs."

Rose and I went into the kitchen to take care of that, since Marian had delivered the programs earlier that morning. The flyer, a half sheet of paper with an attractive design, listed the businesses that contributed goods and services for the support of our endeavors. We made good headway, and finished the task just before I heard a tap on the back door. Betty and her friend, Mike, arrived, so I invited them in, and we did the round of introductions.

Mike had a studious look about him, probably due to his thick horn-rimmed glasses. Tall, thin, and balding, with a well-trimmed mustache, I thought of him as slightly older than Betty, perhaps inching towards 70, and he let Betty do most of the talking. "Everything looks good out there," she noted, "and we saw Amanda and Joe setting up the food."

"What?" I gasped. I glanced out the picture window, but had no direct line of vision. Instead, I bolted out the door, and looked to the right of the barn to see Joe lugging cases of goods to the tables under the canopy, and Amanda showing him where she wanted them placed. I waved but, engrossed in their work, they didn't see me. Nonetheless, I didn't detect any tension between them, which I considered a good sign.

When I returned to the kitchen, I heard Rose explaining to Betty and Mike what took me by surprise. "Yep," she said, "Amanda and Joe had a huge battle, all over a spatula."

"They're working together, and they look OK," I sighed.

"I guess the wedding's back on," Rose chuckled.

"I sure hope so," I agreed, though I could barely wait to hear what brought them back together. "Charlie never told me what advice he gave to Joe when they went out for a beer. Whatever it was, Joe must have taken it to heart, because Amanda fretted about him all week."

"It obviously gave Amanda time to cool down and think about her priorities," Rose said.

"Right," I nodded. "It's good to see them together again. Knowing Amanda, she's now made her expectations clear to Joe, similar to Hildegarde. As a newlywed, she balked at the rules JW imposed, but when she finally voiced her needs and wants to her husband, they gained equal footing in their marriage."

"It's probably typical," Rose replied. "At least, that's how it happened for Paul and me. Don't you ever argue with Charlie?"

"I can't say that we've ever gone to bed angry. Maybe it's different when you marry at an older age, because we don't have to prove anything to each other."

"You still have stars in your eyes," Betty grinned. "Give it time, since it happens to every couple. You'll have some misunderstanding, and you'll both believe the other person caused the problem. I guarantee you'll experience it at some point."

"I think we've had enough gabbing," Rose said, glancing out the window. "I see that some cars have arrived, as well as the news crews, so we'd better head out." She picked up the programs, and promised to make sure each of the guests received one, while I quickly freshened my lipstick.

As the four of us walked outside, I saw that the two TV vans had pulled into our driveway by the side of the house, and I identified one from the local news station; the other, from a major news network in the city. Charlie directed traffic around them as he told visitors where to park.

Betty asked if she could help in any way, but I couldn't think of anything else we needed to do. I suggested that she and Mike take a seat in the second row, although Rose had a better idea. She handed Betty the programs, saying, "Before you do that, perhaps you and Mike could put one of these on each chair. I see that my husband has arrived, and I'd like to give him a little encouragement."

Rose went to greet Mayor Webster, then the two of them sat in the first row. Several of the Sisters walked over from the mansion, including Cathy and Cheryl, who pushed two of the older nuns in their wheelchairs, and they joined the Websters. Father Jim pulled up in the van from the shelter, dropped off a few people I recognized as volunteers from the week before, then he went to park.

Before long, I caught sight of Leon and Althea walking to the seating. Seeing them together made me realize that I may not have initially planned a ribbon-cutting ceremony, but the afterthought brought benefits in more ways than one.

CHAPTER 45

$\mathcal{I}$ welcomed the newscasters as they finished setting up their equipment, then turned on the microphone and tested the sound. Sister Marian and Father Jim, chatting by the podium, reminded me to stay calm, then took their seats in the front row next to Mayor Webster. Although cars continued to arrive, only a few empty chairs remained, so I knew we'd have standing room only.

When the 2 o'clock start time approached, Charlie stopped directing traffic, and came to join me. He gave my hand a squeeze, and whispered excitedly, "I never expected this many people, but I'd say you put *Rock Creek Farm* on the map. You're brilliant!" Charlie's words tickled me, and his presence erased all of my anxieties. As we turned to walk to our seats, we both waved to those we recognized, and I couldn't help but notice everyone's gleeful anticipation.

Once the cameramen gave the signal that we could begin, I nodded to Father Jim. A hush fell over the audience as he walked to the podium and picked up the mic to begin the invocation. As usual, he used no notes. He just gazed at each of our guests, and spoke from his heart.

"Lord, we ask your blessing on this amazing remnant of history that Jonas Willard Smithfield and his wife, Hildegarde, bequeathed to the

Sisters of St. Carmella nearly 70 years ago, and we now share in their bountiful legacy. Although they'd lost two children in the influenza of 1918, JW and Hildegarde didn't wallow in despair. Rather, they used their influential powers of wealth and status to provide for those less fortunate, and they dedicated their lives to helping others. Give us the strength to see beyond ourselves, as in Proverbs 22 we read, 'Whoever has a bountiful eye will be blessed, for he shares his bread with the poor.' Bestow on us the courage to live in dedication and service, as do the Sisters. May we walk with them to experience your final glory. Amen"

Sister Marian walked to the podium, thanked Father Jim for his opening prayer, then said, "We need to recognize that we didn't come today to merely view an old barn or a hidden bootleg operation. All things have a greater purpose, perhaps different from what's visible to the eye."

Marian explained that the Sisters had a mission to care, minister, and support others through their own prayer and works of mercy. "We believe it's fitting that we invite you to observe the story that transpired literally beneath our feet. We have no idea what precipitated Mr. Smithfield's choice to break the laws of Prohibition, but we don't intend to keep his heritage hidden. We want to share what we've discovered, and we also plan to have a working farm that will provide food for the needy, work for the unemployed, and education for those who've never experienced caring for livestock or crops. The Sisters and I want to welcome you to *Rock Creek Farm*."

I watched the faces of everyone in the audience. Those who hadn't heard about the farm nodded their approval. Others gazed intently at the old machine barn, probably wondering how they'd missed seeing it when they drove along the country road, passing by the monastery gates. Regardless, each person showed interest, and I didn't feel nervous when I heard Sister Marian's introduction of me. "Let's welcome Vicki Munley, the director of our non-profit organization. She'll tell you how she and Sister Cathy discovered the secrets of our monastery."

I asked Cathy to join me at the podium, since I considered it her idea to learn about JW and Hildegarde Smithfield, though neither of us expected this outcome of our curiosity. I realized that life often unfolded with twists and turns, yet if we remained open to new possibilities, we'd discover opportunities that we could never have imagined.

After my brief rendition of finding the hidden passage in the basement, ending with the discovery of JWs still, I promised that Sister Cathy and I would remain to answer questions after the ceremony. She thought to add that anyone interested could make a reservation for our upcoming tours, noting the contact information in their programs. I watched as everyone scanned the page when she passed the microphone to Mayor Webster.

The mayor gave a lovely speech about his pride to take part in the Sisters' endeavors, as we witnessed the history of our town and county. He talked from the heart, even mentioning how his wife, Rose, gave her time and effort on our behalf. He noted how much he enjoyed volunteering to prepare the soil for the planting of crops, and he ended by encouraging everyone to become involved. If we all had banners and flags, we'd have waved them, because Paul Webster, a very popular mayor, knew how to work a crowd.

Sister Marian and I stood on either side of the mayor as he flourished his scissors and cut the large neon pink ribbon. Everyone cheered, and it felt as if half the town, and then some, must have come out for the event. Immediately after the ceremony, the media cornered the mayor, Marian, Cathy, and me for interviews. Charlie led folks into the upper level of the barn, while Amanda and Joe served food to others under the canopy.

As people gradually disbursed, Charlie walked over to join me, and we both agreed that the day couldn't have gone better. The two of us had given it our best shot, and everything came off without a hitch. Amanda sprinted across the lawn to give us both a hug, then made sure to show us the engagement ring returned to her finger. "Joe and I have to go," she said, "because so many have decided to have an early dinner at the restaurant. Eeek!"

"We'll clean up here," I smiled. "GP and I are really happy that you and Joe are back together."

"Me, too," she replied with a beautiful expression. "I'll tell you all about it one of these days."

"Good," I nodded, as Charlie squeezed my hand.

I noticed Leon speaking with the mayor, while his friend, Althea, stood talking to Father Jim, Betty, and Mike. Eventually, Leon shook the mayor's hand, then went to stand by Althea. Curious, Charlie and I joined the group, and Betty told us that Leon had some news.

"I accepted the mayor's offer," Leon said simply. Althea smiled her encouragement, so he continued, "I'll need a paying job, because I can't very well support a wife on just a stipend. Anyway, Althea and I will take it one step at a time and see what works for both of us."

We all gave our congratulations, with rounds of hugs and slaps on the back. Father Jim, the only one who didn't appear totally shocked, grinned as he watched us. Besides counseling, I considered him very good at matchmaking.

Betty complained that I'd been so busy, I hadn't kept her informed of the goings-on around here. I promised I'd do better, though I had a hard time staying abreast of the news myself. She would just have to visit more often.

Paul and Rose stopped to chat before they departed to dine at the monastery. "Thank you so much for all you did to make the day such a success," I said. I wanted them to know how much I valued their support, as well as their friendship.

"I've told you before," Rose replied with a smile, "it goes both ways. I've loved working with you, and it's also been good for Paul and me, as a couple. When things settle down, we'd like to have you both over to our place for supper. We'll schedule it on your calendar when I come to work on Thursday."

"That sounds perfect," I grinned.

Betty and Mike asked if Charlie and I planned to eat at the monastery restaurant. He and I looked at each other, and I knew, with one glance, that we both preferred a quiet evening at home. "We'll take a raincheck," I said. "After we lock the barn, and take any leftover food to the house, we plan to call it an early night."

"I can see you're still enjoying the honeymoon phase," Betty chuckled, "so enjoy every moment. By the way, you both make me really proud. As I've often mentioned to Sue, the two of you accomplish great things when you work together."

Charlie put his arm around my shoulder, and gave it a squeeze, then he kissed me. Betty and Mike laughed as they took their leave. Father Jim also waved farewell to us as he ushered his crew into the van, including Leon and Althea.

Finally alone, Charlie took my hand and we walked through both levels of the barn to make sure no one remained. He locked the bolt, checked it for good measure, then we carried the few cartons of iced tea and platter of pastries to the house.

I had a feeling we'd polish those off before the end of the evening.

CHAPTER 46

$\mathcal{T}$he next morning, Leon stopped by after breakfast. Charlie had just made another pot of coffee, since we intended to work on a plan for what we still needed to accomplish as we moved forward with the farm. I invited Leon to join us at the table, then poured a mug of Charlie's brew for him. "I thought you might have gone back to the city with Althea last night," I said with a wink.

Leon smiled a sheepish grin. "No, Father Jim dropped me off at my cabin, but I hoped Charlie might let me use his truck today. Althea wants to show me some things at the shelter, like how much the seedlings have grown."

"No problem," Charlie replied. "I don't think I'll need it for a few days if you want to stay in the city. In fact, this might be a good time for you to take a break, because we'll have to put in the crops next week."

"That's not a bad idea," Leon mused. "If the Sisters don't need me, I'll take you up on your offer."

"Althea seems very nice," Charlie noted. "I guess you've taken a liking to her."

"She's had it rough," Leon said with a sad look in his eye. "Althea lost her husband and three kids in the fire, though she tried to rescue them. In a way, I had a similar experience. You just don't believe that you should be the one to live, when the others didn't make it."

"How long ago?" I asked. I didn't want to intrude, but I sensed that Leon wanted to talk about Althea.

"I guess it's about eight years now," he said. "She'd been living on the streets until she heard about Father Jim's place. Maybe I met her some time back, but I don't recall. She likes it at the shelter because she feels safe."

"It seems to me, you both have a lot in common," Charlie said. "That's important, especially when you're set in your ways. Just don't wait too long. You're not getting any younger."

"Speak for yourself, Charlie Munley," I teased. "I think Leon will know when the time is right. So, tell us when you plan to start on the police job, Leon."

"First, I need the training. There's a police academy at the community college, and the mayor intends to pay my tuition, so it's a pretty good deal. The program starts in July, but I can go part-time through the year."

"That sounds good," I said, "but you'll need a vehicle to get to your classes."

Leon nodded his agreement. "Father Jim's going to see what he can do, and he might be able to get one donated. Even if it's in bad shape, I'm pretty good at fixing cars. Of course, I'll need money for insurance and gas."

I told Leon not to worry about that since the grant will provide funding for his work on the farm. I just wished we could find a way for Althea to move out here, since I knew the challenge of a long-distance relationship. "Do you think Althea will want to live in the sticks?" I asked. "Maybe she'd prefer town."

"She's like me," Leon replied. "She wants space. Father Jim mentioned that she's really good in the kitchen, so I thought the nuns might want to hire her."

"I know Sister Cheryl's looking for reliable help," I said. "You could talk to her about it."

"Yes, ma'am. I might do that today before I go to the city."

"Good idea," Charlie agreed. "While you're here, I'd like your input on some of the things we need on the farm, since we're making a list."

Leon suggested that we add a barn back by the pastures. It should have a few stalls for animals, a feed room, running water, and storage for our equipment. "We're going to need that sooner than later," he said.

I nodded my agreement as I made a note of it, adding that we should put in a driveway all the way back to the barn. In time, we could have it paved, and we'd also want lighting. Charlie mentioned that we had to have a parking lot for visitors, as well as some fenced areas for animals.

"Don't forget about your garage," Leon said. "You could make it large enough to include Charlie's workshop."

"The garage and wrap-around porch are definitely on my to-do list," I said, "but they'll come out of our personal expenses. We budgeted for those last fall when we bought the house, and we could probably get those started in the next few weeks."

Charlie gazed out the window, totally engrossed in his thoughts. Finally, he said, "What do you think about building a caretaker's home to the left of JW's machine barn? It could be in the copse of trees, facing the farm's driveway. We'd want it close enough to provide more security to the place, but not so out in the open."

Though we'd never discussed such an alternative, I knew in a second where Charlie headed with his brainstorm. "It could be an option if Leon would agree to be caretaker," I said. "Of course, it would have to be nice enough that a wife would want to live there."

Leon's face registered surprise, maybe even disbelief. "Are you serious?" he asked.

"It makes perfectly good sense," Charlie said. "It wouldn't be right to bring Althea to live in a rustic cabin built for one person, not that you've made any decisions along those lines yet. I'm just saying."

"I think it's a brilliant idea," I said. "It'll free up a poustinia to provide the nuns more revenue, and we could include your housing as part of your contract to work the farm. I'll plan out the details with Marian and Cathy."

"I don't know how to thank you," Leon exclaimed. "Fact is, I'm speechless."

"We have a lot of wheels to put in motion," I said. "The first step is for you to see if Sister Cheryl will hire Althea. Then, you get on the road, and we'll figure out the rest."

After Leon departed, Charlie and I hashed out the ideas on our list. We knew we'd have to prioritize, since we didn't yet have income from the farm or the tours. "While a barn's high on our list," I said, "I think we could wait on the animals."

"Right," Charlie agreed. He suggested that we could store equipment in our own garage once we had it built. We could also delay further development of a paved road, though we needed a small parking lot by JW's machine barn. "It looks tacky to have guests parking on the grass," Charlie stated.

In the end, we decided that our goal for *Rock Creek Farm* this summer would be to develop the areas that enhanced the tours and our crops. The rest could come later.

CHAPTER 47

*C*harlie and I had decided to have supper at the monastery on Thursday evening. In many ways, we considered it a celebration of all that we'd accomplished with the restoration. With the first tour scheduled for the next day, and Pauline as ready as possible, we just had to wait to see the outcome.

I felt excited, yet anxious about the tours. In fact, I had so many emotions that I could hardly put a name to them. When I thought about it, I'd add that I felt grateful, not because we'd completed this part of the project; but, rather, due to becoming a part of the estate's history.

I tried to express some of my reflections to Charlie as we walked to the mansion, although I didn't think he fully understood what I meant. I knew he felt the connection with the Sisters, as I did, because we kept them in mind with everything we'd accomplished. Charlie and I worked together to enhance their sustainability, and we'd succeeded.

On the other hand, because I'd become so engrossed in Hildegarde's diary, I sensed a deeper connection that traveled through time. Perhaps, I imagined myself as an extension of Hildegarde, since I'd come to know her as a friend, sister, and daughter.

While Charlie and I walked among the fir trees, I wanted to define their strength and beauty as a lasting tribute to Hildegarde. We would always have her Tannenbaums to remind us that life remained on a continuum, even when we no longer walked on this earth. When I gazed at the beauty of the setting sun striking at just the right angle of the mansion's stained-glass windows, I knew the view had captured Hildegarde's spirit as much as it did mine, whenever she stood in this very spot.

I stopped to fully embrace my awe of the scene in front of me. Tears crested, then fell to my cheeks. I brushed them away, but not before Charlie noticed them. He took my hand, then kissed me. "Are you all right?" he asked.

"I'm happy," I said simply.

Charlie nodded, and I thought he might have understood, after all, especially when he said, "Me, too."

"I want to continue Hildegarde's legacy," I remarked. "We don't need wealth to be kind-hearted and generous. We can support others, just as Hildegarde did with the orphans and sick children, even with Adele and Dieter Holtz."

"It's a work in progress," Charlie said, "so we'll take it one day at a time."

"Right," I nodded. "We should tell the Sisters what we've decided about building a home for Leon and Althea. Do you think they'll go for it?"

"I don't see why not," Charlie stated. "They put you in charge, so I'm certain they know that you'll do what needs to be done."

"Are you ready to oversee construction of a house for Joe and Amanda, one for Leon and Althea, and a garage for us?" I asked.

"I can't wait to get started," Charlie grinned.

We both chuckled as we continued our stroll, hand in hand, to the monastery.

CHAPTER 48

*P*auline Holtz arrived just after 10 a.m. on Friday morning. Gunther dropped her off, then met with Charlie to open JW's machine barn and prepare for the first tour. I had to stifle a laugh when I saw Pauline's attire, not that I considered it out of place. Rather, it demonstrated her readiness to play the character since she had on a dress reminiscent of a style from the 1920's, and she wore one of Adele's hats that we'd found in her attic. I thought Pauline chose the perfect outfit.

After I gave Pauline a pep talk, and let her rehearse briefly, we walked over to wait for our guests in the upper level of the barn. Shortly before 11 a.m., Rose led the caravan of ladies from the Women's Guild, and showed them where to park. When they gathered, I sensed the excitement among the 10 visitors, and they cheered when they saw Pauline dressed in all of her finery.

I knew I'd never recall each of their names, though Rose introduced them, one by one. Rose offered to collect their fees for me, while I handed out the vouchers for lunch and the gift shop, then explained that Charlie and Gunther would chauffeur them back to their vehicles. "Just tell Sister Julie in the gift shop when you're ready to leave the monastery, since she'll serve as the dispatcher," I added.

At the appointed time to start the tour, I distributed the flyers, then gave my prepared welcome, although I kept it short, knowing that everyone had come for the tour, not me. I left it up to Pauline to share her story as I said, "Pauline Holtz will serve as your guide today. Please enjoy!"

"Hi, girls," Pauline smiled as she stood by the door of the machine barn. "Of course, you all know me. Still, I'm a little bit nervous. Can you tell?"

Everyone laughed, even as Rose called from the group, "Are you kidding? You're a natural, and I've never seen you at a loss for words." The others joined in to assure Pauline that she'd be fine.

"All right," Pauline nodded. "I know I'm among friends, so let's get started." Pauline took a deep breath, then began.

"I'm really happy that you could be with us today. We're going to take a step back to the 1920's, and have a glimpse of the life of wealthy Jonas Willard Smithfield and his wife, Hildegarde. I also want you to know why this place is significant to me and my family. Did you know that Gunther's grandmother was a servant to Hildegarde? His grandfather was the groundskeeper, and he once worked in this very spot. In fact, the Smithfields gave them the land for their orchard. Isn't that amazing?"

I gazed at the faces watching Pauline. Each of the ladies looked totally engaged, perhaps recognizing that some of their own relatives may also have had connections with Mr. and Mrs. Smithfield. None, however, as far as we knew, could claim the same distinction as Pauline and Gunther Holtz.

After the buzz died down from her introduction, Pauline led everyone into the barn, then pointed out the old wagon used to transport barrels from the still to the creek. "They probably also used it to deliver bottles of whiskey or wine to residents from town in the dark of night," Pauline noted.

"Did they use the creek to wash out the barrels?" one lady asked.

"I guess, in a way, they did," Pauline replied. "Mostly, they needed to dump the mash, which is what they called the residue from the grains or grapes used in the production of the spirits."

"That's interesting," another said, "but what makes you think Mr. Smithfield actually distributed his liquor?"

"Take a look at the displays on the wall," Pauline stated. "They're copies of the pages from the ledgers that the Sisters found, and you can see the prices, as well as the initials of the buyers."

The ladies rushed to view the ledgers, and one said, "Oh, dear. My grandfather's initials were A.J., and it appears that he may have been a steady customer." Despite the titter of laughter, others made similar comments.

"We'd probably all find initials of our relatives on these ledgers," Rose smiled. "Of course, it's all conjecture since JW, as Vicki calls Mr. Smithfield, didn't use full names, but I'd say we all share a part in this history. How did you learn about Gunther's grandfather's involvement, Pauline?"

"Well, let me tell you about that," Pauline replied, "but you'll hardly believe it. During the blizzard last winter, Gunther and I decided to clean out our attic, and we found a beautifully-crafted jewelry box that contained Hildegarde Smithfield's diary. I mean, can you imagine?"

One of the ladies asked, "Why would Mrs. Smithfield have given that to Gunther's grandmother?"

"Even though Adele started out as a servant to Hildegarde, they'd become best friends," Pauline explained. Gathering the women around her, Pauline lowered her voice to almost a whisper and said, "We found a secret compartment in the box, filled with German currency, so we think Hildegarde wanted to assure the Holtzes that they'd have enough money for their growing family."

"Wow, that's amazing," the woman exclaimed, while others echoed her sentiments.

"Right," Pauline grinned. "Anyway, I read the diary from cover to cover, although Gunther had to translate some of it for me because she wrote the first part in German. Between that diary and other letters we found in the attic, we've pieced together the connection between the Smithfields and the Holtzes, and we positively know that Dieter Holtz rolled those barrels up that ramp from the still."

"It would've been a lot easier if they'd just put the still on the upper level," an older woman remarked.

"I know," Pauline agreed, "but the whole enterprise had to remain a secret because of Prohibition. I have a video here to explain that, so let's take a few minutes to view it, then we'll go see the contraption they set up on the lower level."

When Pauline reached for the remote control, I knew the time had come for me to take my leave. Pauline would do a fine job, and she didn't need me hanging on her every word. Rather, without my presence, she could just comfortably be herself. I walked out into the sunlight, down to the creek.

Leaning against a large oak tree, I gazed at the stream that meandered throughout the estate, which I considered the key to JW's profitable enterprise. I picked up a pebble from the bank, and tossed it into the water. The ripples slowly emanated from the stone's point of contact.

The scene made me realize its similarity to what I'd experienced. One little brochure I found on the bulletin board at the post office led me to the Monastery of St. Carmella. One small thought to provide resources for the Sisters had expanded their mission and ministry, while leading me to find deep love and unfathomable contentment with Charlie. One tiny leap of faith allowed me the freedom to discover that I could assist those less fortunate than I'd been. The current had taken me far beyond my dreams or expectations.

Hildegarde could now rest in peace.

ABOUT THE AUTHOR

Kathleen McKee is a retired educator and registered dietitian who enjoys crafting stories that are uplifting and moving. Regardless of genre, she likes to include a touch of romance, history, and mystery, with narratives that bring the characters to life.

Kathleen's heartwarming stories and their settings are often inspired by experiences of people she has met or places she has lived. The Monastery of St. Carmella is entirely fictional, but she based it on her memories of once living in the Drexel mansion when she taught at the Sisters' boarding school for boys. Her understanding of the challenges to develop *Rock Creek Farm* came from watching the start-up of Healing with Horses Ranch in Manor, Texas. Hard work and dedication, soliciting grants, and a cadre of volunteers transformed an empty plot of land to a thriving center for equine therapy.

Kathleen used the diary in *Bountiful Legacies* as the vehicle to share the historical context of Prohibition, the Influenza of 1918, and the experience of German Americans during WWI. She wrote and published the book several years before Covid-19, with no idea that the past would give such shape to the future, as it did in the story.

Kathleen currently lives in southeast Pennsylvania with her springer spaniel, Maggie. You'll find her there, working on her next novel. Visit her website at: https://kathleen-mckee.com/ and sign up for her newsletter at: http://eepurl.com/crzIUv

PRAISE FOR KATHLEEN MCKEE

The Poustinia Series

Poustinia: A Novel

Victoria books a week's stay at a poustinia–a cabin in the woods at a monastery–to discern her future. Besides gaining new friends, she learns an important lesson as she works with Charlie to help the Sisters with their own dilemma. In the process, she experiences something transformative.

Joyful Encounters

Vicki and the Sisters explore the basement of the monastery to learn about Willard J. and Hildegarde Smithfield, generous benefactors who bequeathed their estate. The nuns know about the vintage bowling alley, but never expect that it will lead to an incredible secret that would change their lives.

Bountiful Legacies

Vicki becomes immersed in the history of the couple who bequeathed their estate to the Sisters of St. Carmella. Explore the challenges of a German immigrant during WWI and experience the ravages of the 1918 influenza, while Vicki and Charlie settle into new adventures together.

Honest reviews of my books help bring them to the attention of other readers. If you enjoyed Bountiful Legacies, please post a brief review on Amazon and Goodreads. It's unbelievably important, and I'd be so grateful.

Made in United States
North Haven, CT
01 March 2023

33400972R00134